PRAISE FOR LUCIN

THE BEST OF FRIENDS

"*The Best of Friends* gripped me from the stunning opening to the emotional, explosive ending. In this moving novel, Berry creates a beautifully crafted study of secrets and grief among a tight-knit group of friends and how far a mother will go to discover the truth and protect her children."

—Heather Gudenkauf, *New York Times* bestselling author of *The Weight of Silence* and *This Is How I Lied*

"In *The Best of Friends*, Berry starts with a heart-stopping bang—the dreaded middle-of-the-night phone call—then delivers a dark and gritty tale that unfolds twist by devastating twist. Intense, terrifying, and at times utterly heartbreaking. Absolutely unputdownable."

—Kimberly Belle, international bestselling author of *Dear Wife* and *Stranger in the Lake*

THE PERFECT CHILD

"I am a compulsive reader of literary novels—but this has been a terrible year for fiction that is actually readable and not experimental. I have been so disappointed when well-known writers came out with books that, to me, were just duds. But there was one book that kept me reading, the sort of novel I can't put down . . . *The Perfect Child* by Lucinda Berry. It speaks to the fear of every parent: What if your child is a psychopath? This novel takes it a step farther. A couple, desperate for a child, has the chance to adopt a beautiful little girl who, they are told, has been abused. They're told it might take a while for her to learn to behave and trust people. She can be sweet and loving, and in public she is adorable. But in private—well, I won't give away what happens. But needless to say, it's chilling."

—Gina Kolata, *New York Times*

"A mesmerizing, unbearably tense thriller that will have you looking over your shoulder and sleeping with one eye open. This creepy, serpentine tale explores the darkest corners of parenthood and the profoundly unsettling lengths one will go to to keep a family together—no matter the consequences. Electrifying and atmospheric, this dark gem of a novel is one I couldn't put down."

—Heather Gudenkauf, *New York Times* bestselling author

"A deep, dark, and dangerously addictive read. All-absorbing to the very end!"

—Minka Kent, *Washington Post* bestselling author

THE BEST OF FRIENDS

ALSO BY LUCINDA BERRY

When She Returned

The Perfect Child

THE BEST OF FRIENDS

LUCINDA BERRY

This is a work of fiction. Names, characters, organizations, places, events, and incidents are either products of the author's imagination or are used fictitiously. Any resemblance to actual persons, living or dead, or actual events is purely coincidental.

Text copyright © 2020 by Heather Berry
All rights reserved.

No part of this book may be reproduced, or stored in a retrieval system, or transmitted in any form or by any means, electronic, mechanical, photocopying, recording, or otherwise, without express written permission of the publisher.

Published by Thomas & Mercer, Seattle

www.apub.com

Amazon, the Amazon logo, and Thomas & Mercer are trademarks of Amazon.com, Inc., or its affiliates.

ISBN-13: 9781542022149
ISBN-10: 1542022142

Cover design by Rex Bonomelli

Printed in the United States of America

To domestic violence survivors

PROLOGUE

A loud boom startles me, and I turn to my husband, Paul, instantly annoyed. "Does the Village have fireworks again tonight?" We just started the latest *Succession* episode, and I have to pay close attention, or I'm lost. I can't do that if fireworks are popping off for the next thirty minutes.

He shrugs, brushing his brown hair off his forehead and tucking it behind his ears. "I don't think so. I thought they were done after spring break."

The Village is the outdoor mall at the center of our close-knit suburban community, and they're constantly throwing events in their outdoor space. Most of them end in fireworks.

"I really hope they're not." I've been looking forward to this night all week. Even though Paul and I work together, it's been almost three weeks since we've had any alone time. A surge of desire passes through me. It's hard to believe I can still be attracted to him after more than twenty years together, but he's sexier now than he was when we were in high school.

"It's—" Another blast shatters the air, cutting him off.

"That one *really* sounded like a gun." Fear crawls up my spine. My mouth is instantly dry. I move to stand, and Paul jerks me back to the couch. "It was a gun, wasn't it?"

He shakes his head. "I'm sure it wasn't, but just chill out and wait a second before you start running all over the house like a crazy person."

"Should we get Reese?" I motion upstairs. We banished our youngest son, Reese, to his room for the night, and Sawyer's sleeping over at his best friend Caleb's house.

"No, he's fine. He probably didn't hear a thing with his headphones on, so I doubt he's even worried." He throws his arm over my shoulder. "This is why we need to stay off social media. Reading all that garbage makes us too jumpy." He waits a few beats before pressing play on the remote and pulling me back against him on the couch. We're halfway through the show recap when we hear the sound of approaching sirens.

This time we both fly to our feet.

"Reese!" Paul yells. "Get down here!"

No response.

"I'm going to get him," Paul says as he turns around and thunders up the stairs, taking them two at a time.

Red and blue lights flash through our living room windows. The emergency vehicles turn left. Headed to the street behind us.

The street behind us.

Sawyer.

I race to the dining room table, grab my phone, and quickly pull up his number from my favorites. I wait for the ring, but his phone goes straight to voice mail. I call back.

Same thing.

Reese's and Paul's footsteps echo above me. Their muffled voices move through the house as I wait for his message to end so I can leave mine. "Sawyer, honey, this is your mom. I hope one of you boys heard those noises outside. We think they were gunshots, and now there's lots of emergency vehicles headed your way. So be safe. Okay? Just be safe. Please, honey. And call me."

I press end just as more sirens approach and Paul returns with Reese. His eyes are wild, and his video game headset dangles from his neck. "I'm going over there to check on them," I say, moving past them.

"Going where? What are you talking about?" Paul asks.

"Sawyer isn't answering his phone, and all the police are going toward Caleb's street," I say, slipping my shoes on and then opening the front door. "I just want to make sure they're okay."

"You can't go out there!" Paul yells.

"What if there's a crazy shooter?" Reese asks at the same time.

I ignore them and step outside before shutting the door tightly behind me. Three police cars race down the street and make a left at the corner just like all the others. I take off running. People are coming out of their houses, milling down the street while I sprint past them.

Dear God, please don't let anything happen to my baby.

Around the corner. Almost there. My lungs burn.

Please, God.

Emergency vehicles surround Caleb's house. They're everywhere. The entire block is lit. I run as fast as I can, pushing through the throngs of people gathered outside until I'm almost to their front yard.

"Ma'am, you can't come any closer," a police officer calls out.

"My son!" I point to the Schultzes' house as officers with *SWAT* printed on their backs roll out the yellow tape to surround it. "My son is inside!" I move around him, but he steps in front of me, stretching his arms out wide on each side to form a barricade with his body.

"I'm sorry, but I can't let you pass through." His face is grim, set in stone.

"Please, he's in that house."

He shakes his head. "You're going to have to wait and speak with my supervisor."

I can't wait. There's no time. Adrenaline shoots through me. I turn and bolt, running in the opposite direction.

The back way. I'll go around. Cut through the Hammonds'.

Please, God, let my baby be okay.

Two squad cars block the Hammonds' driveway. I creep behind the sand palms and alongside the shrubs until I reach the porch, feeling like a fugitive. I race up the stairs and rap on the door. Eloise opens it immediately, her dark robe tightened around her waist.

"Kendra?" She raises her eyebrows. "What are you doing out there?"

"El, please, you have to let me go through your house and into your backyard," I say breathlessly as my heart thumps in my chest.

Her face fills with fear. "You can't go in our backyard. The police said to stay inside and not do anything. We're supposed to lock our doors and wait for further instructions."

"Sawyer is over there." Desperation lines every word. "He stayed overnight at Caleb's."

Her hand goes to her mouth. "Oh my God. I'm so sorry, Kendra."

"That's why I need to get over there."

"You can't. It's too dangerous." She shakes her head.

"I have to." I shove her against the doorframe and push past her. Someone grabs me from behind. Muscular arms encircle me.

"I can't let you do that." A deep, gruff voice. The same officer as before.

"Please, my son. I have to see my son." I writhe in his arms. Tears stream down my cheeks. Snot bubbles from my nose.

His walkie-talkie springs to life.

"Coroner on-site in five. Perimeter sealed," it crackles.

Please, God, let my baby be okay.

ONE

LINDSEY

TWO WEEKS LATER

I slam the trash compactor shut and toss my plate in the sink. I'm too angry to eat. My phone rests on the granite countertop, where I left it after getting Dani's text. The screen has long since gone dark—too much time to reply—but what was I supposed to say? We agreed no lawyers. That was part of the plan.

It has only been a day since the funeral. How could she? But it's probably easier for her to worry about lawyers and things like that when her son, Caleb, is safely tucked in his bed at home tonight, unharmed.

The dog's nails dig into my calf. "Get off me," I snap, and he recoils like I've slapped him, tucking his tail between his legs and cowering next to my feet. "Go!" I point to the living room. His ears droop as he slinks underneath the kitchen table to hide. I try summoning up guilt, but I'm too tired. I should've just stayed at the hospital with Jacob, but my husband, Andrew, said that it was important for me to spend time with our other kids.

I glance into the living room, our open concept creating a perfect flow from one room to the next. Wyatt is lying on our L-shaped sectional watching soccer on the flat-screen TV hanging above the fireplace.

He lit the fire even though it's April in California, like somehow the heat will insulate us against what's happening around us. He's focused on the game, oblivious to the mess his younger sister, Sutton, is making with her coloring books and crayons in the middle of the floor. She's probably scribbling on the rug underneath the coffee table with the red one whenever she gets the chance. It's her favorite thing to do when I'm not looking. I let out an exasperated sigh. She's got more attitude than her two teenage brothers combined, and I can't fight with her tonight.

Normally, Jacob would be in there with them, riveted to the game like Wyatt or sprawled out on the floor next to Sutton, but he's not. His nurses should be preparing for shift change right about now, and I hope the new one remembers to put Aquaphor on his lips. They're cracked and bleeding, creating angry sores around his breathing tube. A wave of sadness buckles my knees, and I lean against the kitchen counter for support until it passes.

Andrew is going to be furious when I tell him the Schultzes got a lawyer, even though he's going to pretend like he's not. He wanted to speak to a lawyer before we talked to anyone that night, but I wouldn't let him. Sawyer's death was a terrible accident. Just like what happened to Jacob. Our boys were screwing around. Being drunk and stupid with a gun. That's all. Nobody was supposed to get hurt. It wouldn't look like an accident if we started getting lawyers—only suspicious. I grab my phone to text Kendra. She's been my first call since I was eight. My finger stops midway. None of this matters to her.

Her son is gone—ripped away from her in an instant. But all I could think about when the pair of uniformed officers showed up at our door in the middle of the night to tell us about the tragedy was my own son. Their words came in flits and phrases like liquid moving in and out of me while panic hammered in my chest.

An accident with the three boys.

The hospital.

One of the boys had died.

But not Jacob.

He was alive, and time moved in slow motion as we drove to the hospital. All I wanted to do was throw my arms around him and never let go. Andrew rambled on and on about how we needed Jacob to tell us exactly what had happened before talking to anyone else, but all that changed when we got to the hospital and saw him. The officers had told us he'd been shot in the head and was unresponsive, but that did nothing to prepare us for his condition.

He lay in a curtained cubicle underneath the harsh lights of the intensive care unit. Unfamiliar beeps and buzzes surrounded us as machines kept him alive. His entire head was wrapped in thick bandages, his eyes swollen shut like they had been the day he was born. Tubes moved in and out of his body. Blood filled one of the lines. The air was pregnant with stillness despite the frenetic activity going on around us.

Andrew came to a sudden stop behind me, unable to go any farther. A nurse punched numbers into one of the monitors hanging above Jacob's hospital bed. I shuffled forward. "Can I touch him?" I asked in a voice that didn't sound like mine.

"Of course." She nodded, pointing to his left arm. "That one's free of wires and gear."

I moved to the left side of his bed. My hands shook as I stroked his arm, willing him to wake up in the same way that I used to will him to sleep when he was a baby. It's been that way ever since. I hate leaving him, because what if he wakes up and I'm not there? Kids need their moms when they're sick, so I have to be there when he opens his eyes, and he's going to open his eyes. I don't care what the doctors say or about any of their stupid statistics about where the bullet is lodged in his brain—Jacob is going to wake up. He'll pull through this.

But Andrew is right. Wyatt and Sutton need me just as much as he does. I move my neck from side to side, trying to ease some of the tension pinching my shoulders, but it only makes it worse. Maybe the kids will fall asleep fast if I put on a movie. I'd better let Andrew know about the lawyer before joining them. He won't like it if he hears the news from someone else before me. I grab my phone and quickly text him:

You're not going to believe what's happening now.

TWO

DANI

I inhale the lavender-scented candles and let the bubbles spread over me, doing my best to allow the familiar ritual to relax me, but it's impossible. I'm tied in knots. It's been that way since the knock on the door in the middle of the night. I can't eat. I don't sleep. I'm barely keeping it together in front of the kids. But that's not even the worst part. It's the guilt gnawing away at me, because no matter how awful I feel, it doesn't compare to what Kendra's going through.

Lindsey's rage fills our newly remodeled master bathroom from over two miles away. Kendra is on the cul-de-sac behind us, but Lindsey refused to move when everyone else did. She said she didn't need to trade in what she had for a better model to make it sound like it wasn't about being cheap, but we know her better than that. Not like the distance matters tonight. She might as well be sitting on the toilet, glaring down at me in the tub.

What was I supposed to do? It's not like I had a choice in the matter. Bryan didn't even consult me. How many times have Lindsey and Kendra told me that I need to have a voice in my marriage? I'm as mad at him as she is with me. Couldn't he at least have given me a say in something as important as this? He sprang it on me like it was nothing.

"Ted's coming with us tomorrow," he announced while we were finishing up the dinner dishes.

My back was to him while I scrubbed the last pot, so he couldn't see my shocked expression, and I quickly rearranged my face before turning around. "Really?" I asked.

"He's taking a red-eye out shortly after midnight, and his flight doesn't get in until four thirty this morning. He'll grab a few hours of sleep in one of the hotels by the airport and meet us down at the police station by eight." He pointed to the stack of Tupperware lids in his other hand and asked, "Where should I put these?"

He acts like I'm so dumb. As if he could bypass the bomb he dropped in our kitchen by changing the subject. But I'm not nearly as stupid as he thinks. Or naive. Maybe I used to be, but not anymore.

He didn't need to tell me which Ted. We only have one friend named Ted, and Bryan uses him for anything legal, as if he specialized in all areas of law rather than commercial property. He lives in Upper Manhattan in a bachelor's loft that Bryan swoons over on Instagram whenever he posts a picture of it.

Being single and never married is a badge of honor he wears proudly, and he never misses an opportunity to drop it into conversation. None of his relationships have lasted longer than a year, but he thinks he can give Bryan marital advice. It makes me so angry, and I gave up pretending I liked him years ago. Eventually, he quit coming around, but it didn't stop Bryan from finding a way to make it out there at least once a year. He comes home talking like he regrets being married and tied down with kids. It always takes him a couple of days to come back to reality.

At least Ted's not staying here. He's the last person I want in my space.

My stomach curls in on itself just with the thought of tomorrow. The investigators have been tiptoeing around us until after the funeral in an unspoken understanding to honor the Mitchells' loss, but they've taken their kid gloves off. They made that clear when they called Bryan this morning and told him about the gun.

How many times have we told the kids not to play with the gun?

"What was I supposed to do?" Bryan asked after I got upset that he hadn't consulted me about Ted coming to the police station. "You would've said no even if I'd asked you. Don't even try to pretend like you wouldn't." He sneered at me. "You care more about what your damn girlfriends think than you do your own family. The boys used our gun, Dani—our gun. And the police know it."

The intensity of the grief surrounds us, filling the police department waiting room with thick, suffocating energy. Chairs line each wall in front of the door that I can't take my eyes off because any minute someone is going to walk through it and start whatever grueling process we are about to go through. It's different from any waiting room I've been in before. There are no cheap prints in frames on the walls. No tables with old magazines for us to read while we wait. Nothing to distract us.

Kendra and Paul sit huddled in the corner. Paul's arms are wrapped tightly around Kendra, and her small frame is buried inside his. He had to hold her up when they came through the door. Her sweatpants dragged across the floor, and her baggy long-sleeved shirt was dotted with stains. I tried to make eye contact with her, but she kept her face down, her long blonde hair falling forward like a shield. I shot Lindsey a worried look, but she quickly turned away, clearly ignoring me because she's still upset about the lawyer. I sent her a bunch of apologetic texts last night, begging her to talk, but she didn't respond to any of them, and she never would've done that unless she was mad.

It feels like we're sitting in the principal's office, and I hate getting into trouble. Bryan grips my hand. His palms are sweaty. Ted still hasn't arrived. We got here first and grabbed seats on the row of chairs lining the right wall. Lindsey and Andrew came next and sat beside us, leaving the other wall to Kendra and Paul, like there's an imaginary line separating the parents who have lost their child from those of us who haven't.

Except that line might not be so clear.

Tears fill my eyes. Caleb wet the bed last night, and he hasn't done that since kindergarten. He was too wrecked to even be embarrassed about it. I cleaned his sheets, then lay in bed with him, holding him tightly and running my hands through his hair while he sobbed.

Neither of us fell back to sleep.

He's been out of the psychiatric ward for four days, and each night follows the same routine. His nightmares interrupt his fitful sleep, sending bloodcurdling screams throughout the house and shooting panic through my veins while I race to his room and Bryan rushes into Luna's. Caleb shakes in terror on his bed and clings to me like he'd climb inside me if he could. My pleas are the same every night while I hold him against me, doing my best to comfort him.

"Please, Caleb, just tell me what happened," I whisper.

It's been seventeen days, and he still hasn't spoken. Not one word.

He didn't even speak the night of the accident when Miss Thelma found him wandering down her block covered in blood. She recognized him immediately when she spotted him across the street. She's been walking her poodle, Mitzi, in our tree-lined neighborhood for as long as he's been playing in it with his friends. He has knocked on her door with every school fundraising flyer since kindergarten and practically ran her over on his bike more than once. She called out to him, but he kept walking like he didn't hear her, so she hurried down the sidewalk to make sure he was okay. That was when she saw his face and called the police. Miss Thelma followed behind him without saying anything until the police arrived. She hasn't walked Mitzi since. Her daughter comes every day to do it for her.

We still have no clue what happened that night. The reporters are calling it the worst tragedy since the Lindell fires. The newspapers and media outlets have taken to calling Caleb "the silent child," and some of them have been so bold as to claim he's faking his silence to keep himself out of trouble, but they didn't see him that night at the hospital. He was transported to the psychiatric ward on the sixteenth floor in a wheelchair because he couldn't hold himself up to walk. Andrew and I practically carried him into his locked room. His nurses allowed me to clean him up once the investigators had bagged all his clothes.

I laid him in the tub and bathed him like I haven't done since he was an infant, running the washcloth over his body and face again and again. Every part of his body was limp. His arms dangled like a doll's. He gazed up at the ceiling, eyes unfixed, unseeing, as I washed away the blood of his best friends since preschool.

The front door of the police station opens, interrupting my thoughts. All of us turn to look as Ted strides into the room. There's no mistaking he's a lawyer with his shiny briefcase and three-piece suit. He makes a beeline for Bryan.

"I'm so sorry I'm late, buddy," he says, pulling out a handkerchief from his pocket and swiping it across the beads of sweat on his forehead before sliding it back into his pocket in one swift movement.

Paul lets go of Kendra and leaps to his feet. "You hired a lawyer? What'd you hire a lawyer for?"

Bryan takes a step toward him, holding his hands out in a peaceful gesture. "It's not what you think, Paul. He's just a friend. He's—"

"A friend?" Paul narrows his eyes to slits. "All of us have friends that are lawyers." He waves his hand around the room. "Do you see any other lawyers here besides yours?"

People don't speak to Bryan like that, and his body stiffens in response. I chew on my lip, hoping he'll keep his mouth shut this once.

He expels a deep breath like he's letting go of his anger, and I breathe a sigh of relief.

"We thought it might be a good idea," he says.

That's not what we rehearsed. He was supposed to say that Ted was a family friend and there to help all of us because we were too emotional to think clearly, too close to the situation, so we needed someone to think rationally for us. That was the explanation we'd planned.

"You thought it would be a good idea?" Paul's anger radiates off him, his rage contorting his familiar features into a man I don't recognize.

Lindsey nudges Andrew, and he stands to join them. "Come on, guys. Let's remember why we're here," he says, reaching out and grabbing their arms to form a lopsided triangle in the middle of the room.

Images of the three of them huddled together like that flash through my mind in quick snippets—all the family vacations, school functions, baseball games, and playdates over the years. Kendra, Lindsey, and I have been so lucky. We've gotten to live the life we whispered about when we were little girls huddled underneath our blankets at sleepovers. We always talked about living in the town we grew up in, marrying amazing men, and raising our children together. We couldn't believe it when our three oldest boys were as close as we were growing up. We knew how good we had it and how fortunate we were that our husbands got along so well.

What will happen to us?

"Hey, hey, hey," Ted interrupts, sounding every bit a lawyer, and I hate him for it. There's no hesitation on his part as he moves to stand between Bryan and Paul. "Let's all take a step back and mellow out."

The door opens just as Paul starts to speak, and a detective strides into the room. Everyone stills. It's Detective Locke, the same one from the hospital. He wears a crisp white shirt buttoned to the top with a dark tie and matching jacket. His first name eludes me even though I'm pretty sure he was in my freshman algebra class in high school.

"Everything okay out here?" he asks. He doesn't smile at any of us as he scans the room.

The men exchange awkward glances. I try to catch Lindsey's eye again, but Bryan's body blocks my view. Detective Locke motions to Paul. "Let's start with you and your wife."

THREE
KENDRA

Detective Locke has been bombarding us with questions for over an hour. Maybe longer. I can't make sense of his words. They come from his mouth and float around the room. I don't bother to chase them. What's the point?

My son is gone, and he's never coming back.

Nothing changes that.

I keep waiting to wake up, for Paul to jiggle my arm and tell me I slept through my alarm clock again. I want to wipe the sleep from my eyes, push the horrid images back into the land of sleep, and wake in a world where Sawyer still exists.

"Kendra?" It sounds like Detective Locke is calling me from the end of a long tunnel. "Kendra?"

How long has he been calling my name? I lift my head and try to focus on him as he peers at me from across his desk. His face is a perfect square. Green eyes with specks of gold surrounding his pupils. They're deep, impossible to read. The light coming in through the window behind him is too bright. It makes my head hurt.

"Did Sawyer mention being angry with Jacob or Caleb?" He gazes at me with hawklike precision.

"No, not to me." The Xanax makes my tongue thick. I speak like I have a mouthful of marbles.

"Did you notice any recent changes in his behavior?"

It takes too much effort to shake my head.

Paul answers for me, "We didn't notice anything weird. He was moody, but he wasn't moodier than any other teenager."

Sawyer is our happy one—the easy kid. Reese is our problem child. Always has been.

"Any changes in his sleeping patterns?"

"He slept a lot, but all teenagers sleep a lot."

Except mine. He won't sleep again. The loss claws at my chest, stealing every wisp of air from my lungs. I'm going to scream. That's what happened in the bathroom. Not again.

I grab for Paul's knee next to mine.

"Paul . . ." It's all I can get out. My mouth is too dry to speak. Teeth stick to my gums.

Detective Locke turns his attention back to me. The intensity of his stare is gone and replaced with concern. "Are you okay?" he asks, getting up from behind his desk.

I shake my head. Screams bubble like lava in my chest, exploding in sounds that must come from me, but I've gone behind the glass in my mind, where it's safe. I place my hands on the cool surface as I watch Paul take me into his arms as if it's possible to comfort me.

FOUR
LINDSEY

Detective Locke looks just like he did in high school—square shoulders, angular jaw, clean cut—like he came out of the womb ready to join the military, and that's exactly what he did as soon as we graduated. He was at boot camp the week after our ceremony. I haven't seen him since and had no idea he was Norchester's lead detective until he strode into Jacob's hospital room the first night. We were never friends, but our graduating class was under two hundred people, which meant everyone knew everyone else. Most of us stay in touch, especially those of us who live close, but he's never attended any of our high school reunions, and I haven't seen him at any of the weddings of former classmates.

He had a partner at the hospital that night who followed him around as they hovered in the background outside of Jacob's room, but he's by himself today. I still don't know anything about him. I've scoured social media and can't find anything. He doesn't even have a Facebook profile. What kind of a person doesn't at least have that?

He points to the two chairs sitting in front of his desk while he moves to take the swivel office chair behind it. I slide into the straight-backed wooden seat on the right, still warm from whoever sat here last. Was it Dani? Bryan?

Kendra and Paul were in and out quickly. Kendra's wails cut their meeting short. Her sobs started small and worked their way up to a heart-wrenching crescendo reverberating throughout the building. I've never heard someone cry like that. It took everything in me not to go to her. Andrew sensed my knee-jerk response, and if it weren't for his arm around me, I might not have been able to stop myself. We all stood when Kendra came out like we were honoring the bride at a wedding.

The Schultzes went next. Their session dragged on for over two hours. Dani looked stricken when they came out, but she can't stand anything hinting at trouble, and this room reeks of it. There's nothing on any of the dirty white walls except chipped paint and scratches. His desk is cluttered with papers and files. His meticulous appearance obviously doesn't transfer to paperwork. There's not a single picture frame on his desk. Does that mean he doesn't have a family or that he prefers to keep his personal life private? Gosh, I hope it's the latter, because people without kids have no idea what it's like to be a parent. They think they do, just like I did before I had kids, but they're clueless.

Am I supposed to call him Martin? Detective Locke? I clear my throat, anxious to get started. I can't stand being away from Jacob for so long. He had a terrible night last night. Spiked a 102-degree fever and sent all his machines into panic mode. Andrew's fidgeting next to me isn't helping my anxiety.

"Was Jacob depressed?" Detective Locke asks, wasting no time on formalities and small talk like he did in the hospital.

"Not at all," I answer without hesitation. "I know everyone says that teenage boys are the worst communicators and you can't get them to do more than grunt in response to your questions, but Jacob wasn't like that. We talked every day. Our relationship was open and honest. He came to me with things. All my children do. If he was having problems or feeling down, I would've known about it."

He looks at me like I'm in denial about what he's getting at, but I'm not.

Self-inflicted gunshot wound.

That's what the doctors in the emergency room said when they told us about Jacob's injuries. The same line is listed in his chart, but I skip over it whenever I scan his reports for the latest lab results and neurology tests. He might've shot himself, but he would never kill himself on purpose. Never. Jacob was happy, and happy kids don't try to take their own lives, especially when they have everything going for them.

"Sometimes depression looks different in teenagers than it does in adults. Did you notice any irritability? Change in his appetite?"

Andrew bursts into laughter that's quickly followed by red-faced embarrassment at his poor timing. "I'm sorry. It's just . . . you obviously don't know Jacob." He wrestles with his emotions before continuing. "Our boy likes to eat. There's no problem there."

I reach for his hand and lace our fingers together. He squeezes back. I've never been so grateful to have him by my side as I have been these past couple of weeks. His leave of absence from the medical practice got approved today, and one of the other rheumatologists from Oak Park will see his patients while he's out. This way one of us can keep staying with Jacob while the other manages things at home with Wyatt and Sutton. We're going to work out a schedule later tonight.

"Has he ever tried to hurt himself before?" Detective Locke stares at me like there's a clue hidden somewhere in my face.

"Absolutely not. That's not the kind of kid he is." I lean forward across his desk, pushing a stack of papers aside with my elbows to create space. "I know you're doing your job and that all of this is a part of it, but our son would never hurt himself on purpose." I stare at him pointedly.

"I understand how you feel, Lindsey, and I sympathize with you." He leans across his desk in the same way to meet me in the middle. "However, with all due respect, the forensics taken from the scene paint a different picture. Jacob's injuries and finger placement on the gun are all consistent with an attempted suicide."

"He might have put the gun up to his head and pulled the trigger, but I promise you that he didn't know the gun was loaded, or he never would've done it. He knows better than that." I wait a beat before continuing, making sure my words get a chance to sink in. "And besides, it's not like he was the only one who touched the gun. All three of the boys' fingerprints were on it. Anything could have happened." I throw the information in his face like he wasn't the one who shared the report with us when it came back from ballistics.

Andrew nods in eager agreement with me. We've been through so many different scenarios during the long hours we've hovered at Jacob's bedside. Our ideas range from the relatively mundane, like a truth-or-dare game gone terribly wrong, to things that are more ridiculous, like they were on a whacked-out acid trip that made them think they were in one of their violent video games. But none of them include a suicidal version of Jacob. Something else happened that night, but I don't have time to figure it out. My job is taking care of Jacob. Detective Locke's job is figuring things out. I wish he'd let me get back to mine and start doing a better job at his.

FIVE
KENDRA

I was always on Sawyer about cleaning his room. He was such a slob, and the mess drove me crazy. Not to mention the smell from his sweaty jerseys and socks that he left strewn everywhere. We had some of our biggest fights over it. Now I'm glad he never listened. It's a new house rule to keep his door shut so I can trap his smell in here for as long as it'll stay. His personality fills the space, from the punk band posters taped above his desk to the wadded-up papers in the corner from abandoned homework projects. I try to inhale him as I sit in the middle of his floor, clutching one of his favorite T-shirts against my chest.

Becoming a mom birthed my biggest fear—losing him. Sawyer marked my entrance into motherhood. Pregnancy riddled me with anxiety because his survival depended on me, and I expected immense relief from that burden once I'd successfully brought him into the world. I assumed sharing the responsibility with Paul would give me a much-needed reprieve from my obsessive worrying. My insides expanded with unbelievable love when they placed Sawyer in my arms after a long and difficult labor, and in that same instant, I was filled with the knowledge that the loss of him would wreck me to my core, which brought my anxiety to new heights.

Every fear I've had over the years—each terrorizing thought, every agonizing image of something awful happening to one of my kids—doesn't even touch the utter devastation in my being. And life will go on without him. That's the part I hate the most. It can't. It must stop. Waves of grief strip all concept of time as I disappear into their swirling abyss.

And then I'm returned.

Depleted and empty.

Spent.

My eyes burn. Red fills my left one. My doctor said I popped multiple blood vessels from all the crying. The blood pools in the corner and works its way around my iris throughout the day. That's not the only place seeping blood. My stools are filled with it and with the putrid smell of the pain rotting my insides.

People say they survive this. Millions of children died last year. All of them with parents who somehow managed to go on. Not me.

"Mom?" Reese's voice calls from behind the door. My other son, two years younger than Sawyer.

A flash of annoyance. I don't want to be bothered, but he knows I'm in here. He won't go away if I don't say something.

"Yes?" My throat is raw. Talking hurts. Maybe my throat is bleeding too. Red. Black seeps into the edge of my vision. Did Paul give me another sleeping pill in my tea?

"Mom?"

My head swirls.

Sawyer?

Did I say that out loud?

"No, Mom. It's me, Reese."

Is he reading my mind? Dear God, don't let Reese be reading my mind.

His words are bubbles floating past me. They dance around my head before floating above Sawyer's headboard. I'm on his bed. Wasn't I on the floor? There's another bubble. I stick my pointer finger through it. Pop. It doesn't make a sound as it disintegrates. I want to pop another one, but I'm tired. So exhausted.

My lids are heavy.

Stop fighting.

SIX
DANI

I clasp my purse in front of me and hurry into the hospital, pushing through the heavy glass doors and flashing my license at the security officer standing in the lobby. Guards have been posted up at every entrance and lobby of the hospital for weeks. Everyone wants to catch a glimpse of Jacob, but Lindsey and Andrew are determined to keep them away. They hate being the center of attention and are sickened by the way the media has tried to exploit their tragedy. It's ignited both sides of the gun control debate, but they don't want any part of it.

People's obsession with our story has grown to epic proportions since detectives started crawling all over the school. Kids who barely know the boys are making ridiculous claims just to get their twenty seconds in the spotlight. They're saying things like that the boys planned to blow up the school, that they had a hit list, or my personal favorite—that Bryan and I knew about their plans and didn't stop them. The media has done nothing but crucify us for having a gun in the house. We took Luna's phone away from her yesterday after Bryan found out she'd been on Instagram. She threw a fit over it, screaming that he was treating her like she was still a child even though she's been away at college for almost a year, but it's not our rule. That one came from Detective Locke—no social media.

My footsteps echo behind me as I reach the end of the empty corridor and make a right at the second nurse's station. I scan for **REHABILITATION** signs. Jacob's medical team moved him out of the ICU last week. They consider him medically stable even though machines keep him alive and do everything for him. I assumed visiting him in the new ward would be easier, but it's not because things feel more permanent. Unlike in the ICU, everything is still. Nothing moves fast. People's doors are always closed, and I don't ever look in the ones accidentally left open. I made that mistake once, and I won't do it again.

I tap lightly on room 110's door and wait for Lindsey to respond before going in. She rises from her position in the chair beside Jacob's bed, and I motion for her to sit down. Her jaw is set and she's pasty white, making the dark rings underneath her eyes all the more apparent. She came straight to the hospital after the police interviews this morning, and I bet she'll stay all night.

"Jacob, Dani's here to visit," she says and smiles down at him, reaching to brush the hair off his forehead, but his black curls are gone—shaved before his second surgery. Thirty-two staples form a U shape on the left side of his head. His face is swollen to unrecognizable from all the steroids they pump into him. It was easier to look at him when the bandages covered his head, but there's no need for them anymore. Still.

"Hi, Jacob," I say, averting my eyes and trying to sound upbeat. I understand why Wyatt refuses to visit. He doesn't agree with his parents' decision to keep Jacob alive after the doctors have declared him brain dead. He's not the only one who doesn't agree with them.

Lindsey insists everyone address Jacob when entering and leaving his room. During his first three days in the ICU, she found stories from coma survivors who claimed they felt their loved ones' presence and were comforted by it while they were unconscious. She's been obsessed with their stories ever since and demands we include Jacob in all our conversations. Yesterday she asked one of the nurses to leave because they spoke around Jacob like he wasn't there.

I hand her the grande macchiato I picked up from Starbucks on the way over and take a seat in the tan vinyl chair on the other side of Jacob's bed, marveling at how quickly these visits have become routine. Unlike the general hospital, the psychiatric ward has very strict visiting hours, so I wasn't allowed to stay with Caleb twenty-four seven even though I wanted to. I spent lots of time sitting down here with Lindsey in between my visits with Caleb. I've kept them up since he got discharged because I don't want her to feel like I abandoned her now that he's out.

I search the mural of cards taped on the wall in front of us, trying to spot any new ones since my visit yesterday. There are hundreds of cards, and more arrive every day, each filled with well-wishes and prayers for recovery. Lindsey and Andrew take turns reading them to Jacob, showing him the pictures on the inside like they're reading him his favorite children's book.

#22 is painted in bold red strokes in the center of the mural. Lindsey said it took Sutton two hours to complete it, but she was determined to do it herself. It turned out great.

Jacob has been number twenty-two since the boys started playing Soccer Shots in preschool. They all wanted number twenty-three, but Sawyer got to pick first that day, and he snatched it up before they could. They were left with second best, so Jacob settled for one below and Caleb one above.

#22, #23, and #24.

These past few years we've had to watch Jacob and Sawyer get more and more attention on the field while Caleb is slowly edged out of the equation, but that's how it is when you're the goalie, and they're the leading scorers in the tricounty area. Bryan and I have always told Caleb that, but it doesn't matter anymore. Now it's just him, and something tells me his soccer days are over.

"Did the kids go down easy?" she asks like she used to when our kids were little and getting them to sleep was our biggest worry.

She's really asking about Caleb. Luna has been staying with us since Caleb got out of the hospital, but she's never had a problem falling asleep even when she was a baby. She's one of those people who can fall asleep anywhere and at any time just by laying their head down. Caleb used to be the same way.

"Caleb was still awake when I left. Bryan is sitting in there with him." It isn't exactly a lie. I turned on the baby monitor that I overnighted from Amazon last week before I left and made Bryan promise to check on him. He swore he would, but I'm not sure I trust him, since his expression said differently.

"You've got to give the boy some room to breathe," he said when I set it in front of him on the coffee table. "Maybe all he needs is a little space."

That's not going to happen, because the psychologist's words from the hospital follow me everywhere:

Suicide contagion is a real thing in teenagers. Having someone close to you attempt suicide increases your risk.

It's such an awful term. *Suicide contagion.* Makes it sound like an infectious disease. One that's already contaminated us.

"How about yours?" I ask. Sometimes she goes home at night to put them to bed and leaves once they're asleep to spend the night with Jacob.

She rolls her eyes. "You know Sutton."

Sutton is every bit as spoiled as the name implies, except Lindsey and Andrew call it being spirited. She's their indigo child or something like that. I can't imagine being part of that parenting generation. Everything is so different from when my kids were Sutton's age, and I couldn't handle it. Kendra and I stopped having kids after we had two, and we loved that the three of us each had two kids so close together. It was perfect, but Lindsey was determined to have a girl, and she doesn't give up when she's set her sights on something. It took her ten years to

The Best of Friends

get pregnant again, and I've always secretly wondered what would've happened if she'd had a boy.

"How's Wyatt?"

"Running around trying to take care of everybody else like a good middle child." She smiles at me, but it doesn't reach her eyes. Those are filled with exhaustion and questions she won't allow herself to answer.

That's not what I meant, and she knows it. Wyatt has been as opposed to keeping Jacob on life support as the protestors outside the hospital are. She gives me another smile.

She was obviously mad at me earlier today about the lawyer, but it's impossible to tell if she still is because she acts so differently at the hospital. She keeps a smile plastered on her face like some strange Stepford wife and talks in a high-pitched voice like everything has to be positive. I totally understand why, and I'd be the same way, but it doesn't make it any less disturbing.

"Listen, I just want you to know that we only got a lawyer so we'd have someone to help all of us through this. That's all. We don't want you to think of Ted as just our lawyer. He's here for everybody. Anyone can ask him questions or run things by him." I'm talking too fast, but I can't help it. I fix my gaze on her, and she returns my stare with a strange expression that I can't read despite thirty years of friendship. Our eyes hover above Jacob's body, which is covered with a crisp white sheet. She changes it daily even though the nurses could do it for her and tucks the corners underneath the mattress military style. The beds in her house are the same way. "I wasn't trying to go behind anyone's back or do anything without letting you know. We're in this together."

Those were her words—not mine.

"We're in this together, Dani. We're in this together," she repeated over and over again as her nails dug into my arm while we waited to hear which one of our boys had been shot and was in surgery. Sawyer's death shook us to our core, and not knowing if Caleb or Jacob would be next was a nightmare no parent should have to go through. Just thinking about those moments of sheer terror and powerlessness makes me want to throw up on the tiled floor.

"No worries." Her left eyebrow twitches—her tell since seventh grade. Her light-brown hair is pulled back from her face in a tight ponytail. "We've all got to do whatever we've got to do to take care of our families. I'm over it."

"Please, Lindsey, I really don't want you to be mad at me. I couldn't take it if you were mad at me on top of everything else." I sound desperate. I can't help it.

"I'm not mad at you," she says, but we both know she's lying. I can't count the number of times she's screamed me into tears over a perceived betrayal on my part. Her parents' divorce shattered her childhood innocence, so trust is her most important quality in any relationship. Also her biggest trigger. If we weren't in Jacob's room, she'd be yelling about how I'd gone back on what we said that night in the emergency room when Detective Locke asked us if we wanted a lawyer before questioning.

We all quickly agreed it wasn't necessary and wanted to get started with the questions as soon as possible so we could get back to our kids. None of us were in our right minds. We were stunned. Clueless. Bryan would've answered differently if we'd known how bad things were or that Caleb would be too traumatized to speak about what he'd seen.

"Did Detective Locke tell you that he wants to interview our other kids?" She takes a sip of her macchiato.

I nod. Luna's interview is tomorrow at one. Detective Locke doesn't care that she hasn't lived with us in over a year and has little to do with Caleb anymore. He insisted siblings tell each other things that they don't tell their parents even if they aren't close.

"Did he ask if he could talk to Luna without you guys present?"

I nod again.

Careful, Dani. Don't set her off.

"And?"

I shrug so I don't have to speak the lie. She doesn't have to know. Maybe we haven't decided yet. She can't read my mind. She cocks her head to the side and studies my expression. I force myself to maintain eye contact and smile back at her, doing my best to portray the right amount of compassion and uncertainty.

Lindsey's face mirrors my indecision. "Yeah, we don't know what to do about it either. I can't imagine he'll interview Sutton. Although he'll probably get more from her than he will from Wyatt. He's not much of a talker these days, is he, Jacob?" She pauses to glance down at him. He lies motionless, and she strokes his arm before continuing. "It's a no-win situation. If we say that he can't interview them without a lawyer, then it looks like we have something to hide, but if we say yes, what if Wyatt . . ."

Her unfinished question hangs in the air, but she doesn't need to fill in the what-if. We both know what she's referring to, and we aren't leaving any room for the what-if in our household. Bryan won't allow it. He gripped my arm as we walked out of the police station this afternoon and hissed, "Do not under any circumstances allow Caleb or Luna to talk to the police or anyone else without a lawyer present. Do you understand me?"

SEVEN
LINDSEY

So glad Dani's gone. Being around Jacob makes her uncomfortable, but she's not alone. Lots of people have a tough time being around him. It doesn't help that he looks like a complete stranger. They removed a third of his skull to make room for the swelling in his brain, which adds a nightmarish quality to his already-swollen face. Visitors are tough. It's easier when it's the two of us.

I bring his left leg up and press his foot up against my chest, cradling his calf with my other hand while I slowly count to twelve. I don't even need to look at my cheat sheet anymore for his mobility exercises.

"I don't want you to be nervous about tomorrow," I say, stepping back and extending his leg all the way out once I've finished my count. His ankle is so swollen it rolls over his sock. His day nurse always forgets to remove his compression socks for at least an hour in the afternoon. "It's a really simple procedure, and it'll be over before you know it." I twist his ankles around. First clockwise, then counter. Back again.

A surgeon performs his tracheostomy surgery at seven. I was surprised to learn they can perform it bedside. Andrew will be here by six because he's a nervous wreck about it even though Jacob's lead doctor, Dr. Merck, assured him it was a relatively simple and easy procedure that they performed all the time.

"You're all done with this leg." I return it to the bed and pick up his right leg, beginning the same exercises on the other side of his body. His well-contoured muscles from years of soccer are losing their definition. His skin has developed a weird shine and is velvety to the touch.

I stare at his face, imagining what he'll look like with a tube coming out of his throat. His medical team swears he'll be more comfortable this way and less susceptible to infections. I hope they're right. It's the only reason we agreed to do it. We'll do anything to make him more comfortable. Angry bedsores line his backside no matter how diligent I am about turning him. He deserves some kind of relief. Maybe this will help.

I set his leg down next to the other and move to the top of his bed so I can dim the lights above him. I plant a gentle kiss on his forehead. He smells like stale sweat and rubbing alcohol.

"You're going to be okay," I whisper in his ear. "I promise. Tomorrow is the next step in your healing."

EIGHT
DANI

Bryan grabs me as soon as I walk into our house after my visit with Lindsey at the hospital. I was hoping he'd be asleep by the time I got home since it's so late, and I quickly hide my disappointment before he notices.

"What did she say?" he asks as I slip my shoes off and set them next to the other disgruntled pairs lining the entryway. "I want to know everything."

"Be quiet," I whisper. "You're going to wake the kids."

He snorts. "Nobody's up."

Caleb might be, but I don't say that to him. I smell the whiskey on his breath, which means I can't ask if he checked on him either. He stands in front of me in the entryway, blocking the hallway with his body, his muscular chest puffed out. His eyes meet mine with a menacing challenge. I remind myself what the marriage therapist said at our last session about assertive communication.

"Bryan, I feel like now might not be the best time to talk about this because it's so late, and we're both tired." Did I sound confident? Keep the focus on my needs and what I wanted?

He makes a dramatic production of bowing and moving to the side so that I can walk past him. I step around him, wishing it were this easy, but I can tell from the way he stands with his arms crossed on his chest that he's not finished with me yet. I hurry upstairs, hoping he waits to corner me until after I've checked on Caleb.

His door is still cracked the way I left it earlier, and I peek through the opening. The night-light casts a strange glow on his long body sprawled across the bed. His sheets are tangled around him like he's been wrestling in his sleep. His eyes are closed, and he looks like he's sleeping, but it's hard to tell. I told him fake sleeping works the same as real sleeping because it relaxes your body, so that's what he's been doing for the past two nights. I don't know if it's true, but it made him feel better, and that's all I care about.

How does Bryan expect any of us to sleep in this house after someone died in it? When we left the emergency room that night, we weren't allowed to step foot in our house because it was an active crime scene investigation, but that was totally fine with me because I didn't want to go anywhere near it. I assumed we'd never go back inside. After all, Caleb's best friend had died there, and how could we do that to him? It never occurred to me that Bryan and I wouldn't be on the same page about something so obvious.

"Don't be ridiculous," he said when I brought up selling the house and moving. He talked about cleaning it up like the blood was Kool-Aid one of the kids had accidentally spilled on the floor.

They actually have businesses that specialize in cleaning up crime scenes, and he hired a blood-removal company once the investigation was complete. We walked into a house that was disturbingly clean, as if nothing had ever happened. It sparkled more than the day we'd moved in. There wasn't a trace of anything except the smell of their antiseptic and heavy-duty cleaners.

It doesn't matter how pretty or pristine things look, though. Nothing changes the fact that Sawyer died in our house. I feel it every second that I'm here. I see a puddle of his blood spilled on the wooden floor like flashbacks from an event I never experienced. I can't imagine what it's like for Caleb. His trauma psychologist, Gillian, is usually so good at keeping a neutral face, but even she couldn't hide her disapproval when Bryan announced he planned to take Caleb home when he was ready for discharge.

I shut Caleb's door and head to the master bedroom at the end of the hallway, not bothering to check on Luna. Bryan's perched on our king-size bed waiting for me. His chiseled face is shaved and as wrinkle-free as it was in college when we met junior year. Back then, his Spanish accent was the most exotic thing I'd ever heard. It has lost its charm over the years now that I know he can turn it on and off whenever he chooses. I avoid eye contact and move into the bathroom, grabbing my pajamas from the hook on the back of the door. His stare pierces me from behind as I undress and slip them on without turning around. I draw out washing my face and brushing my teeth for as long as I can until I'm left with no choice but to turn around.

"So?" He pounces immediately. "Are they getting a lawyer too?"

"She didn't say." I take the decorative pillows from my side of the bed and carry them to the window seat, where I stack them in their designated spots. "She asked if we planned on having Ted there when the detectives spoke to Caleb and Luna."

"And you told her yes?"

I grab the pillows from his side and bring them to join the others, holding my breath as I pass in front of him and letting it out when he doesn't grab me. He's tired too. Good. "I told her that we didn't know."

"Why would you do that?" He narrows his eyes to slits.

Because I don't want her to hate me, but I can't tell him that. Instead I shrug and sheepishly look away. Lindsey pretends our situations are the same, like we're both waiting for our children to talk, but they're not. Everybody feels sorry for Jacob, and they feel even sorrier for Lindsey the more she refuses to accept the doctor's grave prognosis for Jacob's recovery, but they don't have the same level of sympathy for Caleb or me. It doesn't help that his fingerprints are all over the gun.

The Best of Friends

And it's our gun. Bryan won't let me forget that. Neither did Detective Locke. That was clear in the way he called out to us as we followed Ted out of his office earlier.

"Did you know that kids over fourteen who commit firearm crimes in the state of California are almost always charged as adults?" he asked. "How old did you say Caleb was again?" He knows exactly how old Caleb is, as well as what he ate in the cafeteria on that awful day. Even though they waited to interview us, they talked to plenty of other people about us.

Bryan started to say something, but Ted hurried us out the door before he had a chance to finish. Ted swore Detective Locke was only trying to scare us, and if that was the case, he'd been successful. Caleb won't survive jail. I never should've let the gun in the house.

I didn't grow up with guns, but Bryan did, and he was convinced we needed one for self-defense. He was raised on the South Side of Chicago, and despite the cul-de-sac nestling our two-story home in a gated community, he still acted like we lived in the kind of neighborhood where break-ins happen all the time. He kept it in a locked safe in our walk-in closet. I've always wondered how much protection it gives us being buried back there. By the time we got to the safe and worked the combination, wouldn't the intruder already be on us? I mentioned it to Bryan once, and he laughed at me like I was being ridiculous.

He wanted to keep it a secret from the kids, but there was no way I was having it in the house without them knowing about it. What if they stumbled on it when they were playing and thought it was a toy? At least I won that battle and we showed the kids the gun. Bryan stressed how important it was for our protection, while I focused on never touching or playing with it. We showed them the safe in the closet so they'd know where it was at all times. We never gave either of them the combination.

Caleb has always been a genius with numbers and taking things apart. He spent hours dismantling his cars and trucks when he was a toddler. Once he took apart an old microwave Luna found in the garage. He was only eight.

That's how I know he's the one who got the gun.

What was he thinking? Why would he do something like that after all the times I've harped that guns aren't toys? It's those stupid video games he plays with his friends. All they do is shoot people, so he's become totally desensitized to it. I hate those games.

They're the reason the boys were over here that night to begin with. Caleb got the latest version of some game they could only play on his Xbox. It was rare to have the three of them sleep over. When they were younger, they worked their way through all our homes in different rotations so we all had our equal share, but in the last couple of years, they've spent most of their time at the Mitchells'. They pretend it's because Sawyer has a better setup in his game room, but it's because Kendra and Paul are rarely there, which makes their place a teenage paradise.

Bryan interrupts my thoughts. "Ted is going to be here at eight so we can prepare Caleb and Luna for their interviews. I want them to have plenty of time to practice their responses. Let's wake them at seven to make sure they're fully cognizant and alert by the time Ted gets here."

He makes it sound like they're taking their SATs in the morning. Caleb doesn't know he's going in front of Detective Locke tomorrow, even though I can't imagine how that interview will go, since Caleb falls apart if you push him to talk about whatever's locked inside him. He's able to acknowledge questions nonverbally, and sometimes he'll indicate responses in writing, but he stops all that once anything moves into uncomfortable territory. I planned on warning him about it when we got home this afternoon, but he was sleeping. Mom said he'd cried for three hours after we'd left. His anxiety pill had done nothing to calm him, and he'd finally fallen asleep out of sheer exhaustion; I didn't want to wake him.

I clear my throat and brace myself, preparing for the verbal assault that's sure to follow what I'm about to say. "I'm not sure we should coach Luna. Maybe we should let her answer the questions by herself. Besides, it's not like she's been around much to know what's happening."

Luna couldn't be further removed from our family. She couldn't wait to leave home and took college-preparation courses in high school so that she could graduate early. These are the first nights she's slept here since she moved out a year ago. I couldn't even get her to stay overnight at Christmas. Her disdain for me started when she was fourteen. Everyone assured me that it was only hormones and I'd get her back in a couple of years after they had leveled out, but she turns nineteen next month, and she's never been more impenetrable.

He scoffs at me. "Of course she needs to be prepared. We're not going to let this incident ruin any of our lives."

My insides recoil like they've slammed into a wall. Incident? That's what he's calling this? One of Caleb's best friends is dead, and the other one is in a coma. We step around their imaginary bodies in our family room. Caleb's life will never be the same. Ever.

"You're right," I say and plaster the good-wife smile on my face. "I don't know what I was thinking."

NINE
KENDRA

"Can you at least come downstairs and try?" Paul asks as he stands in Sawyer's doorway, unable to walk through it. He hates Sawyer's bedroom and avoids it at all costs. I tried going downstairs and throwing something together for Reese to eat, but I couldn't bring myself to do it. The police station visit drained all my energy. I buried myself in Sawyer's bed instead. That's how Paul found me a few minutes ago.

I shake my head. "I can't. I'm sorry. I already tried."

Please go. Why won't he just leave?

"Try again." His voice is strained, pinched.

Last night he hinted that I don't think his grief is comparable to mine, as if we're in some disgusting competition about whose pain is the greatest. I've never wanted to choke him as much as I did in that moment. I've barely cooled off. Clearly, he's in the same boat.

"Just fix him toast. It's way too late for him to be eating anything heavy anyway." I roll over, turning my back to him.

"That's not the point. He needs you. He needs to spend time with you." He shuffles back and forth. He's reached his limit. Too much time surrounded by Sawyer's things suffocates him.

"I know that," I say, not trying to keep the irritation out of my voice.

The Best of Friends

He doesn't bother turning around as he grabs the door and shuts it behind him.

Finally.

I pull out Sawyer's phone from underneath the covers and type in his pass code. The detectives took it for evidence the night of the accident and only gave it back to us three days ago. I've been carrying it with me ever since. I won't even let Paul hang on to it just in case he misplaces it or loses it somehow.

There were 817 unread text messages from after his death, and I answered them all. Even the broken-hearted emoji ones that made me want to slam the phone against the wall. Nobody texts anymore. I miss the notification sounds.

I've started going through his videos, but there are so many it's going to take forever. His goofy, crooked smile illuminates each one. Sometimes I watch to be near him, and other times I watch for clues about what happened. Lindsey and Dani are convinced it was a horrible accident, but I'm not so sure. A gun that accidentally went off? Not just once but twice? You can accidentally shoot yourself in the head—it wouldn't be the first time a kid has done something stupid like that—but how do you shoot yourself in the stomach? That's where they shot Sawyer, or where he shot himself, depending on whose story you believe, but none of it makes sense.

So far, there's not much I haven't seen before, since I go through his phone on a regular basis. Girls were my biggest concern three weeks ago. His athletic scholarship was so close to being finalized, and I've been paranoid about him getting someone pregnant his senior year and ruining it all. It's a pointless worry, but it happens all the time. It happened to Jimmy Krueger, and everyone thought he was bound for the pros. Girls have been after Sawyer since ninth grade, and their attention only increased once the college scouts started showing up at his soccer games.

Sawyer and Jacob were an amazing team on the soccer field. Jacob played center forward, and Sawyer was a striker. They functioned as a pair. A beautifully choreographed pair—that's what the *Post Tribune* called them in the article they did earlier this year. Their competitive streak was clear from their first practice, when they got into my Voyager ruffled and upset after learning the referees didn't keep score at their games. They were appalled at the coach's suggestion that there weren't any winners or losers.

"Mommy, why do we play if nobody wins?" Sawyer's small voice called out from the third row. I always made him ride back there whenever we had friends in the car.

"Because then it's just for fun," I said, sounding like the pamphlet they'd sent home with all the kids before practice. Their website stressed noncompetitive play. It seemed a bit much, and I tended to agree with Sawyer, but it was best to always maintain a united front with the other adults in his life. I learned that the hard way.

"That's dumb," he said.

"Yeah, so stupid," Jacob said, slurring all his *s*'s. He'd start speech therapy next week. Lindsey's pediatrician had made her wait until he was four—stressing lots of kids caught up by then. Lindsey made the appointment the day after his fourth birthday, when nothing had changed.

"Dumb. Dumb. Dumb," Sawyer piped up.

"Hey, you guys, settle down," I said. In another thirty seconds, they'd be shrieking at the top of their lungs, and I couldn't handle it. Not when I had a throbbing headache.

My eyes mist at the memory. I force myself to focus. Recenter.

"Sawyer, talk to me," I whisper to his phone. I hold his world in my hand. There's got to be a clue in it, and I won't stop until I find it. I just wish I knew what to look for.

The Best of Friends

Detective Locke said it'd be easier for the kids and make them feel less intimidated if he interviewed them at their homes. I jumped at the opportunity because I can't stand leaving the house. I don't know about Lindsey and Dani. I've been ignoring their texts and calls. Doubt creeps into my decision as I watch technicians wheel more audiovisual equipment into our living room. It feels so invasive. Reese grinned at me like he was about to go on TV while they hooked a microphone to his shirt, and he's been sitting in the same position on the couch, looking starstruck, while Detective Locke drills him with questions.

He isn't getting anywhere with Reese, but that's what I expected. Reese has no clue what's going on in Sawyer's life or in any of his friends'. Sawyer, Jacob, and Caleb don't have any room for Reese in their trio. There's only a two-year gap between the oldest, Jacob, and Reese, but it never mattered. It might as well have been decades separating them. The boys used to take turns paying Reese not to play with them.

I wanted to be angry with them, but I didn't blame them for excluding Reese. I love him, but he doesn't play well with others, even me, and I'm his mother. Things always have to be his way, and he gets mad if they're not, which doesn't make him an easy person to deal with. It doesn't help that he's socially awkward and blurts out whatever comes to his mind at any given moment.

"Did Sawyer confide in you about things going on in his life?" Detective Locke asks. He's been asking the same thing for the past hour, just in slightly different ways—*Do you and Sawyer tell each other your secrets? Has anyone ever told you anything and asked you not to tell?*—like he expects to trip up Reese eventually.

Reese shakes his huge head back and forth. His head has been off-the-charts big since birth. His former pediatrician told me some kids have their adult-size heads by the time they're five, but Reese surpassed that years ago. His large head only makes his skinny body appear smaller. Emaciated—that's how his current pediatrician referred to him at his last well-child visit. He's as picky about food as he is people.

Sawyer spoiled me by being a perfect baby because I assumed his good nature was about me being a good mother.

And then I had Reese.

He stubbornly refused to come into the world when it was time, and my labor had to be induced. Within hours, he tied my umbilical cord in knots, and my doctor performed an emergency cesarean section. He came out screaming and didn't stop wailing for the next two months. *Beauty and the Beast.* That's what I called them during those grueling days when I was at home with a baby and a toddler. Only to Paul. Never to them. Except now Beauty is gone. There's only Beast.

"Were you fighting with your brother before the incident?" Detective Locke asks.

"Yeah," Reese says like it's not a big deal.

Paul's head snaps up. He's only been half listening, since he knows as well as I do that this interview is only a formality to get out of the way and won't provide helpful information to the investigation. Reese's response surprises us both. Nobody has said anything about the boys fighting. It seems like pretty important information to mention, but that's Reese for you.

Detective Locke raises his eyebrows. "Can you tell me more about that?" Reese gives his classic noncommittal shrug, which came on the scene in fourth grade and hasn't left since. Detective Locke continues gazing at him until Reese's lack of response grows awkward.

"Reese, he wants you to tell him what you were fighting about," I say before it gets any more uncomfortable.

"Oh, me and Sawyer fight every day. Like every single. Day. Of. My. Life." He draws out each word for dramatic effect, finishing with a grin.

Paul laughs and squeezes Reese's shoulder. Reese beams from the attention. I've barely touched him since the funeral, and he's the type of kid who needs lots of physical affection. During the funeral, people kept commenting about how nice it must be to have him to hug when I miss Sawyer or how I must want to hold him tight and never let him go, but it's not that way at all. My thoughts horrify me. I'd never share them with anyone else.

Detective Locke smiles back. He seems to get Reese. He's one of the rare people who do. Probably because he was as awkward in high school as Reese. "What were you fighting about that day?"

Reese shifts his gaze to the floor and mumbles something underneath his breath.

"What?" Detective Locke probes, leaning forward.

Reese shifts his eyes to me, then quickly back down again before speaking. "He was mad because he got ripped off buying pills, and he wanted some of mine."

"What kind of pills did you have?"

"Adderall." Guilt clouds his expression.

Fear squeezes my chest. What was Reese doing with Adderall?

"And that's the kind of pills Sawyer wanted?"

Reese nods.

Paul interrupts, looking confused. "Adderall?"

"It's a stimulant medication prescribed for ADHD," Detective Locke explains as Paul's face pales.

I step out from behind the cameraman and into Reese's view. "What are you talking about?" Both hands go to my hips. "How could you not tell me something like that?"

"He drank all the time. You knew that, Mom."

There's no mistaking the judgment on Detective Locke's face when he turns to see my reaction.

"Drinking is one thing. Drugs are entirely different." I cringe at the hypocrisy.

Reese shrugs. "He liked to party too. I told him he should've come to me in the first place; then he never would've been ripped off. I don't treat my people that way."

This is unbelievable. What is Reese doing talking like he's some kind of drug dealer? I leap around the coffee table and grab him. "Did you give Sawyer drugs? Did you give him any?" I shake him, flinging him back and forth. "Tell me! Did you give Sawyer drugs?"

Paul jumps up and pushes me aside. "Don't say another word, Reese."

TEN

LINDSEY

"Wyatt?" Detective Locke asks, stretching the top of his body across the desk to get closer to him.

Andrew and I are in the same room as yesterday, except this time Wyatt sits between us. I place my hand on Wyatt's knee. At the beginning of the interview, Detective Locke went through a long list of rules for our behavior. He stressed the importance of not intervening in any manner, which included touching, but he quickly relaxed his rules when he saw Wyatt's anxiety and resistance. He hadn't wanted to come, but we'd told him he didn't have any choice. It might not have been the best idea to do the interview at the police station, but Sutton might have overheard something if we'd done it at home. We've been trying to keep her sheltered from all of this, but it's proving pretty impossible. We wait another torturous minute before Detective Locke tries again.

"I know this is difficult, but I'm going to need you to try and answer, okay?" he asks. "Had the boys been fighting in the days or weeks leading up to the accident?"

"Buddy." Andrew can't help himself; the uncomfortable silence is too much. "Jacob can't talk right now, so we need you to tell us anything you can think of that might be helpful, even if it means getting someone in trouble. It's okay to tell. Nobody is going to be mad at you."

"Of course not, honey." I reach over and give him a side hug. His body is rigid and stiff next to mine. I rub his shoulder, trying to help him relax. "Go ahead and tell the officer what you know," I say as if I know what he's going to say. Really, I'm as curious as Detective Locke.

Wyatt pulls away from me and crosses his arms on his chest. "They'd been fighting," he says reluctantly.

Detective Locke nods like he's not the least bit surprised by this information and flips through a pile of paperwork on his desk before pulling out one of the sheets and setting it on top of the others. He skims through it without looking up. "Things were a bit rough for you guys heading into nationals, huh?" he asks.

Wyatt nods. This is the first year he's made the soccer team. He's third string, but he doesn't care, because he's the only tenth grader on the team, and he gets to play with Jacob. Thoughts of Jacob and soccer immediately sober me. I make myself focus on their conversation, refusing to spiral down that hole.

"I spoke with your teammates yesterday, and they filled me in on what's been going on." Detective Locke gazes at him pointedly.

"They did?" He raises his eyebrows in genuine surprise.

What's Detective Locke talking about? Which teammates? Andrew's eyes are laser focused on Wyatt.

"It's like I told you when we got started, Wyatt; nobody is trying to hide anything. All we want to do is figure out what happened so that we can help everyone move through this." Detective Locke nods while he speaks as if he's agreeing with himself. "Everyone had noticed something going on between them. The other captain . . . what's his name?" He scratches his chin. "Josiah?" He peers at Wyatt, and he nods back at him. "Right. Josiah. Anyway, he told me he cornered the three of them in the locker room a week before the incident and told them to work out whatever was going on because it was negatively affecting the team.

He threatened to tell the coach and ask him to bench them for playoffs if they didn't. Whatever it was must've been pretty bad for him to be willing to risk nationals. Any idea what was going on?"

"Stupid stuff," Wyatt mumbles.

"They were always fighting about silly stuff. You know kids," I interject, losing hope that he knows anything about kids, since I finally tracked down someone who keeps in contact with him, and he's never been married or had kids.

Detective Locke never moves his eyes from Wyatt. He gives a slight shrug like what I've said hasn't fazed him. "I don't care if it's stupid. I'd like to hear it."

"Girls." His voice is barely audible.

"A girl? Many girls? Somebody's girlfriend?" There's a shift in his tone.

Wyatt shakes his head a few times in rapid succession. "I have no idea. All I know is it had to do with girls."

"And how do you know that?"

He shrugs. "Because that's what everyone said."

"Everyone being the team?"

He nods.

"But Jacob never told you that himself?"

He nods again.

"How about Sawyer or Caleb?"

He bursts out laughing, just like Andrew does when he's nervous. "I'm sorry." He takes a minute to compose himself. "Those guys told me less than Jacob did about what was going on in their lives."

Andrew cuts in. "The boys fought all the time. That's what happens when you grow up like siblings. It was only a matter of time before they got into it over a girl."

"Did you know they were fighting?" Detective Locke shifts his attention to Andrew.

49

Andrew blushes and nods. Detective Locke asked him the same question yesterday, and he said no. Panic bubbles in my chest. How could he have lied to a police officer?

I whip around to face him. "You knew they were fighting?"

He looks like he'd tuck his tail between his legs and hide underneath the desk like our dog does after he's been scolded if he could. And he should. How could he leave out something like that?

"Honestly, I didn't give it any thought until just now." He keeps his focus on Detective Locke. "Even when you asked me about it before." His face flushes with embarrassment. "I know you must think I'm an idiot, but I didn't lie on purpose. You asked if I'd noticed anything out of the ordinary, and their fighting didn't seem like it qualified because it was so normal for them. How many times have they fought over the years?" He turns to me for confirmation. Worry lines his face as his eyes search mine for understanding. "Please, I didn't intentionally lie. I wouldn't do that. You know me better than that, Lindsey."

All we've done since the accident is go over what could've happened that night. We find our way back to it even when we try to give it a rest. He didn't think to tell me they'd been fighting? But I can't stay mad at him. I don't have space for the anger. I need to get back to Jacob.

I turn my attention to Detective Locke, eager to get out of this room. Jacob's surgery went well this morning, but he usually struggles in the afternoon. "The boys fought all the time, so it's not surprising they were fighting that week too. I'm sure it was nothing, and that's why Andrew left it out. Can we move on?"

ELEVEN

DANI

I stare straight ahead in the back seat of my Uber so I don't get carsick. Normally, I would've hopped in the front, but my driver is sketchy looking, and I'm not taking any chances since I'm by myself. Bryan's already texted twice from the restaurant. Hopefully he'll be more forgiving than usual tonight since leaving the house takes longer than it did when the kids were little.

Caleb freaked out right as I was leaving. It was one of his inconsolable sobbing episodes that come out of nowhere. At least that's the way they seem to us. One minute he was on the couch flipping through trashy magazines with Luna, and the next minute he was crying in the way we've started calling his "somewhere-else cry." It's different from his other cries. This grief sends him somewhere, and it takes him a long time to get back. That's how Bryan explained it to Gillian and the hospital psychiatrists. He does a better job explaining his episodes than me.

Luna swooped in as he started pacing the living room, trying to save him before he disappeared. The episodes make him so agitated. He rubs his hands down his forearms while he walks, like he'd step out of his skin if he could. She walks beside him without touching him. I tried it once, and he came at me, so I keep my distance, but he allows it with her in the same way he allows her to give him his medicine without a fight.

It's been amazing watching her take care of him. I've seen glimpses of the Luna I didn't think I'd ever get back. We used to be so close. She was my best friend, even though you're not supposed to say that about your kids. I've never felt so betrayed as I did when she suddenly wanted nothing to do with me and everything I said was the most annoying thing in the world. Just because it's a normal part of being a teenager didn't make it any less heartbreaking, and she's further away from me than she's ever been.

But we've been caring for Caleb like we used to care for him when he was a baby. She was barely over two when he was born and just an itty-bitty thing herself, but she was determined to help me with everything. She didn't just want to be his big sister—she wanted to be his second mommy, and she told that to anyone who'd listen. It's been so nice having her around and not bristly.

"Right here!" I call out to the driver as he's about to miss the valet parking entrance. He jerks to the side, almost hitting the car pulling out behind us, and cusses at the driver underneath his breath even though he's the one at fault. I hop out as soon as he pulls to a stop. Definitely no tip.

I smooth down the front of my dress and tug the arms of my jean jacket down. Am I overdressed? Underdressed? It was impossible to get a good idea of the restaurant's dress code in any of the pictures. I hate when that happens. Bryan picked the latest hip and trendy place on Fairfield since we're having dinner with Ted, like we're still up on what's cool even though we rarely go out on this side of town anymore.

I push through the door into a dimly lit and heavily crowded room. It takes a minute for my eyes to adjust from the outside. Throngs of people push by me, most of them talking loudly. A circular bar stands as the room's centerpiece. Maybe it'll be better this way since I'll barely be able to hear Ted speak over the music. My phone vibrates again.

Upstairs. I see you.

I raise my eyes, noticing a second floor for the first time. Bryan smiles down at me from the balcony as Ted talks with the server. He's probably ordering another round of drinks. It's why I got a ride. Bryan drove here, but there's no way he'll be in any condition to drive home, although we'll pretend like he's going to all the way to the valet. We'll put on a good show—we always do—as he drives around the block, and then we'll switch spots. He barely got out of his last DUI. We're not taking another chance.

I've never met a drunk like Bryan. I have plenty of drunks in my family, but they act like drunks. Some of them are super sloppy and embarrassing, while others get emotional. We even have a few of the angry kind who look for a fight whenever they have more than two drinks. But nobody like Bryan.

Alcohol turns him into a special kind of monster—a perfectly articulate and well-poised monster. He doesn't slur his words or stumble over his sentences. He walks straight and appears aware of himself and his surroundings. You'd never guess he was drunk. It's why they'll give him his keys tonight, because they won't see the darkness that's taken over his insides.

I smile and wave back before moving through the crowd as I scan the room for stairs. They're all the way on the other side of the restaurant, so I don't bother using the restroom before hurrying to join them, since Bryan's patience has reached its limit. They both stand when they see me approach, and I hand my purse to Bryan as Ted leans in to greet each cheek with a kiss. Bryan slips his arm around my waist.

"Glad you could finally join us, sweetheart," he says. There's a barely detectable edge to his tone.

"Me too. I'm so sorry," I say, turning to look at Ted before shifting my attention back to him. "Caleb had one of his fits before I left, so I couldn't leave until Luna had things under control. I—"

"She sure has grown up this past year," Ted interrupts with a disgusting smirk on his face as we slide into our seats.

I flash him an annoyed glance. "Anyway, like I was saying, we probably won't be able to stay long because I don't want to leave her alone with him for too long when he's having a rough night."

A sharp pinch stings my upper thigh. My back straightens against the chair. What did I say? Did I insult him? Ted?

Bryan increases the pressure on my skin, twisting slightly. The first time he pinched me flashes through my mind, like it does every time he hurts me. I didn't stop him that night, and that's what you're supposed to do when your husband physically hurts you on purpose. You draw a line in the sand—put your foot down and say *never again; leave.* But I didn't do any of those things. I fixate on that night as if all it would take to fix our problem is to go back in time and make a different choice.

Caleb was only a few weeks old at the time, and my mom was staying with us to help me with him even though she only lives a few miles away. It was easier having her with me because I've never felt so clueless as I did during those early days with a colicky baby. Luna cried when she was a baby, but never the way Caleb did, and she slept like a champ, which didn't prepare me for the sleep deprivation that accompanies a difficult infant. The hormone surges only made things worse. My mom's presence irritated Bryan, but I needed her close to keep me from losing it.

I was in the middle of feeding Caleb when he had a huge diaper blowout on my lap that soiled us both. Bryan scooped him from me, and I hurried to the bathroom in our master bedroom to clean up while he cleaned Caleb. When I got back to the living room, my mom pointed out that Bryan had snapped Caleb's onesie wrong. He'd put both legs through the same hole, and they looked like two fat sausages squeezed together. My mom and I burst out laughing. As soon as she left the room, Bryan scooted down the couch to sit beside me and pinched my arm as hard as he's pinching me now.

"Don't you ever embarrass me like that again," he hissed. He never yells. He always speaks in an even, calculated tone, which makes it worse, colder.

"Stop it." I jerked away, but he didn't let go. "You're hurting me," I cried.

"Oh, please," he scoffed and slowly released his hold on my arm.

Tears filled my eyes. "I can't believe you just did that. Why would you do that?"

"Quit acting like I punched you in the face," he said.

My insides twisted at his response, but I started feeling overdramatic when he immediately began talking about the golf scores without missing a beat like nothing had happened. I'd almost forgotten about it until I noticed the purple prints on my triceps the next morning in the shower. I thought about saying something—telling him that he'd left a mark, really hurt me—but I didn't. I assured myself he hadn't done it on purpose and it'd never happen again. Besides, he was right. I've always been a bit on the dramatic side.

But it's never stopped.

I realize my mistake and smile at Ted. "I'm sorry for giving you a nasty look. I don't know what I was thinking. It's been a rough day, and I'm exhausted."

"Oh, please," Ted says, waving me off. "Don't even worry about it."

Bryan's pressure on my skin releases.

TWELVE
KENDRA

I shut the sliding glass door behind Paul and me. Reese is upstairs playing video games again. He's spent so much time playing them that his brain is going to turn to mush, but I don't know what else he's supposed to do. What are any of us supposed to do?

We haven't spoken about the interview since Detective Locke and his crew left. Reese stayed by our side the rest of the day, obviously waiting for us to tear into him about the Adderall so he'd find out what type of punishment was coming his way, like he does every time he gets in trouble. This is about so much more than getting into trouble. Why can't he see that?

I don't even know where to begin with the Adderall. My head is spinning with all my questions. Was he really selling drugs at school? Where does he get them? God, I hope he's not taking them too. But what if he is? What will I do then? I'm going to have to tell Paul what I did. He's going to be so angry.

He interrupts my worrying. "God, I need a cigarette," he says as he paces the concrete patio in front of the pool. He hasn't smoked since college, and even then, it was only when he was drinking. I always hated the smell and the way it clung to his clothes afterward.

I've never smoked, but I want one too. I can't take this. "What are we going to do? What happens if Reese gave Sawyer or one of them drugs? What if they were all messed up? Does that make Reese responsible? Will they come after him? Could he end up getting in trouble for this? Why—"

He presses his fingers up to my lips. "Stop. Just stop."

"Stop?" I push his fingers off my face. "I'm not stopping. What if I lose both my boys in a matter of weeks?"

"You're not going to lose both the boys." Paul shakes his head. "You need to calm down."

"Really? Our kids are liars, and apparently, Reese is the high school drug dealer. But you want me to calm down?" I glare at him.

"At least keep your voice down so he doesn't hear you." He points to the house like I need to be reminded Reese is inside. He finally told Reese to do something by himself after dinner and said we'd have a discussion about his drug dealing tomorrow.

"I want him to hear me. Every word of this. What if he gave them drugs that night? That changes everything. Who knows where they get any of it, and they could've gotten bad stuff that made them completely lose their minds."

He shakes his head. "You can't put that on Reese."

"Who else should I put it on if he's the one who gave them the drugs?" Kids pop pills all the time, and every high school has its drug dealer. I just never expected him to be my fourteen-year-old kid.

"First of all, you need to slow your roll because we don't even know if he gave them anything. That's what we need to find out before we go any further. If he didn't, then we're wasting our time and energy spiraling down this path." He runs his hands through his hair. "I still can't believe this is happening."

"God, how could he have been such an idiot?" I snap. Paul recoils, and it takes me a minute to realize he thinks I'm talking about Sawyer. "I mean Reese. How could Reese be so stupid?"

57

The look of horror doesn't leave his face. We don't call our children names. Not even when we're mad at them. But we did everything right—spoke to them in affirming language, followed the best parenting advice, sent them to the greatest schools, surrounded them with positive things—and look where it got us.

"He doesn't need to hear you say that," Paul says underneath his breath.

"Obviously."

Paul holds up his hands in a peaceful gesture. "I don't want to fight. Can we just talk about this and figure out what we're going to do?"

"I don't want to fight either." My voice fills with emotion. The fight in me is gone that quickly and replaced with tears. I step around him and plop into one of the chairs lining the outdoor dining table, wrapping one of the blankets around my knees. Paul hesitates for a moment before walking over to the bar and opening the wine fridge underneath. He pulls out the bottle of cabernet we opened last night and takes a huge pull like he's drinking hard liquor before pouring it into one of the dirty glasses on the table. He hands it to me, and I take it, grateful to have something to hold in my trembling hands.

"What are we going to do if it turns out Reese gave them drugs?" He doesn't wait for me to answer before continuing. "I feel like such a hypocrite because of how I went after Bryan about getting a lawyer, but I don't think it's smart to go any further with this on our own. I mean, we're talking about our kid's life here, and we're in way over our heads."

"Do you think they're looking at Reese like he's some kind of suspect?"

He shrugs and takes another drink. "They're obviously looking at him as more than just a source of information. Today went nothing like Detective Locke presented it as yesterday—that was clearly a police interview, and he knew way more than he let on. Detective Locke isn't as naive as he comes across. He knew exactly what he was trying to get at in that room today . . ." He pauses a moment and stares up at the sky. The moon's half-hidden behind the clouds.

"What do you mean?" Thoughts are getting fuzzy and starting to blur around the edges like they do after I take my pill at night. I hate those pills, but I hate the attacks more.

Paul narrows his eyes. "Detective Locke's keeping secrets and knows way more than he's telling us."

"You sound paranoid," I mumble.

"Maybe we should be paranoid."

THIRTEEN

DANI

I shift in my seat. Bryan places his hand on me like he's done every time I've moved an inch or done anything hinting at wanting to leave the restaurant. I gave up on getting home early an hour ago. At least my phone's been silent. Luna would've texted me if she needed my help with Caleb. The minutes are crawling. We've eaten our way through every painful course, and the men have mostly ignored me. Suits me fine. It's easier to stay out of trouble that way.

"What did you think about the interview today, Dani?" Ted asks halfway through his huge piece of chocolate cake. It hasn't occurred to him to ask if I might like a bite. Not that I would take one, but most men would offer.

I wouldn't describe what happened between Caleb and Detective Locke as an interview. Ted had insisted we do it at the police station, so we all traipsed into the interview room that grows more familiar each day. We never got to the part where we each take our seats, because as soon as Detective Locke said hello to Caleb, he collapsed into hysterics, and it wasn't long before he moved into one of his episodes. Nothing we did brought him back. Ted didn't even need to step in and make Detective Locke stop his questioning like I'd spent all last night worrying about, because seeing Caleb's wrecked state was enough to get him to reschedule Luna's interview too.

"I just wish someone could help Caleb talk." He holds the key to what happened, but it's buried within, and Gillian says he might not ever unlock the memories even if he starts speaking. Bryan thinks Gillian is too soft and full of crap, even though she's got a doctorate in psychology, but he says the same thing about our therapist. He just doesn't like therapists.

"Did you get him to settle down once you were home?" Ted asks.

I nod. I've never seen Ted shaken up before, but Caleb disturbed him today. I had a similar reaction when I saw Caleb in the emergency room after the incident. He sat on the edge of the hospital bed wearing the same ripped jeans he'd had on when he'd left for school that morning. His legs hung over the bed, dangling above the dirty linoleum floor, while his arms hugged his stomach like he was in pain. Bryan and I stalled in the doorway. Everything moved in slow motion.

"Caleb?" I whispered. I hadn't meant to speak so low or move so slowly, but something about the way he held himself sent a wave of fear down my spine. He turned toward us and cocked his head to the side. Blood painted his face in freckles.

But it was his eyes that stopped us in our tracks. They were wide open, frozen in a moment of terror, but there was nothing behind them. It was like looking into a hollowed-out tunnel. Gillian and Caleb's team of mental health professionals diagnosed him with acute stress disorder and assured us that it would go away over time, but it's been nineteen days, and it hasn't gone anywhere.

His eyes are still too glassy and wide. They look right through us without seeing or connecting, like he's run away somewhere outside himself and we have to find him and bring him back. But how do we do that when we can't even get him to come out of his room?

He stays in the same position when he's in there—curled into a ball with his red comforter pulled over his head. The food I bring him on breakfast trays sits untouched on the floor next to his bed. Bryan and I take turns coaxing him out, but our efforts are useless. He refuses to move. Won't speak.

"I've never seen someone that scared." Ted interrupts my thoughts. "What do you think he's so afraid of?"

His question catches me off guard. Isn't it obvious? He saw two of his best friends get shot. He was probably involved in whatever they were doing with the gun beforehand. One bled to death in front of him, and the other probably won't ever wake up. But I can't say any of that without angering Bryan. "Their goofing around killed someone," I say evenly, making sure the sarcastic tone in my head doesn't bleed into my words.

"You're convinced it was goofing around?" he asks.

Bryan's grip tightens on my knee.

"Of course." I nod my head and force myself to maintain eye contact with him. "It was just boys being boys." Disgust churns my insides at what I've said. It's no wonder Luna hates me.

"Let's say you're right and Caleb's too freaked out by what he saw to speak. But here's the deal." He pauses to shovel another bite of cake into his mouth. "Your kid didn't look traumatized in there. He looked terrified. Why's he still so afraid?"

Bryan leans forward in his chair. "What are you getting at?"

"I mean, nobody else was in that house." He shrugs like what he's implying isn't a big deal. "That's the one thing we know for sure."

The police reviewed all the video footage from the security cameras at our front door and around the exterior of our house. Bryan built our home security system himself with one of the local alarm companies, and the police were impressed by the level of sophistication. After the boys had stumbled in the door at shortly after ten, nobody had entered or exited until Caleb had fled out the back-patio door at 11:37.

Ted continues. "And the boys' fingerprints were the only ones on the gun besides Bryan's."

"Of course my fingerprints were on the gun," Bryan interrupts like he's insulted his name has been brought into the equation. "It's my gun. I take it out to the range all the time."

The police have a training camp nestled between two of the mountain ridges behind our house, and one of his favorite Saturday activities is to go out there and shoot a couple of magazines. I figured the police made similar assumptions.

"It's too bad you didn't call me immediately for advice, because I would've told you not to admit anything about the gun, but it's too late now." Ted shoots me an icy glare because I was the one who originally told Detective Locke that it was our gun.

It's not like they wouldn't have found out anyway. The gun is registered to Bryan, and they found it on the rug in our family room. I grip the edge of the table to keep myself in check and the unwanted images at bay.

Ted pushes his plate aside and lays his hands out on the table like he's spreading out his poker hand. "Listen, I don't want to have to do this to the two of you, but I'm just going to come right out and ask—is there any chance that Caleb's afraid of himself?"

Is there any chance my son is a murderer? That's what he's really asking us.

Bryan leans across the table at eye level and peers into his face. "There's no way Caleb did this."

FOURTEEN
LINDSEY

Andrew rubs his face like he does when he has a sinus infection—starts at the nose, works all the way up the forehead and back down, and then starts the process all over again. He doesn't handle stress well. Never has. His skin has been red and inflamed with stress-induced psoriasis since the night at the hospital. This is more than he's ever had to deal with. Who am I kidding? It's more than any one of us has dealt with. Things like this don't happen in Norchester.

He leans against the wall on the other side of the hallway in front of Jacob's room. We stepped outside so Sutton could have some alone time with him and we could talk privately. She's reading him the children's version of the second Harry Potter book. She loves anything related to Harry Potter, but Jacob has no interest in any of it unless it's one of the rides at Universal Studios. We've been listening to her read for almost twenty minutes in the same bubbly voice she uses when she reads to her stuffed animals.

"This is awful. What was I thinking? How could I have been so stupid? I lost all my credibility today." He works his jaw while he speaks. "Detective Locke is going to look at me totally different now—"

I cut him off. "No, he's not."

"C'mon, Lindsey. You know it's true no matter what he says. That's how it goes when somebody lies to you. You never look at them in the same way again." He's on the verge of panicking like he did when we came out of the police station this afternoon. It took me over ten minutes to calm him down. I've never seen him get so worked up.

I walk over to his side of the hallway and pull him off the wall. "Come on; let's walk."

He reluctantly follows me down the empty corridor. The other patients are tucked in for the night, and the nurses have dimmed the hallway lights. They never did that in the ICU, but I like it. Makes me feel like there's a difference between day and night rather than all of them blending into one continuous blur.

"You didn't screw anything up. We're not criminals. Neither is Jacob. Nobody's done anything wrong here," I say with more confidence than I feel.

"Really?" he scoffs, raising his eyebrows at me. "That might work with the kids, but it doesn't work with me. Maybe you should've listened to me the first time I said we should get a lawyer," he snaps before quickly changing his tone. "Sorry."

A frustrated sigh escapes me. "Don't be sorry. You should be pissed." I crave a good fight. Nobody understands that. My girlfriends rave about his kindheartedness. His patients at the rheumatology practice love him. They constantly gush about his listening skills and how he must be such a wonderful husband since he's always so kind and thoughtful during their appointments. But I want him to yell and scream at me. His emotional control infuriates me. "I totally screwed up. We should've called a lawyer as soon as we found out."

I wasn't thinking straight. None of us were. How could we after our world had just been flipped upside down, and we'd found ourselves thrust into a nightmare without any warning?

"We've gone as far as we can go in this alone. We're getting a lawyer tonight," he says and pulls out his phone.

"What are you doing?"

"Finding us a lawyer."

There are people who have lawyers at their beck and call, but we're not those kinds of people. Our lives are entirely too boring for that. "It's nine o'clock on a Thursday night, so maybe now isn't the best time to start making calls? Do we really want to put our son's life in the hands of someone based solely on the criteria that they happened to return our phone call?"

"Good point." He slides his phone back into his pocket. "I'll wait until morning."

We reach the end of the hallway and circle back toward Jacob's room instead of making the turn in the other direction. Sutton would stay all night if she could, but Wyatt needs to get home and study for his algebra test tomorrow, and he's waiting at the coffee shop in the reception area. That's as far as he'll step foot in the hospital, and most of the time he waits in the car, but he was starving when we got here, and the coffee shop food is better than the cafeteria's.

"How'd you know the boys were fighting? Did Jacob tell you?" We haven't been alone all day, and it's been driving me nuts. I work hard at not being jealous when Jacob tells Andrew things and not me, but sometimes I can't help myself, especially if it's something important.

"Remember when he shattered his phone screen last month?"

I was the one who took him to the mall and got the screen fixed. Two hundred dollars. It was his second one in a month, and it never occurred to me to ask how it had broken. I assumed he'd broken it like he'd broken the last one—stepping on it in his backpack.

"It broke because he threw it on the kitchen floor after he got a text from Sawyer. He was livid, and when I asked him what it was about, he said, 'Sawyer is being a stupid fuck.'"

"Really? He said that?" I'm not ignorant enough to think my kids don't swear, but they don't swear like that in front of us. Ever.

"He did. I asked what they were fighting about, and he gave me one of those you're-so-stupid-and-you'd-never-understand-anyway looks, so I left it alone." Sadness clouds his expression. "I shouldn't have left it alone."

"That's all?" I don't have time for him to get emotional. I need the full story before we get back to Jacob's room. We can't bring any of this negativity in there with us.

"There was another incident about a week or so later. I scooped the three of them up after practice, and nobody said a word the entire ride home. Again, nothing huge, but I noted it at the time because I couldn't remember when they'd ever been quiet that long."

That's definitely strange. The boys were never quiet when they were together. Caleb made sure of that because he couldn't stand silence. Dani used to say he even talked in his sleep. It's one of the reasons his silence is so disturbing.

"Did you ask him about it afterward when they weren't around?"

"Of course."

"And?"

"He shrugged it off like it was nothing."

Typical Jacob. Getting him to talk about his emotions was tough. Really wish I'd known something was going on. I might've been able to get it out of him, since I can pull things out of him that others can't. It's one of my gifts.

Sutton's voice calls out to us. "Mom!" She doesn't wait for us to respond before she calls out a second time. It's only a matter of seconds before she comes looking for us. We speed up, hurrying to tend to her, and pause the conversation until tomorrow.

FIFTEEN

DANI

My feet pound against the pavement. I don't care how Lindsey tries to play this off—it's weird. This morning Kendra group-texted us to see if we could come over tonight. We both said yes, but when I wrote Lindsey earlier to see what time she'd be by my house—thinking we'd walk over to Kendra's together—she didn't respond. I poked her around four, and still nothing. I waited for as long as I could before heading over without her. My phone vibrated with her text as soon as I reached the end of my driveway.

Already here. See you soon. Xo

How long has she been there? Is that why she didn't answer my text? I glance at my watch: 6:10. She's had over thirty minutes alone with Kendra. It's one of those weird moments when the fact that Lindsey and Kendra were best friends first comes into play, creating all kinds of weird tension and jealousy—their weddings, my wedding, birthdays, special vacations when we were kids. It's so silly that fourth-grade girl drama would follow us into middle age, but it's here, rearing its ugly head.

I pick up my pace, rounding the corner and hurrying down Kendra's cul-de-sac. The Madisons haven't finished their landscaping.

The front yard is covered in piles of dirt and gravel, which has been driving Kendra nuts for months. She swears it brings down the property value of every house on the block, which I thought only mattered if you were selling your house, but I guess not, and she'd know since she and Paul own the top real estate firm in our area. Her house looms at the end—the largest one on the block. Unlike the Madisons', her landscaping is a mosaic of bold colors meticulously maintained. Solar garden lights dot the sidewalk, illuminating the path to the front door. Paul opens the door to greet me before I knock.

Grief can't hide his stunning looks. The scruff he wore on his face a few days ago has grown into a dark beard, and I've always liked him best unshaven, but Kendra is obsessed with smooth skin, so he rarely grows it out. His perfectly tanned skin matches his light-brown hair, which is so dirty I can see specks of dandruff in it, but even that doesn't detract from his model features.

I search for words. None feel right. I clear my throat and come up with, "Hi, how are you?"

"Hi, Danielle," he says, using my childhood name. The one that followed me all the way into seventh grade, when I started referring to myself as Dani in an attempt to be cool, since that was the most important thing in our world at the time. He started playing sports then for the same reason. We got what we wanted, but our relationship was never the same.

Bryan knows we were friends in elementary school. It'd be impossible not to have been, since our class size was so small, but he has no idea that Paul was the one who told our first-grade class he'd spilled his orange juice on the floor so nobody would know that I'd accidentally peed my pants, or that he kicked Jeff Williams in the shins after he pulled the ribbon out of my ponytail on Valentine's Day. Kendra asked me if it was okay to go out with him when he asked her out for the first time in tenth grade, and I said yes without a second thought because I never thought they'd last past a few dates, since Kendra was so boy crazy. They split up for a while after graduation, but it didn't last long, and they've been together ever since.

He points to the massive staircase behind him. I spent hours perusing Pinterest boards and interior design blogs with Kendra while she tried to decide on the perfect railing. "They're upstairs in the master bedroom."

"Thanks," I say, realizing I haven't moved through the doorway yet. I duck my head in embarrassment and mumble something about wanting to get caught up on what I've missed before hurrying up the stairs and down the hallway to Kendra's bedroom. I knock before opening the door and going in.

Lindsey and Kendra are huddled on the four-poster bed in the center of the room. Balled-up tissues surround them. Long, flowing drapes hang from the windows lining the east side. Their pale-blue design emphasizes the twelve-foot ceilings. A plush rug in a slightly different shade of blue circles the space between the door and the bed. Back when the rug graced the smaller bedroom in the Mitchells' house on Windsor Street, Luna used to run upstairs whenever we came over and throw herself on the rug. She'd wiggle around on it like dogs do when they're trying to scratch their backs.

I sit down on the bed next to them, and we come together in a group hug. Our hands twist and turn, rubbing and soothing each other. In junior high, our teachers called our parents in for a conference and said we were too close, that we touched too much, spent too much time doing each other's hair. The school guidance counselor said it wasn't healthy for us to be that dependent on each other, but what did she know? We've carried each other through every important milestone in our lives, from buying our first training bras to buying our first houses. This one is big, though. Much larger than anything else we've dealt with, and the weight of it descends on the bed, filling the room with darkness despite the gleaming, sunlit walls.

The Best of Friends

"I can't take this. I really can't." Emotions coat Kendra's voice, making it thick. My hands meet Lindsey's on her back. "I'm not going to make it."

"Shh... shh... it's okay. Yes, you are," I say.

Lindsey quickly follows with, "Somehow, you'll find a way. You're stronger than you know, hon."

"But I'm not, you guys. I'm really not." Tears flow unchecked. Her face is wasted with grief and devastation as she struggles to continue. "It's like I'm a shadow getting sucked into darkness, but I don't care. That's the worst part. I want to disappear. Reese needs me. He's in all kinds of trouble, and I'm just like, *Oh well*. I'm a terrible mother."

"Well, if you're a terrible mother, then I don't know what I am," I interrupt before she can spiral any further downward.

"Don't even try." She shakes her head, intent on destroying herself. She points her finger at Lindsey and me. "I know you guys think I'm the worst mother."

"No, we don't." Lindsey immediately jumps to her defense.

"You're only saying that because you're my best friend."

"That's not true," Lindsey and I say together.

"Please, you guys, I know all the things people say about me and how much I work."

They've been awful to Kendra in the local press about her devotion to her career as if her strong work ethic is somehow related to the accident. There's no mention of Paul as a workaholic parent like they've labeled her, even though they work similar hours and both have devoted equal time to building a thriving real estate company.

"When Luna left home, she said that she would spend the rest of her life making sure she never turned into me." I blurt it out without thinking. "She said she had no respect for me because I did nothing but cater to Bryan's and their needs like my needs didn't matter. She was upset that she didn't have a role model to look up to when she was growing up because I didn't have an identity outside of my family."

They shift their attention to me. I've never told them that. I haven't said it out loud to anyone. But just because I haven't said it out loud doesn't mean I haven't thought about what she said every day since or cried about it in the shower when nobody could hear me. Luna doesn't know the girl I used to be—the one who went to college and was on target to graduate summa cum laude until she got pregnant her senior year—even though she's seen the pictures. Sometimes my life before Bryan seems like a made-up story to me too. I always intended to go back and finish my degree, but fear stole my choices one at a time until I didn't have any left.

"The thing about it is that she wasn't even mad. She's said plenty of nasty things when we were fighting. Honestly, she's probably said worse, but we weren't in a fight or an argument. Nothing like that was going on. She said it in the most calm and calculated way, like she'd thought about it and decided being me was the worst thing she could possibly be. You want to know the worst part?" I don't wait for either of them to respond before continuing. "She never apologized or said she didn't mean it."

"Really?" Kendra asks. My confession is enough to pull her out of herself for a second.

"Yep. So you're not the only one who's not winning any mother-of-the-year awards." I smile for her benefit, not because anything about my disclosure makes me happy.

Kendra grabs a tissue and blows her nose hard. "God, this sucks." She points to the walls of her beautiful master bedroom. "I'm barely in this room. I hung out in here today because you guys were coming over, but I haven't slept in this bed since Sawyer died. I spend all my time in his room digging through his stuff for anything I missed. How did none of us notice anything strange? There had to be something."

The same question tortures me, especially since I was the last one of us to see them. "I've obsessively gone over every detail of that night for any clue about what they were up to, but I was so preoccupied with dinner that I barely paid them any attention. Bryan was trying to land a new client, and he needed me to impress his wife. You know how that goes." It's my least favorite part of his job, and I spent all afternoon trying on outfits and practicing things to say to her. I'm not even sure Sawyer was there when I left. If he was, I didn't see him. I remember seeing Jacob briefly as he passed through the kitchen, but I'm not sure we spoke. Our kids move freely through our houses. It's the best part of living so close.

"I asked Jacob about their plans before he left for Dani's, and he didn't say anything about a gun, so I'm really confused about how things went so wrong in such a short time," Lindsey adds matter-of-factly.

I shoot her an annoyed glance. I can't help myself. Like Jacob would say, *Oh yes, Mom, we're planning on messing around with Caleb's gun,* when she asked him about his plans for the night. She prides herself on how well she communicates with her kids. It wasn't always that way, but she changed after she had Sutton, and it became all about conscious parenting. She tells anyone who will listen that her kids can come to her about anything because she talks to them like they're real people with their own thoughts and ideas rather than some weird extensions of her and Andrew. It's a subtle dig targeted at the rest of us, hinting that we treat our kids that way, but whatever. She's always thought she was the best parent—she's not. She's just got easy kids. I tuck away my irritation. This is about Kendra and our boys.

Kendra grips Lindsey's wrist and speaks in a fevered pitch. "Do you think he knew he was dying? He was dead on arrival. Did you know that? There was nothing the paramedics could do for him. All their attention went to saving Jacob."

I hear Lindsey's sharp intake of breath at the mention of Jacob's condition. She's as silent about him as Kendra is vocal about Sawyer. I can't imagine she isn't torn up inside, but I haven't seen her break down once. Not even while we waited in agony to find out which one of our boys had been shot or during Jacob's twelve-hour brain surgery.

"Does that mean it was quick and he didn't suffer? Or was it agonizing and slow?" A strangled sob escapes Kendra's lips, and it takes her a few minutes to compose herself. "I can't stop thinking about it. I play different scenarios over and over again in my head. There's no relief. Not even sleep, because it's all I dream about too. I can't live like this. I have to know what his final moments were like." She glances at Lindsey, who gives her an approving nod. "I told Lindsey I want to talk to Caleb and see if I can get him to talk. How's he supposed to feel safe when the person asking him all the questions has a gun strapped to his belt?"

There have been a lot more people who've tried getting Caleb to talk besides the police and Detective Locke. Me, for one, not to mention Gillian, who went to school for ten years to work with traumatized kids, and if Caleb hasn't spoken to us, I'm pretty sure he's not going to speak to her, but I give her a sympathetic nod. "That's one of the reasons they called in a specialized trauma therapist to work with him. Remember Gillian?" I briefly mentioned her before, but I don't expect Kendra to remember with everything she's going through. "Detective Locke is setting up an interview with her soon. Hopefully, they'll get somewhere."

Kendra shakes her head. "Yeah, but he still doesn't know her. How do they expect him to talk to a total stranger?" She wipes her face on her sleeve. "I think he might talk to me because it's not going to be so weird for him, and it would just be the two of us."

"You want to talk to him alone?" I assumed I'd be there. What will she do if he gets upset? There's no way she can comfort him. Besides, I can't remember the last time she talked to Caleb alone. Probably not since elementary school. She nods like it hasn't occurred to her that it'd be any other way. "I'm not sure about that." Getting Bryan to allow Caleb to speak with Kendra with me there would be a stretch. He's definitely not going to let him do it alone.

"Oh, honey, I'm so sorry you're going through this." Lindsey leans in and kisses Kendra on her left cheek. "I wish Jacob could be more helpful. If the shoe was on the other foot, I'd be more than happy to let you talk to him. You know I'd do anything for you."

That's easy for her to say when there's not any possibility he can. They both turn to look at me expectantly.

"Dani, can I talk to Caleb?" Kendra's eyes plead with mine.

"I mean . . . it's just . . . I'd—"

"Please?" There's so much desperation in Kendra's voice that the only answer I can give is yes.

SIXTEEN
KENDRA

"I can't believe she agreed," Paul says. He knows how hard it is for Dani to make decisions by herself. I've complained about it for years. I called him upstairs after Lindsey and Dani left and quickly filled him in on everything.

"She's one of my best friends. What kind of a horrible person would she be if she said no?"

"I think I should be there too," he says.

I shake my head. "No way."

He's instantly insulted. "I want to know what happened that night just as badly as you do."

"I know that," I say, not bothering to keep the irritation out of my voice. "But he's more likely to talk if it's only me, and that's the most important thing here, remember? Getting him to talk?"

Why is he bothering to argue with me? He doesn't have that kind of relationship with Sawyer or any of his friends. He never has. It's the recurring joke in our house that Sawyer and his friends go mute in serious conversations with him unless a ball is involved. Then you can't shut them up, but beyond that, they mostly just sit there.

Sawyer and his friends talk to me, though. They've spent most of their time here since the end of middle school, and I wouldn't have it

The Best of Friends

any other way. Lindsey and Dani think it's because Paul and I are never around—even though they'd never say it to my face—but that's not the reason. Our house is the most comfortable. I don't hover around the boys like their lives are teetering on some precarious edge, and for some reason, they come to me when they want to talk without me having to do anything, but I'd never tell Lindsey and Dani that. Especially not Lindsey. She wants everyone to see her as being the best mom, and I conceded the title a long time ago because it's the only thing she's got. I'm not being mean. It just is what it is. She's never worked, and she turned into someone I barely recognized after she had Sutton. She kept a journal of Sutton's poop for a week because she was afraid she wasn't getting a proper diet and brought it to her pediatrician to analyze. I'm still waiting for her to come back. Sometimes I worry she never will.

Paul lets out a deep breath, conceding my point even though he doesn't want to. "Are you nervous about being around him? Remember the funeral?"

He doesn't need to remind me. It was one of my worst moments that day. I hadn't seen Caleb since the accident because it'd only been two days since he'd been discharged. I had no idea I'd react the way I did when I saw him for the first time, but all I wanted to do was shake him and ask if he'd killed my son, demand he tell me what had happened. Paul spotted the fire in my eyes immediately and pulled me aside before I could do anything. I broke into hysterics, and it took him over ten minutes to get me calmed down again.

"I'll be fine," I say with determination. I have to be if I want him to talk, so I can't push him away. He has to think I'm on his side. Same as Dani. She and Lindsey are equally invested in calling the whole thing an accident, but there's no denying the possibility Caleb shot them both. How did he walk away from something so horrific without a single scratch? Nobody can explain that or anything else that's happening with him. Dani keeps going on and on about how his therapist says he's struggling with survivor's guilt on top of everything else, but what if it's just plain old guilt?

"How do you plan on getting Caleb to talk?" Paul asks.

"The same way I always do."

"And that is?"

He's never around during any of my serious talks with the boys. They clam up if he comes in the room. Our talks usually happen in the kitchen while he's asleep. That's how it is with all the boys. I stumbled into my role as adult confidant by accident when I discovered the secret late-night world of teenagers—they binge eat in the middle of the night just like me. Busting me in front of the refrigerator with my mouth full of whipped cream or my hands buried in a bag of Cheetos was almost as shocking as finding me smoking crack. Discovering my secret gave them the freedom to share theirs. There's something to be said about the intimacies that are shared over a pint of Ben & Jerry's ice cream at three a.m.

I sit up and reach for the water on my nightstand. It feels strange being in my bed. Paul's been on me about moving back into our bedroom, but I'm not ready. "I'm going to ask him how Sawyer died, and then I'm going to wait for him to answer." I take a sip. I've been in this room too long. I want to get back to his. "I'll sit in silence for as long as I have to until he talks."

SEVENTEEN
DANI

Bryan's lips curl into a sneer as he grips my arm. "How could you be so stupid?"

I fight the urge to pull away, raising my eyes to meet his instead. I try to keep the trembling out of my voice as I speak. "You should've seen her. She was wrecked. Completely destroyed . . ."

You would have to be cruel to say no to her. That's the last part of my sentence. The one I want to say but hold inside like all the other secrets I keep.

"Caleb isn't meeting with Kendra. He's not talking to her or anyone else." He increases the pressure on my skin, twisting slightly. There were four empty beer cans in the garbage when I got home. A bottle of vodka is probably hidden somewhere in this room. His breath smells like old cottage cheese.

"Please, stop. You're hurting me," I cry.

He snorts. "Oh, please." He slowly releases his hold. "You're so attention starved."

"I'm sorry." The apology rolls easily off my tongue, even though it couldn't be further from the truth. Years of apologizing so ingrained in me that I can't stop even when I want to.

"You should be." He points to my mascara-smeared face. "Clean yourself up. You look disgusting."

I sit on the edge of the bed, too scared to move. *Just let it be over.*

He walks to his closet and grabs his leather coat. "Oh, by the way, I'm going out tonight." He slips on his coat and struts back to me. I haven't moved from my spot on the bed. He flicks my chin up with his fingers so his eyes meet mine, then peers at me within inches from my face. "And you need to tell Kendra it's not happening with Caleb by the time I get home."

I nod. A sinking sensation in the pit of my stomach. Nerves frayed, on edge. I'm sick of feeling like this. *Please go.*

"I mean it. By the time I'm home," he says as he turns to leave, then shuts the door behind him.

Every sense is attuned to his movements as he passes through the house. Footsteps in the kitchen. Toilet flushing in the guest bathroom. The sound of his car in the driveway, and loud rock music filling the neighborhood. The roar of his Benz down the street like he's racing.

And then he's gone.

I sink into the bed, and relief floods my body.

"So you still let him talk to you that way?" Luna's voice startles me from the doorway like a scene out of her childhood. How many times did I wonder how long she'd been standing there and what she'd heard?

"Please, Luna. I can't do this with you right now. I can't." I turn my back and swallow my tears. She can't see me cry. She already thinks I'm pathetic.

"Are you okay?" There's a hint of kindness in her voice that hasn't been there in years, and it almost makes me break down.

"I'm fine. Just trying to decide what I'm going to do about Caleb's appointment." I get up and start busying myself with grabbing the dirty clothes from the floor and tossing them into the hamper so I don't have to see the pity in her eyes.

EIGHTEEN
LINDSEY

I tap my foot, anxiously waiting for Jacob to come out of his MRI. It's been almost two hours since they wheeled him away. I hope that doesn't mean something's wrong. I'm not a fan of this rehabilitation unit. The doctors treat him like he's one of the other stroke patients, and I've complained numerous times about the nurses' lack of urgency, but nothing has changed. He's on the wait list for a bed to open up at Prairie Meadows, a long-term residential facility for traumatic-brain-injured patients, and I'm hoping they'll treat him better there.

Andrew's been working on finding a lawyer all morning. Turns out it wasn't as easy as making a few phone calls, and his anxiety pulsed through the phone every time we talked. I'm glad he skipped his morning visit. It's not good for Jacob to be around all that negativity. But now I haven't heard anything from him since eleven, and he was supposed to pick Sutton up from a playdate at noon. She and Wyatt go back to school full-time on Monday. It'll be good for her to hang out with her friends and act like a normal kid again. Same with Wyatt.

Feels like all I've done all day is wait, since I'm waiting to hear from Kendra too. I can't believe Dani agreed to let her talk to Caleb. I could tell Kendra was surprised, too, when she texted me about it last night. Dani was supposed to go over there with Caleb at nine, and it's almost noon. There's no way they met for that long. Kendra FaceTimed me this morning while she was scurrying around her house like she was having the prince over for tea. She was a wreck, but it was wrecked like she used to be before all this. It was the first glimpse I've seen of her old self in a long time. Kendra feels further away from me than she's ever been, and the distance started long before the accident with Sawyer. I miss being able to talk to her without feeling like she's judging everything I say.

I check the volume on my phone for the third time, making sure it's not on silent. Maybe I should just text Dani. If it didn't go well, Kendra will disappear into Sawyer's bedroom, and I won't hear from her until at least tomorrow. I pull Dani from my favorites and tap out a text:

How'd it go at Kendra's? Haven't heard from her . . .

I pause before hitting send. Looks good. Send.
Delivered. Read. The three dots.
Why is she taking so long? Finally:

I'm so sorry.

My chest constricts. No. She wouldn't. Dani promised Kendra she could talk to Caleb. She wouldn't go back on her word. Not on something like this. Something else must've happened. Maybe Caleb got sick or something came up with Luna.

For what?!?

Please, no. This will divide us. We'll fracture, split, and this time it'll be the end. There will be no coming back from this. We won't survive it.

Bryan won't let him.

NINETEEN
KENDRA

The doorbell chime echoes throughout the house, sending the contents of my stomach shooting up and back down, leaving a bitter taste in my mouth. The last time it rang was the worst night of my life. I want to rip the entire system out of the wall and burn it in the backyard. Reese rushes into Sawyer's bedroom without bothering to knock and hurls himself on the bed, half his body landing on top of mine.

"What's happening?" he asks. There's no mistaking the terror in his eyes. He remembers too.

I shake my head. Too nervous to speak. I fold my hands, whispering to a childhood god I abandoned long ago, begging him not to shatter us again.

"Kendra, can you come downstairs?" Paul's voice calls out from below. The marble floors throughout our house ensure nothing goes unheard. He sounds clear. Calm. Not fake calm for me but genuine there-isn't-anything-wrong calm.

I shove Reese toward the edge of the bed. "Go see who's down there."

He shakes his huge head back and forth, making his long blond hair fall in front of his eyes. I'm not sure how I ended up with such dramatically different boys. Not just in looks but in personality too.

"I said, go down there and see who it is," I say, refusing to move from my position on the bed.

"Fine," he huffs before getting up and rushing downstairs. It's only seconds before he's back. "Luna's here," he announces.

"Luna?"

"Yes, Luna," he says, speaking more slowly, like I didn't comprehend him the first time.

Dani texted earlier that Caleb wasn't coming today like we'd originally planned. I haven't texted back. I'm not going to. I might not ever speak to her again. At some point she has to take a stand against Bryan, and if this isn't the thing that motivates her to do it, then nothing will. She made her choice.

"Tell her to come up here."

"Luna, come up to Sawyer's room!" Reese screams at the top of his lungs.

I cover my ears. "I could've done that."

He grins. His smile still lopsided despite two years of braces.

I smile back. "I love you." He beams right as there's a timid knock at the door. "Come in," I say.

Luna walks in, shifting her eyes back and forth around the room, refusing to make eye contact with me or Reese. She's been in my house many times but rarely in Sawyer's bedroom. At least not when I've been home. She's transformed in the last two years, and I barely recognize her as the girl who sold me Girl Scout Cookies every year. She used to be the perfect embodiment of a California girl—flawless tan and taut, strong legs and a flat stomach, like she'd stepped out of an Abercrombie & Fitch ad. Today her small frame is hidden underneath baggy clothes draped on her body. A half-shaved undercut marks her part, and the long hair hanging on the other side of her face is streaked purple. Piercings dot her ears, and a barbed wire tattoo encircles her tiny neck.

The Best of Friends

She stands in the doorway, unsure of what to do with herself or where to sit.

"It's okay." I pat the spot on the bed next to Reese. "Come sit next to us." Maybe it's a good thing that he's here. She sits tentatively next to Reese, who promptly makes a weird grunting sound rather than saying hello.

"I'm sorry Caleb didn't come today," she mumbles as she pulls her legs up to her chest and wraps her arms around them. "Mom should've let him."

"Don't worry about it. That's not your fault. You didn't have anything to do with it," I say. Her face crumples like she might cry. I reach for her hand and give it a squeeze. "Sweetie, it's okay. Really it is."

"It's not that." Tears move down her cheeks, and she tries to talk, but that only makes her start sobbing. It's impossible for her to speak while she cries, so we wait as the torrent of emotions passes through her. The dark makeup lining her eyes drips down her face. Reese keeps glancing at the door like he's thinking of a reason to bolt from the room without looking rude. I could sit here all day. Intense emotions no longer make me uncomfortable.

I hand her a glass of water from Sawyer's nightstand after she's settled a bit. "What's going on?" I ask.

"Sawyer would still be here if I hadn't been so lazy and selfish," she cries as she wipes her nose with the back of her sleeve. "It's all my fault."

Reese tosses her one of the Kleenex boxes on the bed. She pulls out a handful and blows her nose. Her eyes are red rimmed from crying so hard, and the dark eyeliner smeared all over her face makes her look ghoulish.

"My interview with the detective is this afternoon, and I want to tell you what I'm going to tell him. You should hear it from me first." Her voice trembles with emotion. I wait for her to go on, but she doesn't. I place my hand on top of hers, working my thumb in circles on top of her soft skin. Sawyer's skin was never this soft.

"Mom, can I go now?" Reese asks, edging his way off the bed and away from Luna. The color's drained from his face at the seriousness of her visit. He's not interested in what she has to say. Not now.

I nod my approval and motion for the door without taking my eyes off Luna. I'm scared to move in case it spooks her and she stops talking. He quickly scurries away, shutting the door behind him and leaving us alone in Sawyer's room. It's where I planned to talk to Caleb if he made it today. Luna's the last person I expected to see.

"I don't want you to be mad at me or think I hid anything on purpose." Her voice catches in her throat. "I'm sorry."

She's making me nervous. What's she getting at? The walls pulse and throb around me.

"I was with them that night."

"You were home?" Lindsey told me she'd moved home after the accident. Not before.

"Yes, but no." She shakes her head. "I'm sorry I'm not making any sense. This is so hard."

"It's okay, honey, really. Whatever you have to say is okay." I give her the same smile I give my real estate clients when I'm trying to land a huge deal.

"They showed up at the Delta Tau house, and I—"

"Who's 'they'?" She can't leave out any part of the story. Every detail matters.

"Sawyer, Caleb, and Jacob."

"Was there a party?" Delta Tau is the only fraternity house at Hamlin College. Hamlin's one of the oldest and smallest colleges in Southern California. I used to sneak into Delta Tau parties with her mom and Lindsey when we were in high school.

She nods, bringing her hand to her mouth and nibbling on her fingernails. They're chewed down to nubs. "They made a huge scene."

"What kind of a scene?" I try not to sound too eager.

"I wasn't there when they got there, so I missed out on the beginning of the drama. But apparently, they'd already been drinking before they got to the party." She looks away, embarrassed to be telling on them, even though there's no way around it and she's doing the right thing by coming forward. Besides, we already knew they'd been drinking. There was no mistaking the smell of alcohol on all their clothes. "They were already pretty drunk, and Sawyer started doing shots in the kitchen with a couple of the other guys as soon as they got there. The Delta Tau boys can drink. They do it every weekend, and Sawyer tried to keep up with them. He got wasted super fast. Way too fast. That's when he got belligerent and started picking fights with people for no reason. He gets like that sometimes." She quickly glances up. Conflict twists her expression. "I'm sorry. Are you sure you want to hear all this?"

"Absolutely. Please, don't leave anything out." I lean into her like a heroin addict about to get their next fix.

"Sawyer got into a scuffle in the kitchen because he offended someone by using a racial slur—"

"A racial slur?" Sawyer wasn't racist, and I've never seen him belligerent. He must've been really drunk. "What'd he say?"

"I'm not sure what he said."

She knows, but her expression tells me she's too embarrassed to say. It must've been really bad. "Sorry I keep interrupting you," I say, even though I'll probably do it ten more times before this conversation is over.

"It's okay." She gives me a timid smile. "Anyway, I got to the party right as they were throwing them out. Caleb and Jacob had jumped in, and a big brawl was about to happen in the front yard. Honestly, I'm not sure what would've happened if I hadn't shown up. A couple of my friends were there and helped me break it up. I called them an Uber and ended up getting in the front seat because I didn't trust them not to act like idiots, which they pretty much did even with me in the car as a babysitter. I was so irritated with them, especially Caleb." Guilt stalls her story at whatever part comes next.

"Was Caleb drunk too?"

"Yes, and he was angry, too, but Caleb being angry drunk is way different than Sawyer."

"It is?"

She nods. "Sawyer is, like, dumb-jock drunk." She puts her hand over her mouth. "Oh my God, I'm so sorry. I didn't mean—"

I put my hand on hers again. "Don't worry about it." Sawyer could act like a dumb jock when he was sober, so I can't imagine what he was like drunk. "Nothing you say will offend me."

"Caleb is angry and mean when he's drunk. He immediately started in on the driver over nothing, and our driver wanted to cancel the trip because he was super annoyed with all of it. I barely talked him into taking us home. Jacob and Sawyer were screaming at each other in the back seat, and I just kept telling them to shut up while we drove." She gnaws on her nails while she speaks. "I've replayed that stupid car ride over so many times I'm sick of it. Honestly, they sounded like a bunch of drunk frat boys who didn't make any sense. There were a lot of 'bruhs' and 'dude, no.' I was more annoyed than anything."

I don't like thinking about him drunk. It's one of the reasons I left him and his friends alone when they came home after they'd been out drinking. I could tell they'd been drinking whenever they tried to be quiet because they never worried about being quiet any other time, but I wouldn't confront them about it. I was glad they came home and passed out in my basement. Kids who stayed out all night without a place to crash were the ones who got in real trouble.

"Did any of them have a gun?" I ask like it's the most normal question in the world to ask a person.

"No, there wasn't any gun." Offense clouds her eyes for a brief second, as if my question implies that she left that piece out on purpose. She resembles Dani when she's offended—same squinty eyes and slightly turned-up chin. "Getting them out of the car and into the house was a spectacle, and I couldn't get out of there fast enough."

"That's it? Did you hear anything else from them?"

"No, I had no idea anything happened until I got the call from Mom around midnight. I knew something was wrong as soon as I saw it was a call and not a text." She takes a deep breath before continuing, obviously trying to clear those memories from her mind—the moment the world shifted underneath her feet. "I went back to the party and tried repairing the damage they'd done. That was my biggest concern, and I'll regret it forever. I should've stayed with them . . ."

Maybe none of this would've happened if she had, but I can't say that to her. "It's okay. You couldn't have known what was going to happen."

She hangs her head. "The last thing I said to them was that they should leave partying to the grown folks who could handle it. It was such a nasty thing to say rather than find out why they were acting that way."

"Honey, you have to let yourself off the hook. We all say stupid things and stuff we regret. This just reminds us how important it is to treasure the time we have with people." I sound like a Hallmark card, but she's gobbling it up. Her body slowly relaxes into the bed. She deserves the absolution she came for. I put my arm around her shoulders and pull her frail body close to mine. She's skeletal underneath her clothes.

"That's everything I'm going to tell Detective Locke today, but I'm sure he's heard most of it by now anyway."

I raise my eyebrows. "What do you mean?"

"He's been interviewing everyone who was at Delta Tau when Sawyer got into a fight in the kitchen."

"He has?"

She nods.

Detective Locke hasn't shared any of this with me. We speak every day, usually multiple times a day, and my questions are the same every

89

time. I never waver. *Are there any new leads? Where are we in the investigation? Anything I can do to help get information?* There's been no mention of a party. Nothing to speak of with drinking other than the full toxicology report that we're waiting to come back from the lab. He hasn't said anything about the boys being somewhere else besides Dani's that night or about other kids—college kids, for that matter—being involved.

We're not on the same team. It's never occurred to me that we weren't on the same team, even when Paul hinted at it the other night. What else does Detective Locke know that he's not telling us? More importantly, why is he hiding it?

TWENTY
LINDSEY

Wyatt and Sutton went back to school today. They've missed almost three weeks, so it will be good for them to get back into the routines of their daily lives. Sutton couldn't wait to go and got insulted this morning when I put my hands over her face to shield her from any of the media that might be lining the intersection before the school. Thankfully, they were gone. Maybe they're finally ready to leave us alone.

"But we're famous, Mommy," she said as she sucked in her cheeks and gave me her best pout.

I explained that the media hounding us are different from the paparazzi, and we aren't any kind of famous that anyone ever wants to be, but it didn't matter. Right before I dropped her off, she proudly announced that she'd selected her printed pink romper with her favorite Mary Janes in case any of the photographers managed to get into her school.

Wyatt's a different story. He complained all last night about having to go and insisted he should be able to finish school online this year. Andrew wouldn't hear of it, even though I was open to the idea. He thinks online education is a joke.

"Seriously, go around back. I don't care if they said you can't drop anyone back there," he moaned from behind me when I was dropping him off. Normally, he would ride in the passenger seat, but he had no interest in getting his picture taken.

"Once you're there and inside, nobody's going to care," I said, glancing at him in the rearview mirror. He hid in the back seat the entire ride. "Mr. Williams sent an email to all the parents and kids stressing the importance of no smartphone use during school hours and absolutely no pictures." They threatened to take away the phone of anyone caught breaking the rule. I couldn't think of a worse punishment.

He rolled his eyes. "They always say that like it's going to stop anything. Remember Stacey Meid?"

She'd been last year's scandal. She'd hid her pregnancy all year and given birth after gym class in one of the showers in the locker room. One of her lacrosse teammates had helped her. They'd disappeared from school for a month, and we'd gotten the same email the day they'd returned to class, but pictures of them had been smeared all over social media within hours of their arrival. Teenage girls can be especially cruel, and they'd ripped Stacy and her friend to shreds. Neither of the girls had lasted more than a few weeks before transferring to a different school on the east side.

"This is different. They'll respect the fact that someone died," I said, but I didn't believe myself any more than he did. I haven't read anything about the case, and I won't. I don't need other people's lies and fabrications swirling around in my mind, and once they're in there, my brain grabs them and doesn't let go. Nope. Social media warnings are wasted on me.

His face paled as the school came into sight.

"Find Reese. He'll help you."

Reese and Wyatt are in the same grade. They're exactly six months apart, but they've never been friends. Kendra and I were thrilled to be pregnant together for a second time, since Jacob and Sawyer are only two months apart, but Reese and Wyatt never bonded like their older brothers. Reese has a hard time bonding with anyone.

Wyatt snorted. "I'm better off alone."

I pulled into the car pool lane. A horn sounded behind me as someone grew frustrated with how long it was taking me to get over. "I don't know why you can't give Reese a chance. You're always so hard on him," I said as I stopped alongside the curb.

"Maybe if he put any kind of effort into being a regular person, I would." He opened the door and hopped out before I could respond.

I wanted to roll the window down and tell him I loved him, that he'd be okay, but he would've been mortified, since people were everywhere, so I kept my mouth shut.

He wasn't any happier when I picked him up. He said he'd only gone to first period and then had hidden in the library for the rest of the day. At least he'd gone. Hopefully, things will go better tomorrow.

I wait in our driveway as he hurries up to our front door, anxious to get inside and away from this day. He gives me a quick wave and heads in. I shoot him a text reminding him to set the alarm before pulling out and heading back to the hospital to relieve Andrew. He'll pick Sutton up from ballet and grab dinner on the way back to the house.

Dani texted earlier and asked what time she should come today, but I haven't responded. We've had zero communication since she told me Kendra couldn't talk to Caleb because Bryan won't allow it. We used to joke about his controlling behavior to make light of it because it embarrassed her so much, but it stopped being funny a long time ago. Thoughts of her upset me, and I don't want her to visit. I just can't see her. Not today. Andrew thinks I'm overreacting, but he'd say that no matter what because he hates conflict.

Kendra's name flashes on my screen, and I quickly transfer her to my Bluetooth.

"How'd school go?" she asks when I answer.

"Lovely," I say, and she laughs at my obvious sarcasm.

For a second, things feel normal, but it's gone in the next second when she asks, "Any press outside the school?"

"Nope, and Sutton was really disappointed." She doesn't laugh this time. Maybe I've overstepped. It's so hard to tell. I quickly switch gears. "The security will do a great job keeping them out. You know how they are."

We were one of the only private schools that didn't have security when the kids started high school at Pine Grove, and we moved freely around campus, but all that changed once we got our first celebrity kid. Easy accessibility was on the top of their list of things to change. Pictures and social media use at school were a close second.

"That's good." She pauses a second before continuing as I pull into the parking lot of the hospital. "I had an interesting visitor over the weekend."

"You did?" I put the car in park. "Who?"

"Luna."

"Luna? Why'd she come to see you?"

She waits a few beats before continuing. "She was with the boys the night Sawyer died."

"Really? Are you serious?" What would Luna have been doing with them? They never hung out together. Not even when they were little.

"Yeah, the boys went to a party at the Delta Tau house, and Sawyer got really drunk. Apparently, he got into a fight with some guys in the kitchen, and they got kicked out of the party. Luna showed up right as they were leaving and helped get them home."

I wait for her to go on, but she doesn't. That can't be the end of the story. "So then what happened?"

"She doesn't know. She dropped them at the Schultzes' and went back to the party."

"Did you tell Dani?"

"No."

"Are you going to?"

"No," she says quietly. "Luna needs to trust me."

Which means Luna's trust is more important to her than Dani's. Guilt tugs at my conscience even though I'm mad at Dani. I'd want to know if one of my kids were talking to them about what happened. It doesn't feel right keeping it a secret. But maybe that's why she's telling me. Maybe she wants me to be the one to tell Dani.

"They were all wasted that night."

"Are you sure? Jacob drank, but he didn't like to get drunk." He's like me that way, but I don't expect her to understand that. Kendra's always liked to party hard. They probably got the alcohol they were drinking from her bar in the same way we used to break into her parents' liquor cabinet when we were teenagers.

"Right." There's a strange tone in her voice. "Except sometimes he did."

"What do you mean?" A knot of anxiety balls in my stomach. Static air stretches between us. Is she trying to torture me?

"I've found him in the bathroom throwing up before," she finally says after what feels like an eternity has passed.

"Maybe he was sick." He's got a sensitive stomach. Dairy can do horrible things to him.

"He wasn't sick. He was drunk." She says it like there's no mistaking it's true.

My head swirls with possibilities. None of them good. "When did it happen?"

"Once after homecoming last year and another time after the spring formal."

"Twice? It happened twice, and you never told me?" How could she not tell me that? I'd call her immediately if I found Sawyer drunk enough to throw up in my bathroom. In fact, I don't think I'd do or say anything to him until I'd consulted with her about how she wanted me to handle it. That's the adult thing to do, but she's way more invested in being the cool mom than she is in setting limits.

"I didn't think it was that big of a deal."

"Not that big of a deal?" I want to lunge through the phone and grab her, shake her, tell her to wake up. Grow up. But I rein myself in. It's wrong to fight with someone when they're at their weakest. That's been my mantra with her these past few weeks.

"I'm sorry. He made me promise not to tell you." I detect a hint of smugness.

Ignore it, Lindsey. She's been through a lot.

I draw in a deep breath and roll my shoulders, trying to calm myself before speaking. "Well, what happened?"

Both nights were school formals, and I love everything about the dances. I have the best staircase for pictures, so everyone meets at my house beforehand. All of them slept over at Kendra's afterward, and I thought nothing more of either event besides creating a reminder to add a picture of Jacob in his tuxedo to our Christmas card this year.

"The night was fine. They came in a bit earlier than I'd expected. Remember we gave them a later curfew?" She doesn't wait for me to answer. "Anyway, I got up at three and heard noises coming from the guest bathroom. It was obvious someone was sick, so I went in to check on him. He was hugging the toilet like it was moving and holding on for dear life," she jokes, then giggles to ease the tension. "I sat with him for a few hours, rubbing his back and getting him to drink water. He was fine by the morning, especially after I gave him a Bloody Mary for breakfast." She laughs again, but there's nothing funny about it.

How could she not tell me something like that? But I already know the answer. It's the same reason she didn't tell Dani about Luna.

TWENTY-ONE
KENDRA

I shocked them both today. Turns out their boys' stainless lives weren't so clean after all. I drain what's left in my wineglass and scan Sawyer's room for my bottle. His room tilts and images blur in front of me.

Dani's terror was palpable through the phone after I told her Luna had sneaked over to my house. I wasn't going to tell her. I don't know what changed my mind. She swears Bryan doesn't hit her. Something about psychological abuse and gaslighting, but come on—he can silence her with a look, make her completely tongue-tied. There's no way he doesn't smack her around at home.

Shame on me.

Pretty sure I called Detective Locke too. Oh well. He's a traitor.

There it is.

The auburn glass peeks out from underneath a pile of Sawyer's flannel shirts. He had a better collection of bottles than me. It must've rolled. I don't remember putting it there. I crawl over to the clothes and dig out my bottle. Screw off the top. This one is empty too.

I stand. The world spins with my movement. I steady myself against his dresser.

"Make sure you don't drink on the pills." That's what the doctor said. She was worried about this?

This is wonderful.

I'm not going downstairs for another bottle. Paul will say I've had enough. That's what he'll say. He hates seeing me like this. I don't care.

Sawyer's closet door is open. I make my way to the back, where he keeps his old toys. He still has his Little League mitt. He was talented enough to play soccer or baseball. I toss the mitt aside and rummage through old superhero figurines until I get to the bin of LEGO. Red lid off. Bottles inside.

Two fewer.

He'd been busy.

Is that what they drank that night?

I pull out a bottle. Château Margaux. Expensive tastes.

Mine.

Uncorked.

I take a pull.

Mine.

TWENTY-TWO
DANI

I hold the ice pack up to Luna's split lip, and she pushes it away, cringing. "It's too cold," she cries out in pain. Her face is streaked with tears and blotchy red spots.

"It doesn't matter. You have to put this on it to keep the swelling down." Years of soccer injuries have turned me into a skilled nurse. I gently place it on the opening again. The bleeding has finally stopped. The trembling in our bodies hasn't. My insides are jumping like there are a thousand volts of electricity shocking me. I'm doing my best not to cry. She just stopped, and she'll start all over again if I do. I have to keep it together.

Oh my God. What am I going to do?

I apply light pressure. "Is that too much?"

She shakes her head.

Bryan has never hit me or the kids. Kendra and Lindsey don't believe me when I tell them that, but he hasn't. He told me once that I was too pretty to hit, and I felt flattered at the time, like I was somehow better than other abused women. He spanked the kids when they were toddlers, but that's different. I didn't like it and asked him to stop, but he swore he had a right to discipline his kids in whichever way he saw fit, and who was I to argue with that?

But tonight?

He slapped her. Hard.

I'll never forget the sound of the smack when his hand connected with her face or the horror in Luna's eyes when she realized what he'd done. For a minute, she was too stunned to speak, and then she crumpled to the floor in tears.

It started when she strutted into the house after her meeting with Kendra. Her eyes immediately met Bryan's with a challenging glint that I've seen before, but she's never come at him with it. I knew where she'd been by the look in her eyes before Bryan ever asked the question. Why couldn't she have been like every other teenager and lied when he asked if she'd gone to Kendra's and talked to her about the accident?

"What are we going to do, Mom?" She sits on the toilet, holding the ice pack to her lip and searching my eyes for an answer. I'm her mom, and it's my job to have answers. I'm supposed to make them up if I don't have them, and most of motherhood feels just like that—pretending like I have a clue what I'm doing.

"I don't know." The words feel foreign coming out of my mouth, but tonight has stripped me down to nothing but raw honesty.

"What about Caleb? Are you going to tell him?"

I've never been so grateful that he barely leaves his room as I was tonight. He slept through the argument and missed the whole fight. This will break his heart. How do you shatter someone's heart when it's already in pieces?

"I'm not sure, honey." I kneel beside the tub and start running her a bath. I put my wrist under the faucet, making sure it's the temperature she likes. I can't remember the last time she let me take care of her, but it comes at too great of a cost. I turn my head so she can't see the tears making their way down my cheeks again. "Why don't you take a nice long bath, and then I can lie with you until you fall asleep?"

Her back straightens with anger. "Sleep? That's what you want to do? Put me to bed? Jesus, I'm not two." She pushes my hand off her face and storms out of the bathroom. She stomps down the hallway into her bedroom and slams the door behind her.

I quickly grab a towel from the rack above the tub, roll it up, and tie it around my mouth like I'm about to kidnap myself, then cry as hard and as quietly as I can. Gagging into the terry cloth as I sob. I flush the toilet to muffle the sound and let out one more wail before turning off the bath and hurrying to the sink.

I turn on the faucet, refusing to meet my eyes in the mirror. None of this is supposed to be happening. I splash cold water on my face and pat my skin dry, hurriedly applying concealer underneath my eyes even though it's after midnight. I take a deep breath and head down the hall in the opposite direction of Luna's bedroom and into ours.

Bryan lies at the top of our master bed with his arms casually folded behind his head. His eyes are glued to the TV screen hanging on the wall in front of him above our mahogany dresser. I've outgrown the dark wood and have been begging him to replace it for years. A bloody scene from *The Walking Dead* blares from the speakers. I hate the show—the zombies, the killing, being scared, all of it. Normally, I'd work on calming myself down, realizing how important it is to show an interest in the things he likes, but I can't muster the strength.

Tonight he hit my daughter.

"Can you turn off the TV?" I ask. I don't even say please. He ignores me and maintains his focus on the screen. "Bryan?"

He turns his head slowly, like my presence has just registered. "Oh, hey, baby." He pats the spot next to him on the bed. "Come sit next to me. I don't want you to miss this."

I can't take my eyes off his hands. Two hours ago they broke the skin on Luna's face. I'm rooted to my spot in the bedroom doorway. He cocks his head to the side. "Come sit next to me," he repeats himself, like I might not have heard him the first time.

There has to be a line. That's what my therapist says. Not the one he and I see together for couples therapy but my individual therapist,

Beth. The one I see in secret, whose fees I pay for with the cash I take out in weekly increments as cashback from Target so Bryan doesn't notice. She tells me that women leave abusive relationships when they're ready and not a second before, and that it's usually once some final line has been crossed.

My line was pathetic—when he hit me in the face. I hated myself for it, but hating myself didn't make it any less true. Whenever Beth asked me about my line in our sessions, I never once considered the possibility that it'd have anything to do with the kids. If she would've asked me the question when the kids were toddlers, it would've been a different story. Back then, I worried about Bryan losing his temper and flying off the handle when they were running around like tyrants and almost impossible to control. I was secretly glad he traveled so much during those early years, but I haven't given any thought to him harming them in over a decade.

"No." I can't believe I'm refusing. The words feel unreal coming out of my mouth. How many times has he told me not to defy him?

Bryan sits straight up in the bed, his body a perfect ninety-degree angle. "What did you say?" He swings his legs over the bed in one swift movement before I can answer.

He's going to make me say it again. I can't say it again. Yes, I can. I said it once. I can say it again.

"No." Not any louder, but I've told him no twice.

He rises from the bed, and everything moves in slow motion as he steps toward me. Each step is methodical and deliberate. His impact on the wood floors reverberates in my head, making my insides cringe while I struggle to hold my body still. He thrives on my weakness. His eyes never waver from mine as he reaches me. I hold my breath as he enters my space. He's too close. I fight the urge to push him away.

"Don't you ever do that again," he hisses through gritted teeth. His chest inches from mine. "Do you understand?"

I'm too scared to speak. *Nod. Do something.* Can't move.

He points to the bedroom door behind me. "Get out of here. I can't stand to look at you." The room tilts. Spins.

"Go!"

His scream shocks me into my body, and I bolt for the door, fumbling with the handle as he looms behind me. I stumble into the hallway like I'm drunk, and he slams the door shut. I fall into a heap in front of our door, shoving my fist in my mouth to stifle my cries. I never even got to say it wasn't okay—that he can't hit the kids. Did I get out words? Anything?

Fear brings me to my feet. I saw the look that came over him when his backhand connected with Luna's face, and it wasn't one of instant guilt and regret. A fire was lit. There was a hunger. Some kind of thirst. Luna didn't see it because she was too stunned to process anything, but my eyes were frozen on his while I held her against me and slowly backed us away from him. It wasn't until she lifted her face and he saw the blood that he showed an ounce of remorse. It might not have even been that. He could've just been worried he was going to get in trouble. It's hard to lie your way out of a busted lip.

I scurry to the other side of the house and down the hallway to Luna's room. I knock timidly at the door. I wait a few moments for her to answer and then knock again. Louder this time.

"Luna, please, open up. It's your mom," I whisper-shout. She probably has earbuds in. I wiggle the doorknob. Normally, I don't go into my kids' bedrooms without asking or being invited, but there's nothing normal about this. The door is locked. "Please, honey, let me in. I don't want to fight. I need to sleep with you."

Her feet patter across the wooden floor as she moves through the room. She opens the door a few inches like she hasn't decided whether she's going to allow me in, but she takes one look at me and pulls the door open wide. "Mom, what's wrong?" Her eyes cloud with worry and concern. "Did he hit you too?"

It's the *too* that breaks me, and sobs erupt from somewhere deep inside. Luna grabs me and pulls me into her room, quickly shutting the door behind us. She wraps her arms around me and rubs my back, holding me while I cry like I've done for her so many times in the past. "It's okay, Mom."

"No, it's not, Luna. Your dad hit you. That's not okay. None of this is okay." I shake my head. "I'm so sorry I couldn't protect you. I didn't know he'd do something like that. I swear I didn't."

"Don't worry about it." She swallows her feelings for the sake of mine. "What happened in there?"

I take a seat on her bed. Fatigue seeps its way into me. "After you left the bathroom, I went into our bedroom to tell your dad to leave. Hitting you is unacceptable, and he needs to know that." I swallow hard. "I don't know what I expected, but it totally shocked me to find him watching TV and acting like everything was fine. I was so stunned that I didn't say anything, and he took it as a sign that I'd gotten over what he'd done to you." Because that's what I've done for years. Let the argument or fight disappear into the air as if it never happened. I play along because nothing good comes from confronting him. I learned that back in the years when I still believed he could change. I shouldn't be having this conversation with my daughter, but I'm left with no choice. "He asked me to come sit by him, and I said no. Then he made me get out of the room."

"And you just left?" Disappointment joins the concern in her voice.

I can't give her answers that make sense. I don't know how he can move my body without laying a finger on it. How his physical presence becomes so large I can't see around it and everything inside me shrinks to nothing. How it happens so fast that I don't even know when I've fallen underneath his spell—the one that makes me fall in line with him.

"I wasn't always like this." I burst into tears again. She doesn't know a mom who existed before the fear, but I used to be strong. There were days when I was fierce. I want to explain this to her. Give her a picture of someone besides this mess. But I can't. I lost that girl a long time ago, and I don't know how to find her.

TWENTY-THREE
KENDRA

I grip the shopping cart and stare down at the apples like I'm performing a careful inspection before I buy them. The reds swerve in front of my tear-filled eyes.

Focus. I can do this. I've gone grocery shopping hundreds of times. Probably thousands. Besides, I came super early so there wouldn't be many people shopping. I reach for a prepackaged bag of apples and toss it in my cart. Move on to the bananas. Panic claws at my chest while the other customers' eyes bore holes into my back.

And then I remember.

I'm in Carlsberg. Nobody knows me outside of our insular suburban community, so I won't be recognized. Most of these people have probably seen my picture on the news and plastered on social media, but I look nothing like those pictures at the moment.

The bananas are too ripe, so I move on to the cheese. Sawyer's hated cheese since he was two. He said it smelled like puke. I quickly grab the provolone slices for Paul's lunch and move along before the memories overwhelm me.

Why am I doing this? I don't want to be here.

Paul wants me to close on the Fords' house next week. He insists it has to be me since I'm the only one who can deal with Mr. Ford. He's a cranky old billionaire who has more money than he could spend in two lifetimes, but he's one of the most miserable people I've ever met. The other was Estella Viore. She wanted to buy an island.

I can't do this. What was I thinking?

The thing nobody tells you about grief is that time moves on. Or my personal favorite that nobody stops telling you—time heals all wounds. As if I want time to go anywhere. I want the world to stop. For every person to quit moving around me. For the screens to quit flashing and the zombies to stop walking so slowly down the streets that they almost get hit by cars. I don't want the cars to drive or the buses to come, because every minute feels like I'm leaving Sawyer behind and living the life he was supposed to have.

It's swirling. It's coming. Not here.

I release my cart, turn on my heels, and race for the sliding glass doors at the front of the store. I burst through them into the sunlight and try not to sprint when I hit the blacktop parking lot.

Where's my car?

I twirl in circles as I press the fob.

All I hear is the loud buzz in my ears. The rest of the sound in the world is turned off.

Press again and again.

Brake lights flashing.

There.

I hurry toward it, but the animal sounds are forcing their way out. My head swirls. Stomach heaves. I fumble with the handle. The world thrums around me as I slam the door. I can't breathe. Where's the air?

The empty halls reverberate the sound of my shoes as I make a beeline for the office. The high school looks nothing like it did when I roamed the halls as head cheerleader and homecoming queen so many years ago. They're on their fourth remodel, and all the traditional brick is gone. They've replaced it with a new modern and sleek design. The school secretary, Mrs. Newton, called me on my way home from my breakdown at the grocery store to come get Reese because the janitor caught him vaping in the bathroom before first period. I'm glad it was only vaping and he didn't get busted with anything else. Paul and I still haven't talked to Reese about selling drugs at school. Neither of us has brought it up again, like we somehow agreed to mutual denial on the topic, but it was the first thing that popped into my mind when Mrs. Newton called me about the incident. He was probably waiting to sell somebody pills or some other drug the teenagers are doing that I don't know about.

The principal and vice principal are at a conference in San Diego until tomorrow. Their assistants suspended Reese until they get back, even though they didn't want to. They kept stressing how they wished they didn't have to do it because of everything going on, but they couldn't go against school policy. Pine Grove has a certain image to maintain, and they don't take lightly to anyone tarnishing their reputation. Vaping in bathrooms is for kids in public schools.

I whip open the office doors and immediately spot Reese in the farthest corner. His entire body is curled in the chair like he's trying to hide from me or anyone else who might walk by and spot him through the shiny glass windows. I hope the entire school sees him. Maybe it'll shame him into never doing it again.

"Hello, Kendra," Mrs. Newton says with a forced smile from behind her U-shaped desk in the center of the room. Her salt-and-pepper hair is cropped short, and fifty extra pounds hang on her frame, but I recognize her wide-set champagne-colored eyes and flat, freckled face from the days when she was Ms. Raph. She didn't like me then, and she likes me even less now.

I flash her my most apologetic smile and reach for the three-ring binder to sign Reese out. I quickly scribble our names in their designated spots. "So Dr. Charles will be emailing me, or should I expect a call?"

"Probably both." The smile has disappeared from her face. She looks at me like I was the one vaping in the bathroom.

I turn around and shoot Reese a serious glare, hoping he heard what she said. This isn't the first time Reese has gotten into trouble, but everything else he did was annoying and immature stuff like belching loudly in someone's ear during a test or hanging smelly socks outside of his best friend's locker. I motion for him to get up before turning back to Mrs. Newton.

"I'm sorry about all this," I say like she has any way to save our reputation. She nods with her best fake understanding as I hurry Reese outside, and we move through the parking lot as fast as we can. Neither of us speaks until we get in the car.

"How could you be so stupid?" I snap as soon as we pull out of the school parking lot and head toward the boulevard. Fury pounds my forehead.

He slinks down in his seat. "Sorry, Mom. I wasn't thinking."

"No, you weren't thinking—you weren't thinking at all! You were only worrying about yourself." I smack the steering wheel. "Everybody's already talking about us, and now you've just added all kinds of fuel to the fire. Can you imagine the things they'll say?"

"That's what you're worried about?" His eyes ignite with anger. "What people are going to think about us?" Disgust twists his face. "I might be dumb, but you make me sick."

Anger surges through me. I can't look at him. I'm dangerously close to the edge. My hands shake on the wheel. I have to find a way to calm down. Images swerve in front of me as I drive.

Reese fumes in the passenger seat. His school uniform is already untucked, and the shorts will be off within minutes of our arrival at home. His white Converse rest on the dashboard in defiance. I don't give him the satisfaction of asking him to take them down. He stares straight ahead, eyes in hostile slits.

"You are making a difficult situation worse," I say after a few minutes pass.

"Why are you crying?" Irritation fills his tone.

I wipe the tears off my cheeks; I hadn't realized I was crying. I hate that I cry when I'm angry. "Things are pretty tough right now, Reese, or haven't you noticed?" I snap.

"Yeah, I bet it's really hard losing the good son and getting stuck with the bad one. That must be really difficult for you."

All the air is sucked out of the car.

It takes me a second to find my voice.

"How could you say something like that?"

"You know it's the truth. Everyone does." His voice is sad, resigned.

"Don't you say that!" I unleash a scream. "Don't you ever say that again!"

"Mom, pull over! You're going into the other lane!" Reese shrieks.

My hands grip the wheel as I shake. I can't control the trembling in my body any more than I can control the swirl of emotions whipping through me.

"Mom!" He tugs on my arm. "You're too upset to drive."

I signal right and turn into the Ralphs parking lot. My hands grip the wheel even after the car is parked. Anger and hurt throttle me. There's no telling where the hurt ends and the anger begins.

"God, you almost got us killed," Reese says. "You should let me drive."

"I'm not going to let you drive. You don't even have a license."

"Well, let's get an Uber home, then, because I'm not driving with you when you're acting all crazy."

"I'm not acting crazy," I say, but the hysteria still lines my voice. I take a deep breath, slowly releasing my hold on the wheel. "We're not going to get an Uber either." I put my hands in my lap.

"What are we going to do?"

"We're going to sit and take a minute to get ourselves together." My head pounds in rhythm with my heart.

"I'm together."

I rub my temples. "Okay, so I'm not, and I need some time." The silence only lasts for a few beats before Reese starts messing with the radio and trying to get his phone to play through the speakers. I place my hand on top of his to stop him. His music annoys me. It's not even music—just mostly made-up words and ridiculous sounds. My touch softens him.

"I'm sorry that I always screw up, Mom," he says.

"You don't always screw up."

He nods. "It's okay. I know I do. I just—"

I put my hand up to his lips to stop him from talking. "Please, Reese. Stop." I fumble with his seat belt, releasing him from its hold. "Just come here." I pull him against my chest and circle my arms around him. He clings to me and starts crying. The parking brake digs into my ribs, but I ignore it. "I'm the one who is sorry," I whisper into the top of his head while he cries. "I'm so sorry."

TWENTY-FOUR
DANI

My hand trembles on the spoon as I stir the creamer into my coffee and wait for the rest of the house to wake up. I've been up all night. I lay still as a statue next to Luna until Caleb's nightly screams sent me to his bedroom. I was terrified Bryan would come out while I calmed him down, but he never did. Luna slept through it too.

My eyes sting like they've been rubbed with sandpaper. Before Luna fell asleep last night, I told her to stay in her room this morning until Bryan leaves for work. I said it like I have some master plan in place for us as soon as he's gone, but I'm as clueless this morning as I was last night. What am I going to do if he goes into her bedroom and tries to talk to her? Do I try to stop him? That's never worked. What if he doesn't go to his office? It's already past nine. Anxiety grips my chest.

How am I supposed to kick him out of the house he pays for? That's what he'll say. It's what he's said before. My head swirls with possibilities. None of them good. This is why I've been too scared to leave. Nobody ever talks about the logistics of leaving, like getting out of an abusive relationship is simply working up the courage to go. But I have to find a way out for Luna. She'll never speak to me again if I stay. Memories from last night pummel their way into my consciousness.

She put her hand on her left hip and jutted out her chin in defiance as she announced, "I went to Kendra's and talked to her about what happened the night Sawyer died." If she were five, she would've stuck out her tongue at him.

Bryan flew off the barstool. "What did you say?" He peered into her face.

Her expression filled with righteous indignation and pride that she'd stood up to him. She quickly glanced at me as if to say, *See, this is how you do it*, before bringing her eyes to meet his challenging stare. "I said I went to Kendra's and told her everything." She was as proud to say it the second time as she was the first.

"After I forbid anyone in this house from doing that?"

"Forbid?" She burst out laughing. "Please, Dad."

The back of his hand smacked her before she knew what was happening. I never saw it coming either. At first, she was too stunned to cry. She'd never thought he would hit her. That was all she kept saying last night while she cried. The sound of it hasn't stopped playing in my mind. I saw him coming at her every time I closed my eyes and tried to sleep last night. I hate being in this house. Too many bad things have happened here.

I sense Bryan's presence before I hear the sounds of him whistling as he comes down the stairs and into the kitchen, tightening his tie around his neck. He's freshly shaved and washed. "Can you make sure this is straight?" he asks, giving me a huge smile. "I can't seem to get it right. It's like I have two thumbs this morning."

I grip my coffee mug and plaster myself against the counter, putting as much distance between him and me as possible. All I have to do is tell him to leave. That's the first step. Say the words.

He raises his eyebrows in mock surprise at my response to him. "I see someone is still upset this morning."

"Upset? You hit our child, Bryan!" Adrenaline surges through my body despite my resolve to stay calm.

"A child?" He smirks. "Please, she's almost nineteen years old, Dani. She's hardly a child."

My thoughts grow smaller and race in tight circles. "It's still wrong." That's all I get out. It's so weak. I want something more—more powerful words to describe the magnitude of what he's done—but I have none.

"I don't have time for this." His smile disappears and takes his fake mood with it. "I have to be in a meeting at ten." He grabs a travel mug from the cupboard above the sink and fills it with coffee from the pot I brewed at six. "Luna purposefully went behind my back and spoke with the Mitchells without a lawyer present. She knows what she did was wrong, so I'm not sure why the two of you are so angry with me."

His ability to twist things is unnerving. He won't make me question my sanity this time. There are bruises on Luna's face proving he's a monster.

"You have to leave." I force myself to sound strong and confident, just like I practiced in the mirror. Beth told me to get used to saying the words until they rolled easily off my tongue.

"I have to leave? For what? Protecting my family?" He throws his hands in the air. "All I've done is protect you guys since day one. We're all under an incredible strain, and I bear the most burden because I'm responsible for keeping us afloat during this chaos, or have you forgotten that?" He points to our kitchen with its marble countertops, stainless steel sink, and concrete tiled floors. "I gave you this. All of it, and I'll do anything to protect it. Why?" He walks toward me. I steel myself as he gets closer. "Because I love my family more than anything else in the world. You guys are the most important people to me. I might have lost my temper last night because I was so frustrated, and I shouldn't have done that, but it's natural instinct to protect your family when they're being threatened."

"You didn't just get frustrated and lose your temper—you hit Luna." *Stay firm. Speak clearly.*

"Excuse me for caring so much." He shrugs like he's the one insulted.

My heart thumps. "Don't come home tonight after work."

He lets out an exaggerated laugh. "Of course I'm coming home after work, darling. This is my house, and I don't have a problem with anything going on in the house. If you have a problem with things here, then by all means, please leave."

He turns on his heel and walks out the front door, leaving me standing in the kitchen with my coffee mug in my hands. My phone vibrates on the counter with a text from Luna upstairs:

Is dad gone yet?

TWENTY-FIVE
LINDSEY

I fold the last towel and set it on top of the stack before tucking the pile in the cupboard underneath the sink. Jacob got two sponge baths today instead of his usual one. His nurse gave him one in the morning before his physical therapy appointment, and I like him to bathe after a workout, so I just gave him his second. The physical therapist only comes every other day no matter how much I insist on daily sessions for his mobility. The hospital won't allow it because that's all our medical insurance covers. Andrew offered to pay them cash, and they still refused. They've probably been burned too many times, so they're not willing to budge. I fill in the other days and do my best to mimic the exercises, but I have no idea if I'm applying the right amount of pressure even if I'm doing the right stretches.

"What did you think of your physical therapist today?" I ask, gazing down at Jacob. It didn't take me long to get used to his tracheostomy like I expected. The tube looks more natural in his neck than it did in his mouth. His misshapen head still bothers me, though. The incision will heal once the tube's taken out and leave a scar, but his head will forever be concave, like a spoiled pumpkin the day after Halloween. I stroke the side of his cheek, missing the hair I've been brushing out of his eyes since he was two. "Yeah, you're right. I don't like him as much as

The Best of Friends

Sean either. We won't have time to get too used to him anyway. They're going to move you to Prairie Meadows soon."

I can't wait to leave this floor. I'm glad we're out of the ICU, but we've never settled into this place, and I don't think we're going to. There's a lack of enthusiasm for his care, like we're in a holding cell, even though it's supposed to be the next step in his rehabilitation.

I move to the other side of his bed. New flowers arrived this afternoon from the moms on his soccer team. They never miss a week. "Is it hard not being on the field?" I ask while I adjust the foliage around them. Even though the soccer moms send flowers every week, the visits from the players on his team are dwindling. During the first week, they kept a twenty-four-hour vigil in the ICU waiting room, but as time moves forward, people grow more and more uncomfortable being around him. They don't want to say it, but they've given up hope, and his presence depresses them. That's fine with me. I'd rather they stayed away, then.

"Your team was pretty mad at you, huh? I wish you would've told me what was going on with you and your friends. I know you told your dad, but I hate to break it to you—he's not very good at things when it comes to girls. I mean, I'm the one who had to ask him out first." I smile at the memory and how many times we have shared it with the kids. They love hearing how I bid on him at a charity auction hosted by my sorority house. "You had a lot going on that you didn't talk to me about. Why didn't you feel safe coming to me with whatever was going on between you guys?" I scan his body for movement like I'm the MRI machine. I'd give anything for a twitch. "Did you lie to me about your drinking?"

It's not like we haven't talked about his drinking. Last summer, they all got busted downtown after they sneaked out to watch a fight between the star quarterback of the Lyons football team and the pitcher from their baseball team. Half their class had done the same thing, and things grew rowdy quickly. The police busted up the gathering after a group of kids flipped over a car in the gas station parking lot. They threatened to write all of them tickets for underage drinking and vandalism. The police brought the boys back to Kendra's smelling like alcohol, and Caleb had puke on his shirt.

I stormed into Jacob's room when he got home. He tried to sneak in by using the back door, but I'd been waiting for him all morning. Kendra had called me earlier and filled me in on everything. She probably would've kept that instance a secret, too, but she had to tell me because half of Norchester knew about it, and word travels fast. I waited for Jacob to get comfortable in his bed so it would really punish him when I ran into his room and flung the covers off his body.

"Get up!" I yelled.

He struggled to grab the covers from me, but I yanked them back each time he tried. "Mom. Stop. What are you doing?" His voice was pained, like it hurt him to talk. "Give them to me."

"I said get up." Anger coated each word. I wasn't messing around.

Jacob can't afford to get into trouble, or he'll lose his scholarship. We can't afford private school for three kids without some help. Nobody knows we get financial assistance. Not even Jacob. Everyone always assumes we're loaded because Andrew's a doctor, but rheumatologists are one of the lowest-paid specialties. It's why I worked so hard at talking him out of it during medical school, but he wouldn't budge, and he loves working with old people. People naturally assume I have this luxurious life, which couldn't be further from the truth.

Jacob scuttled against the headboard, drawing his knees up to his chest and bringing his arms around them in a tight hug. I grabbed one of his pillows and flung it at him. "You were drinking last night!" I shook my finger at him.

"I wasn't." Righteous indignation lined his face. Did that mean he was lying or mad because he was being falsely accused?

"Caleb says you were." I wasn't wasting any time playing games. Caleb hadn't admitted to anything, but one of the best ways to get kids to confess was to make them think someone had told on them. There was a flicker of something in his eyes, and then it was gone.

"They were the ones drinking." He grabbed the covers from me again. This time, I loosened my hold.

"Caleb and Sawyer?"

He nodded.

"You didn't have anything to drink?"

He lowered his eyes and stared at the striped design on his comforter. "I was fake drinking." Red crept up his neck and worked its way through his ears, just like his dad's response when he's embarrassed.

I waited for him to say more, but he didn't go on. "I'm sorry, but if I'm supposed to know what that is, I don't."

"I don't like drinking. You know that, but everyone looks at me like I'm a freak if I don't, so I take a few sips and pretend to drink the rest." He shrugged. "The girls do it all the time, and that's what we call it when we're making fun of them. I'm just better at it than they are, so nobody knows I'm doing it."

"And that's all?"

"Mom, why do you keep asking me the same question over and over again? That's super annoying." He rolled his eyes at me.

I would give anything for him to open his eyes and give me a dramatic eye roll. I take a seat on the edge of his hospital bed and will him to open them. Every day a doctor lifts his eyelids and shines a light into his eyes, and every day it's the same—unresponsive. His pupils are fixed and dilated; they don't shrink at the light like they're supposed to.

Did he have more than a few sips to drink that night? The full toxicology report still isn't back. Detective Locke said it should be back any day. Part of me hopes he was drunk. At least it would make what happened easier to understand if none of them were in their right minds.

"Dad got a lawyer today. Did I tell you that?" I can't remember if I did. The days run together, and sometimes I can't remember if I'm talking to him out loud or in my head. Being in the hospital this long is like living with constant jet lag. "We meet him tomorrow for the first time. It feels strange to have a lawyer. I feel like a criminal just saying it." He's the only person I've told. I don't want Dani to get all high and mighty like she does whenever she's been right on something we've fought about. "It's perfect timing since Detective Locke wants to see us again. They've gone through your laptop and want to fill us in on what they've found. He made it sound so serious, said it couldn't wait. He's always so dramatic about everything." I roll my eyes. He left me two messages about an "urgent matter" within a half-hour span. "That's why we're meeting the lawyer tomorrow." I lean down and press my lips against his forehead. It feels waxy and stiff, like an expensive doll. "Is there anything on your computer that I should know about? If there is, you should probably tell me now," I whisper.

TWENTY-SIX
KENDRA

Every noise cuts through my brain, making my stomach heave. I've already puked twice. It didn't make me feel any better. Not like it used to in college. This is why I don't get drunk anymore. Moving my eyes makes my head spin. I'm done taking those pills. I can't stand feeling like this every morning.

I untangle Sawyer's sheets from around my legs. I have to quit sleeping in here. I tell myself the same thing every morning, but by the end of the night—who am I kidding? Usually by the middle of the afternoon—I find myself underneath his covers. It's the only way I feel safe.

"It's not healthy," Paul yelled at me last night, and I couldn't argue with him. I never said what I'm doing is healthy.

My body screams at me to lie back down and sleep for another two hours, but Reese is suspended, so I have to get up. Paul will drill him with questions when he gets home from work, and Reese won't hesitate to tell him I stayed in bed all day again. The two of them have no compassion.

Paul gets angrier every day. I've never seen him like this before. He grinds his jaw so hard that it sounds like he's going to crack his teeth. Anger radiates from him, and last night was no different. He kept saying it was about Reese vaping, but Reese being in trouble at school isn't exactly a surprise. We've joked since his first day of kindergarten that we'd be lucky if he graduated high school. Not because he's not smart. Reese is brilliant in his own way. He simply doesn't care about school or being told what to do. He doesn't understand other people's behavior or why people pretend to like each other when they don't. That's why I know Paul's anger wasn't about that. Besides, he didn't get that upset when we found out Reese was selling pills, so his anger obviously isn't about Reese vaping.

I'm not even mad at Reese for vaping. It's not like any of the PSAs on the billboards and the sides of buses do anything except increase your curiosity about them. How could they with the main tagline:

TASTES LIKE CANDY. WORKS LIKE POISON.

I never get past the candy part either. Still. He shouldn't have done it, especially not at school.

I drag myself into Sawyer's bathroom, avoiding my image in the mirror as I pass. Sawyer's phone lies on the floor next to the toilet. I must've been going through it before I went to bed last night. That's another thing I hate about the pills—I can't remember the last thirty minutes before falling asleep. I pick up his phone and take a seat on the toilet, quickly typing in his pass code. The motion makes me dizzy again. A wave of nausea passes through me. Deep breaths.

Jacob's face fills the screen instead of Sawyer's. His midnight-black curls. Dark-brown eyes framed by arched brows. His eyes were always so intense, like he was thinking hard. He was by far the most serious of the boys. Both boys were so handsome. Sawyer was attractive in the traditional Southern California way—blond hair, blue eyes, tan skin, and perfect white teeth—but Lindsey's olive skin and Andrew's German background gave Jacob an ethnic flair that you couldn't pinpoint, making him appear mysterious and aloof.

His quiet and reserved self shows through in the pictures. It wasn't that he was shy. He was simply an observer. He stood back and watched before he ever made a move or a decision, which is why we always put him in charge of things. He was the responsible one. We relied on him to give us the real story whenever there was a questionable situation or someone was in trouble.

People tiptoe around Lindsey's denial about Jacob attempting suicide. They pity her refusal to accept it. Nobody comes right out and says that to her, but it's in their eyes and the way they speak to her. I'm the only one who believes her, but they pity me more than they do her. They write us off as a pair of grief-stricken mothers. It's easy to do, but just because I'm mourning doesn't mean I've lost the ability to reason. And here's the thing—suicide is an impulsive act, and Jacob never did anything without thinking about it first. He was the oldest of the three—two months ahead of Sawyer—and he functioned like their older brother, always the voice of reason. He also didn't have a selfish bone in his body, so there's no way he'd leave his family and friends behind to cope with such a huge loss. An attempted suicide doesn't make sense.

"Mom?" Reese's voice calls from outside Sawyer's bedroom door. "Are you okay?"

"I'm okay. I'll be out in a second." I do my best singsong mom voice even though it makes my head start throbbing all over again. I'm committed to showing up for him and being nice. Yesterday's breakdown in the car was awful. He needs me now. More than ever.

I scroll through more of the pictures on Sawyer's phone. Sawyer captures Jacob in a way I've never seen him before, and it's startling how manly he looks in some of them. His usual serious expression is drawn into a playful smile. The last photo in the album is a stunning side profile shot of him. There's a gentle expression to his face that's usually not there. His hair is tousled, and he's gazing into the distance like there's something really beautiful just over the horizon.

"Mom! Are you coming? I'm starving."

"Fix yourself a bowl of cereal." He's fourteen. The child should know how to make himself breakfast.

"I don't want cereal." He's moved into a full-on whine.

"Jeez, Reese, I said give me a second." I force patience into my voice. I set Sawyer's phone on the vanity next to the toilet. I'm going through those pictures again tonight and forwarding the best ones to Lindsey.

"It's already been a second. You've been in there like forever. Are you taking a poop? What are you doing?"

It takes all my willpower not to scream at him to shut up. I wash my hands, glancing down at the wallpaper that's taken over Sawyer's screen. It's a goofy cartoon drawing of him making a goal and couldn't be more different than the album I just went through. I had no idea Sawyer was such a gifted photographer. He never expressed any interest in it to me. Did he have other hidden talents?

Maybe I didn't know him as well as I thought.

TWENTY-SEVEN
LINDSEY

Andrew shuffles into Detective Locke's office with his head down and takes the chair beside me, mumbling apologies about being late. He's almost never late. He wears a crisp white shirt buttoned to the top with a dark tie and matching jacket, but despite his freshly pressed clothes, he still looks disheveled. His thin lips are pursed in a straight line.

"Hi, honey," I say, reaching out and taking his hand. "We haven't gotten started yet, so you haven't missed anything."

Andrew loosens the tie around his neck. "I got caught up with a patient emergency at work." Red creeps up the back of his neck. He's a terrible liar. How long has he been lying? I should've been paying better attention.

Detective Locke doesn't notice, or if he does, then he doesn't care, because he moves right into business without acknowledging Andrew's tardiness or the fact that he was late too. I sat in the waiting room for twenty minutes by myself waiting for these guys when I could've stayed for the first part of rounds this afternoon. I'm as irritated about having to wait as Andrew is about being late.

Detective Locke tilts his computer so that all of us can see the screen. Our new lawyer's face fills the screen. His name is Dan, and he wasn't able to attend the meeting in person on such short notice since he doesn't get back from Toronto until Wednesday. He doesn't look or sound like any lawyer I've ever met, and I'm afraid Andrew might have gotten him because his retainer was cheap. Andrew suggested we reschedule until he could be here in person, but I'm not willing to wait that long.

"I'm going, and there's nothing you can do to stop me." That's what I declared in our conversation yesterday. It was directed toward Andrew, but it sounded like I was threatening them both, since we were on a three-way call, and it came out sounding much harsher than I intended.

Andrew wouldn't let me go alone, so Dan agreed to be available via webcam at the scheduled time, even though he wasn't pleased about it. It definitely wasn't the best way to start a new relationship, but the circumstances didn't leave much choice. Dan spent the last thirty minutes of our phone call half-heartedly rattling off advice like he didn't expect us to follow it, and I run through it again quickly while I prepare for Detective Locke's questions.

Let him tell you what he knows.
Don't offer him any information.
Don't lie, but don't tell the truth if it will get you in trouble.

The last rule bothers me because it's another reference to us being criminals. How can a lawyer represent me if he thinks we've done something wrong? I'm anxious to get started. At least the formal introductions are out of the way. That's one good thing about Andrew being late.

"First, I want to thank you for being so kind and helpful by giving me access to all of Jacob's accounts. We were able to save so much time in our investigation by you voluntarily handing the computer over for a search and giving us his passwords," Detective Locke begins. I already notice a difference in his manner from having someone else present with us during his questioning.

Andrew shoots me a pointed glare that's impossible to miss. Most of our conversation with Dan was centered on how we willingly gave the police access to Jacob's laptop and his online accounts. He said we never should've given them up without a court order. He was adamant that we receive an itemized list of everything they'd taken from the house. But that's the thing—we don't have anything to hide, so why act like we do? We're behaving like guilty people, and we haven't done anything wrong. I wasn't about to give the police a reason to doubt me by refusing to turn over Jacob's personal stuff.

Detective Locke smiles at us from across his desk. His eyes are warm and kind. He likes us, and he's been working with us. What's he going to do if we turn into stone walls during this meeting? Because that's what Dan implied we should do with his questions. He said they were going to pump us for information that they could use against us later, so we shouldn't give him anything to work with.

I return Detective Locke's smile. Andrew doesn't.

"Our technical team has run a thorough search on his laptop, and we've turned up the basic stuff that you'd expect to find on anyone's computer. Nothing set off any major alarms or raised any red flags for us. Jacob has a pretty normal online presence." He clears his throat. It's what he does when he's uncomfortable. I brace myself for whatever is coming next.

"What kind of stuff did you find?" I lean forward in my seat.

"Very usual stuff for a teenage boy living in a digital age." A half smile turns up the corner of his lip.

"Could you be more specific?" I ask.

"Porn," Andrew says. "He means they found porn, Lindsey."

"Oh." I quickly sit back in my seat, embarrassed.

"Was there anything . . ." Andrew rubs the spot between his eyes like the question is painful. "I don't know how to ask this . . . did you find any, uh, disturbing porn?"

Why would he ask that? What's wrong with him? Who cares what kind of porn Jacob was into? I don't want to hear about it. I raise my hand like I'm in elementary school and need the teacher to call on me before speaking, except I don't wait for Detective Locke's approval like I would a teacher's.

"I, um . . . don't really want to be here for that answer. If you guys are going to talk about porn, could you maybe do it when I wasn't in the room?" I ask.

Detective Locke laughs. I've never heard him laugh before. Is he doing it for Dan's benefit? "I didn't bring you in today to talk about Jacob's porn history." He shifts his gaze to Andrew. "And to set your mind at ease, there wasn't anything out of the usual realm."

Andrew's shoulders sag with relief, and he settles into his seat.

"I called you in because there's still a hidden account on his laptop that we can't get into with the username-and-password combinations you gave us earlier. We got lucky with the others, but no matter what we do, our team isn't able to get into this account. It's been used as the primary account to access other sites, and we need to see the account history."

What are they trying to find buried in his search history? The secret life of a depressed teen? They've already found his secret social media accounts. That wasn't a big surprise, since I found them over a year ago. I pay more attention to those than I do the public ones. Kids are brutally vicious these days, and I was pleased to see that Jacob maintains his integrity even online when he doesn't think he's being watched. It has never occurred to me to search his laptop, since he only uses it for school-related stuff. At least that's what I thought.

"Are there any other passwords you can think of? Anything that might be helpful?"

Andrew and I turn to each other, communicating without speaking like couples do when they've been married for almost twenty years. We racked our brains when they asked permission to go through all his electronics, and I can't imagine there's any we left out, since we stretched things the first time with pretty obscure possibilities. I can't believe none of them worked. We turn back to Detective Locke at the same time with matching shrugs.

"Shoot. I was hoping you guys would be able to help us out." He looks disappointed.

"Does that mean you won't be able to get into those accounts?" Andrew asks. His face is pinched with worry.

"No, we can still get into them. It just means we have to send his laptop to our bigwig team, and they're in Los Angeles with caseloads a mile long. It'll take forever to get back." He lets out a frustrated sigh. "But I guess we've got to do it because we don't have any other choice in the matter. We have to see what's in those accounts. If he went to such great lengths to hide them, then it's probably exactly what we've been looking for."

I swallow my dread. It leaves a nasty taste in my mouth.

Andrew slips his hand from my hold and clears his throat like he's about to give a speech. "Don't waste your time. The accounts are mine."

I whirl around in my chair to face Andrew. "What do you mean, they're your accounts?"

"I mean they're mine." He refuses to look at me. His eyes roam the room with nowhere to land. He's obviously shaken. "I created them with Jacob's information."

Alarm bells go off inside me. "I don't understand. What for? Why would you do something like that?"

The color is gone from his face. Sweat breaks out on his forehead.

"Oh my God." It hits me like I've been stunned with a Taser gun. "This is what you've been so worried about? All this time I thought you were freaking out over Jacob, but you've been scared that you were going to get caught. What have you been doing?"

"I was going to tell you. I've been trying to find the right time." He spits it out fast, like the words have been stuck inside him for a long time just waiting to get out.

The room spins. I feel sick. This can't be happening. I grip both armrests. My body goes rigid with fear like I'm about to plummet on an amusement park ride. I can't swallow.

"I haven't been doing anything in real life. All of it is online. I don't even know who she is. She just wanted a friend. Same as me." He's speaking too fast for my brain to catch up.

"I assume it's safe to say that you can provide access to those accounts?" Detective Locke breaks into our conversation.

I forget he's in the room. Humiliation burns my cheeks. Dan clears his throat, reminding us of his presence too.

"Do you really need to see it? How does that help Jacob?" There's no hiding Andrew's embarrassment. He picks at the irritated skin on his hands.

It's sex stuff. It's got to be. That's the only thing that would elicit this type of reaction from him.

Dan jumps in. "If we provide you with the IP addresses and history so that you can verify all accounts, will that suffice?"

Detective Locke is as calm and collected as he was at the beginning of the interview. "As long as everything checks out, that should be fine."

How long did it take him to be able to sit in the midst of people's crumbling lives and remain unaffected? Why couldn't he have had this conversation with us over the phone? Suddenly, the realization slams me—he set us up. Detective Locke set us up. I can't believe it. He wanted to be present so he could see our reactions.

TWENTY-EIGHT

DANI

I tug on the glass door of the police station and quickly scan the empty waiting room. There are too many options. Does Bryan expect to walk in and sit next to me? What will he do if I tell him not to? But what's it going to look like to Detective Locke if we sit apart? My thoughts overlap as they chase each other. I flash the receptionist my ID, and she barely glances up from behind her Plexiglas window in the corner of the room.

I pick a chair in the center of the room: completely neutral. I'll leave the decision up to Bryan and do my best not to freak out during whatever surprise Detective Locke has in store for us. He left a harried voice mail right before lunch about coming in to speak with him as soon as we could because there'd been an interesting turn in the case that he wanted to discuss. He refused to say anything more when I called him back to confirm. I was extra careful to schedule it at a time when Bryan could attend. I haven't heard from him all day. His assistant was the one who confirmed our four o'clock appointment.

My thoughts summon his presence, and he walks through the door arm in arm with Ted. His head is thrown back and he's laughing in the ridiculous, over-the-top way that he does when he wants people to notice him. Ted's strides match his as they take spots on the opposite wall. Ted shifts his eyes from me to Bryan, then back again. I shrug as if I owe him an explanation for our distance.

Thankfully, we don't have to wait long before Detective Locke calls us into his office. He never takes us in the interview rooms lining the hallway like the ones I've seen on TV. I'm not sure if that's a good thing or a bad one. I trail behind Ted and Bryan, following them into the room. I slide into one of the chairs in front of Detective Locke's like we usually do, but Ted and Bryan stay standing behind me, as if to imply that they don't expect this meeting to last long. Detective Locke is unfazed and settles into his normal seat behind the desk. He takes a minute to shuffle through the papers on his desk, and Bryan does his impatient throat-clicking thing behind me while we wait. I try not to cringe. He hasn't looked at me once. It's like I'm not even in the room. Ted's following his lead.

"Good to see you again, Martin," Ted says, breaking the tension.

"You too." He finds the paper he's searching for and sets it on top of the stack. "I won't take up too much of your time, since I know we all have things we'd rather be doing. I've had the opportunity to interview many of Caleb's friends and classmates as well as some of his teachers. They've all been very accommodating in helping us get to the bottom of things." There's a perceptible shift in his tone. "Would you describe Caleb as having a temper?"

Here we go. It was only a matter of time. I take a deep breath before speaking. "You have to understand—"

Ted places his hand on my shoulder to stop me and interrupts. "What are you getting at?" he asks Detective Locke.

"An idea of Caleb's temperament. Does he get angry easily?"

"He doesn't have a temper." The lie easily rolls off my tongue without a conscious thought. I can sense Bryan's pleased expression without turning around.

"Would you agree?" Detective Locke glances at Bryan.

"Caleb isn't an angry kid," Bryan says without any hesitation.

"Hmm . . . that's interesting because his teachers and classmates painted a slightly different picture. All of them described Caleb as being quick tempered." He skims his paper. "In fact, someone called him a 'hothead.' Why do you think so many people described him that way? Was he only that way at school?"

"He wasn't that way anywhere. He might've had a strong personality, and he stood up for himself if he felt wronged, but that doesn't mean he was a hothead. That implies something completely different." Bryan maintains his stance.

"So he didn't get in trouble for . . . let's see, 'threatening behavior toward a teacher' last year?" he recites from what I'm assuming is the disciplinary report in his hand. We have the same one in our files at home.

We've already been through this with the school, and I don't want to go through it again with the police department. Caleb never threatened a teacher. Period. I'm not one of those mothers who acts like their child can do no wrong. That's not what this is about. I can admit when I'm at fault, and I've taught my children to do the same. But Caleb had every right to stand up to Ms. Arias when he was being accused of something he didn't do.

"One of his teachers got upset when Caleb didn't agree with a grade he'd gotten on his midterm," I explain for what feels like the thousandth time.

Detective Locke shifts in his seat and raises his eyebrows. "He got an F for plagiarizing, didn't he? Isn't that what the dispute was over?"

"Technically, yes, but Caleb got angry when—"

Ted interrupts Bryan. "We've established that Caleb has been in trouble at school. What kid hasn't? Can we move on?"

"Very well." Detective Locke gives him a clipped nod. "Can we talk about the time Caleb was suspended for spitting in someone's food?"

I push my chair back. "This is getting ridiculous. Are we going to go through every incident Caleb's had in school since kindergarten?"

This is starting to feel like a witch hunt, and I don't like it. Bryan's anger radiates from behind me. He doesn't like this any more than I do.

"No, but we are going to talk about the ones that involved violent behavior toward other students." He looks so pleased. He's one of those people who's never had any real power in their life, so once they get even a little taste of it, they totally let it go to their head.

Bryan speaks to Ted rather than addressing Detective Locke. "He's making it sound like such a bigger deal than it was. That's exactly how the school handled it, too, like Caleb was some vicious bully who tormented kids on purpose, but that couldn't be further from the truth. All he was doing was trying to make his friends laugh. Nothing more."

I nod my head in eager agreement. Caleb is a clown, and making people laugh is his favorite thing to do in the whole world. Does he step over the line occasionally? Yes, but his intentions are always good. He would never hurt anyone on purpose.

"I'd like to bring Caleb in for questioning again but this time with his trauma therapist. I've already reached out to her, and she's agreed to join us." Detective Locke doesn't bother pretending like he needs my permission. His gaze is focused on Ted.

"We're more than happy to cooperate with the investigation. All the rules previously created will apply to this interview too, of course." Ted doesn't skip a beat.

"Caleb still isn't talking, so I'm not sure what good that will do," Bryan says.

Detective Locke dismisses him with a shrug. "You'd be surprised what kids will disclose once they know that you already know their secrets."

I duck my head and hurry through the Denny's parking lot, shoving down the leftover worry from our meeting with Detective Locke this afternoon. Nobody from Norchester goes to Denny's except as a last-resort breakfast venue, but we aren't taking any chances with being spotted. Lindsey and I picked one ten miles away just to be careful.

I push open the heavy glass doors and scan the tables for Kendra. I quickly spot her sitting in a booth at the center of the restaurant. She couldn't stand out more from the truck drivers and crew of twentysomethings that just left the bar, in her paisley-flowered sweater and pink scarf tied over her head. The smell of booze and stale cigarettes mingles with the smell of bacon grease and pancakes. We might as well be holding signs that say we're out of place. It just increases my sense of being a criminal, and I scurry to our table, avoiding eye contact with everyone.

She moves to stand and greet me, but I motion for her to stay seated. There's no reason to draw more attention to ourselves. I slip into the other side of the booth.

"I ordered you coffee." She motions to the thick ceramic mug in front of me before untying her scarf and wrapping it loosely around her neck. The top half of her blonde hair is pushed forward in a bump, secured with a clip, while the rest hangs over her narrow shoulders. It's the most put together I've seen her look since it happened.

"Thanks." I lace my fingers around my mug.

We stare at each other from across the booth. She has a petite face and perfect round lips. Natural lips. Not those fake ones that make women look ridiculous. Hers are the real deal. We've probably sat this way thousands of times in hundreds of places over the thirty-plus years of our friendship, but it feels like an awkward first date, and I have no idea what to say. I haven't been alone with her since before the accident, and so much hangs between us that I don't even know where to begin.

I take a sip of my coffee. Kendra put in the perfect amount of cream and sugar for me. If she's starting to pull any part of herself together, then I don't want to screw that up, so I choose my words carefully. "How are you feeling after Luna's visit?" I skirt by the fact that she was supposed to be meeting with Caleb.

"Thanks for letting her come see me," she says, sidestepping the issue right along with me. "Did she tell you what we talked about?"

I nod. Luna's story came out in pieces while I tended to her the other night. I wasn't surprised to learn she'd been at the same party or that the boys had gotten kicked out for getting into a fight over something stupid. All of it sounded like pretty normal teenage behavior to me—exactly the kinds of things that happened when we were in high school and were probably happening tonight.

"What did you think?" Kendra returns my question.

I size her up like she's been doing to me, each trying to figure out where the other stands like neither of us can be trusted. I have no reason not to trust her. Well, except for that one time. There was that one time, but we don't talk about that. Ever. Not even the night it happened. Anyway, she has no reason not to trust me. I'm not a dishonest person.

"Sounds like they were more wasted than we thought, and none of this probably would've happened if they weren't," I say, staring at her pointedly.

Luna also told me that the boys got the alcohol they were drinking that night from Kendra's bar. I knew it hadn't come from me because the only alcohol that gets into our house is the bottles Bryan sneaks inside. The blame can no longer be pinned solely on the gun, and I'd be lying if I said there wasn't a certain amount of relief in not bearing so much of the responsibility.

This time she's the one to nod. "So what kind of stuff has Detective Locke been asking you?"

Kendra's boldness takes me by surprise, even though it shouldn't. "Um . . . well, he asks things like how much time Sawyer spent at my house and how much time Caleb spent over there, if I'd noticed anything different or strange in the days leading up to the accident," I respond, then quickly add, "Except he doesn't call it an accident. Did you notice that?"

She makes air quotes while she says it in Detective Locke's deep voice. "The night of the incident."

"Exactly." I smile despite the seriousness of the situation. "But he asks way more questions about Caleb and his behavior than he does Sawyer. How about you guys?"

"Pretty much the same. He always circles back to whether or not the boys had gotten into an argument recently or any kind of disagreement." Kendra pauses, taking a minute to mull over what she wants to say before continuing. "They weren't fighting or anything, were they?" Her eyes cloud with doubt.

"No. Not at all. They were fine. Everything was fine."

"Right." She nods her head in agreement.

We both sip our coffee. I look away first, glancing at the door for Lindsey. She should be here by now. The silence stretches out between us. "Lindsey texted right before I left and said she'll be here as soon as Jacob's asleep," I announce to break it up.

Kendra leans across the table and grabs my hand conspiratorially. "Okay, can I just say to you before she gets here that I think some of the stuff she does with Jacob is super creepy?"

"Oh my God, me too!" I squeal, trying to keep my voice down. "I haven't been able to talk to anyone about it, and I've felt like the biggest bitch for even feeling that way."

"Trust me, you're not alone. Like tonight. She'll come after Jacob's asleep." She raises her eyebrows. "I feel so bad for her, though."

"I do too. At some point she's just going to have to accept his condition. It can't be good for her to hold out hope like this. I mean, it's been over three weeks."

We all count how many days have passed since our worlds changed forever. There should be a measure of relief at having survived the first few weeks, and hopefully there is for them, but it's still ground zero for me. I want to open my mouth and spill what it has been like these past few days, to unburden myself of the pain attaching itself to me like a cancer, but I'm supposed to be her emotional container, not the other way around.

"How are you doing?" I ask, bringing my attention back to her.

It's the only permission Kendra needs to open the floodgates. She grabs tissues from the Louis Vuitton purse sitting next to her in the booth and launches into a description of her emotional turmoil. I can't concentrate on anything she's saying. I nod my head at the appropriate moments and do my best to look interested, but I'm gone. All I can think about is what happens when I get home. Bryan and Ted left the police station without saying goodbye to me this afternoon. Whatever weird sort of alliance we'd developed while inside was gone that quickly. I haven't heard anything from Bryan the rest of the day.

I'm scared to go home because I don't know what lies in store for me there. Luna was gone this afternoon when I came home from the police station. She left a letter in a sealed envelope on my pillow that I can't bring myself to read. Not yet. I've tried texting her, but she doesn't respond. I want to tell her that I told her dad to leave. I said the words—*get out*. But that's the thing: they meant nothing. My words mean nothing to him, and he's probably lounging in our bedroom watching *SportsCenter* without a care in the world.

My therapist is convinced he's a narcissist. She says he doesn't have the ability to feel empathy for others. I argued with her about it for a long time. After all, you can't have the kind of chaotic and abusive childhood that he did and expect to come through it unscathed. But that's just it. She says that's what makes him the perfect candidate for narcissism. I don't care what it's called. I just want him to go away without hurting us.

All of this is happening so fast, and I don't know what to do. Beth said baby steps were okay, that I didn't have to do everything all at once, so that's what I've been doing. One thing at a time in the direction of leaving him, but I can barely scrape up the money to see Beth every week, and I'm nowhere near being able to provide Caleb and me with a stable home. I don't even have enough money saved for a deposit on an apartment yet.

I haven't had access to our finances in over twenty years, and I rely on my monthly allowance to pay for things. I thought it was so cute and romantic in the beginning when Bryan wanted to take care of me the way that he did. Back then, that was how he framed it—taking care of me—because that was how he framed everything, and it seemed so sweet. As soon as we got engaged, he put himself in charge of our finances. I was still working at Macy's, and I gladly turned over my biweekly checks because I've never been good with money and was more than happy to have someone else do it for me. In those days, I didn't know about the other Bryan. I'd yet to meet him, so I just felt like a pampered princess.

Now I'm a prisoner.

TWENTY-NINE
KENDRA

I find myself in front of the Delta Tau house. Thankfully, there's a steady stream of Uber drivers pulling up alongside the curb, so nobody notices me parked on the other side of the street. I meant to go home after my Denny's date with Dani and Lindsey, but I drove here instead. An unconscious desire to retrace Sawyer's last steps drew me.

I can't be home without taking those pills, and I don't want to take those pills anymore, so I needed somewhere to go. Normally, I'd go to Lindsey's or Dani's, and if that wasn't an option, I'd beg one of them to go out with me until they relented. But none of that's feasible.

I haven't been to Dani's or anywhere near it yet, and I'm pretty sure I never will. I don't know how she lives there. How do you stay in the same house where someone died, especially someone you loved and cared about? Neither of us brings it up. We skirt around it like expert dancers. That's what tonight's meeting felt like too. At least she sat and listened to me ramble and cry before Lindsey showed up.

Lindsey wasn't any more relaxed than Dani. She was so anxious she barely stayed in the booth long enough for a cup of coffee. As it was, she jittered her legs, occasionally bumping the table and making the silverware clang, throughout the entire time she was there. Her face is gray like it was the summer she got mono and slept through all of June. She needs to get outside of the hospital more. I told her that but then immediately felt like a hypocrite, since I barely leave my house and spend all of my time holed up in Sawyer's room.

My legs are shaking harder than hers were at Denny's. Sweat trickles down my back. At the same time that I desperately want to flush the poison from my body, I'm frightened of what will happen once it's gone. I'm not an addict. I partied hard when I was a teenager and in college, but all that stopped after I had kids. I get tipsy after two glasses of wine, and I can't remember taking anything stronger than a Tylenol PM in the last decade. I don't like the pills or the way they make me feel, but the only alternative is the debilitating emotional pain. It's the loss of control and the groundlessness when they overtake me that are so terrifying. Feeling nothing is preferable. Maybe that's how addicts get started.

What will the kids inside of Delta Tau do if I barge in and ask if anyone was there the night Sawyer died? Will someone take pity on me and come forward? Will they answer my questions if they do? Doubtful, but they will record me and post it for all the world to see. The video of me coming out of the hospital that night has gathered over 500K likes. Reese brags on our stats like it's something to be proud of.

I bring Sawyer's phone out of my purse and swipe it to life. I don't go anywhere without it, guarding it more carefully than mine. I pull up the series of videos I've been watching under the file with the skilled photography pictures. I push play on the latest one.

Again, it's Jacob. Always Jacob. This time he's standing in Sawyer's closet with his back toward him. He's shirtless, and muscles ripple their way down to the elastic waistband of his boxers. Ripped jeans are slung from his hips. Barefoot.

"Jacob . . . ," Sawyer calls to him from behind the camera.

He turns around and smiles.

Video ends.

My chest constricts. I press play again. Another time. Same thing. Nothing changes. A chill runs down my neck. It's not the images in the video that disturb me—it's the desire. Sawyer's throat is laced with it when he says Jacob's name, and Jacob's eyes return the fire.

I drop the phone in my lap.

THIRTY

LINDSEY

I don't bother being quiet coming into the house. Andrew said he'd wait up for me no matter how long my meeting with the girls took because we need to talk about what happened in Detective Locke's office. That's my Good Andrew. My Always-Doing-the-Right-Thing Andrew. *Of course we'll have a nice chat about your secret online world before bed, because today I met Bad Andrew.*

He's perched on the couch in the living room like an anxious parent waiting for their child who's out past curfew. There are two glasses of water on the coffee table in front of him. His thoughtfulness irritates me. I take a seat on the armchair across from him, refusing to sit next to him and putting the coffee table between us so there's no way he can touch me. I cross my arms and legs.

"We need to talk," he says. His dark hair sticks up all over the place. He coats it with gel in the morning to keep it straight and off his face, but no matter how much he uses, it all separates by the end of the day. He's wearing his office clothes instead of the sweatpants he dons whenever he's settled in for the night, which means he's prepared to leave if he needs to. Good.

I nod, signaling for him to continue.

"A couple years ago, I—"

I almost come out of my chair. "Did you just say a couple years ago? How long has this been going on?"

"Almost two years." His expression tells me it doesn't get any better from here. I brace myself for whatever he's about to say next. "I created a profile on an online site for married people who are looking for companionship." He reaches across the table and grabs my wrist, trying to hold my hand. "Please, it's not a dating site. I told you it's not what it looks like, and believe me, I know how bad this looks."

I jerk my hand away and glare at him. I've never wanted to spit at anyone, but I'm angry enough to spit, and for a second I consider hocking a loogie in his face. It's disgusting and crude, just like what he's made our marriage into. Almost twenty years, and we're a joke. A cliché.

His voice is strangely flat as he continues speaking. "The site is set up specifically for people who are interested in friendships without any sexual involvement. It's for people who want friendships outside of their marriages, but their spouses won't allow it—"

"What do you mean, their spouses wouldn't allow friendships outside of their marriage? I've always let you have friends." I'm not the jealous type. Never have been—at least with him. I didn't need to be because I trust him, wholeheartedly and completely. His trustworthiness was one of the main reasons I married him. He walked the straight and narrow through all of high school, no matter what anyone else did around him. He was the treasurer of the student council and president of the MATHCOUNTS team. It's why I didn't pay him any attention then, but when it came time to start thinking about my future, he was the perfect candidate.

He shakes his head as if I'm not understanding what he's trying to get me to see. "If I would've told you about it, then you would've asked me questions about it."

"So now I'm being punished for asking questions? Are you serious?" I'm done keeping my voice down. I don't care if I wake the kids.

"The conversation would've turned into this, and I didn't want to have this argument with you. I wanted a relationship that was mine and only about me so I could feel like a separate person again. I didn't feel like I had any part of myself left. I'm sorry if this hurts you." He looks genuinely apologetic, like he doesn't want this to be happening any more than I do. His kindness makes it hurt more. I'm not sure how that's possible. "I lost myself along the way with being a dad and a husband. I wanted to find out who I was again. Meeting other people helped me do that."

"There was more than one?" I've had enough. I don't wait for him to answer before stomping out of the living room and heading for the stairs. He grabs me from behind.

"Please, Lindsey. Stop. Just look at the site. You'll see what I mean." He frantically pulls his phone from the back pocket of his pants. He pulls up the site and hands it to me.

Married Friends. With a tagline: *Looking for companionship outside your marriage without the guilt of an affair?*

He isn't lying. At least not about the site. Sadness builds in my chest as I quickly skim the site. It's geared toward men and women who are missing intimacy and friendship in their marriages but don't want to cheat.

"Now do you see?" I keep his phone, mindlessly scrolling while he talks. The site boasts of having thousands of members worldwide who are longing to get in touch. You can choose what you're looking for like on any other dating site, with options ranging from exchanging information to "affectionate companionship," which sounds borderline sexual to me.

"Everything I do and every relationship that I have is about you or the kids. I don't have a friend who's not connected to you in some way or hasn't known me since preschool. This gave me a space that was mine. Allowed me to explore who I was again. It was fun."

"Did you meet anyone"—I pause as I search for the right word—"special?"

He nods. "Last year right around this time. We were in lots of group chats and other meetings, but we never did any instant messaging for a long time until she came on one night really upset and nobody else was on but me. We ended up talking, just the two of us, and we've been close ever since."

"Close?" What does that even mean? We're supposed to be close. I'm his wife. He doesn't need to be close with other women. There's only one reason men want to be intimate with women, even the best ones. "What's her name?"

"I don't know her name."

"Come on, Andrew. For this to work, you have to be honest."

"No, I'm serious. That's the point. You don't know any of the real details about each other's lives unless you choose to disclose them, and we never did. Neither of us wanted that. I only know her as MayDay39. I call her May." There's a hint of affection in his tone when he says her name.

"What does she call you?"

"L."

"She called you L? A letter? Why'd she call you that?"

"Lindsey, please, don't. Some of this you shouldn't hear. It will only hurt you more." His eyes plead with mine.

"Now you're worried about my feelings?" Anger floods my body. "Why did she call you L?"

He drops his head and his voice. "Because my profile name is LonelyInLondon."

"You don't live in London." I state the obvious before letting his response register. He gives me time to remember when we were in London. "Oh my God. Then?" I grab the railing and steady myself as I slide down to the step, taking a seat on the wood. It was our first international trip. I thought it was magical, but apparently he was so lonely while we were there that he went lurking on websites for female friends.

He takes a seat on the stair below me and places his hand on my knee. I watch him do it, but my legs don't feel connected to me. "I'm so sorry about all of this." He struggles not to cry.

"When did it get sexual?"

He balks and moves against the stairway wall. "I told you. It wasn't about that. Trust me, it wasn't. We never even exchanged pictures. I couldn't pick her out of a lineup if I tried."

"But earlier today you said you were going to tell me about her and that you were just working up the nerve to do it. Why would you be so worried about it if she was only a good friend? That doesn't make any sense."

He shrugs. None of this makes sense. I'm not an idiot.

"What's your log-in?" I ask, bringing up the box on the site.

"Um . . . it's . . . I mean, do we need to log on to my profile? It's kind of embarrassing. I can tell you everything that's on there. What do you want to know?"

I narrow my eyes, daring him to challenge me. "I want to see for myself." I hand the phone to him so he can enter the information. He takes it reluctantly and makes no move to enter digits. "Andrew, let me see your profile."

He shakes his head like an animal caught in a trap, except he set this one for himself. "I don't want to hurt you."

"Why would it hurt me? You said it wasn't sex." His eyes fill with fear and foreboding. What could hurt more than sex? And then it hits me like I've been punched in the gut.

"Did you have feelings for her, Andrew?"

THIRTY-ONE

DANI

I tiptoe into Caleb's room so I don't wake him up in case he's asleep. His eyes spring open before I reach his bed. I put my finger to my lips so he doesn't move around and make too much noise. Bryan's only a short distance down the hall, and I still hear his TV on, so I'm not sure whether he's sleeping or not. The last thing I want is for him to get up and start storming around the house.

I crawl into bed next to Caleb and wrap my arms around him. The front of his shirt sticks to his chest, dampened with sweat. "Did you have one of your nightmares?" He nods against my chest. "I'm sorry I wasn't here when you woke up. I met Lindsey and Kendra at Denny's in Chatsfield, and there was a huge accident on my way home. How bad was it?" He holds up eight fingers. We've developed a rating system with Gillian for his attacks. It has something to do with creating his anxiety hierarchy. I hug him tightly and try to send every ounce of my love into his body. "Well, I'm here now, and I'll sleep right next to you for the rest of the night if you want. Will that help?"

He nods and forces a half smile. His collarbone pokes through his athletic frame. The weight has fallen off him in these past weeks. Getting him to eat is impossible, and I've resorted to making him huge protein drinks like the wrestlers use when they're trying to bulk up.

I force him to suck down at least two a day. I've tried cooking all his favorite foods, but nothing brings back his appetite.

I rub circles on his back, and his body slowly melts into mine. It's still early enough that he might be able to fall back to sleep and get a few decent hours of rest before the sun comes up. When his nightmares wake him after three, he almost never falls back to sleep, and those end up being horrible days for him because he can't keep it together at all. All his doctors agree that sleep is the most important thing for him, but it's also the most elusive. I'd be scared to sleep too. The sounds he makes during his dreams don't sound human.

Sometimes when I'm lying in the darkness next to him, I wonder if Sawyer's ghost haunts our house. He took his last breath lying on our family room floor. Where did his spirit go? What if he's still here?

Caleb shifts position against me. What is being in this house like for him?

Cruel.

That's the word that immediately pops into my mind.

Is that what Luna's letter will say if I read it? She came close to saying as much when she found out we were coming back home after the accident. Pretty sure that's why she came home with us—so that she could be there to buffer Caleb against the memories. I hate that I went along with Bryan and didn't fight more, but I didn't know what else to do. It was an awful decision, and look what happened. I might not love myself enough to demand to be treated better, but I love my kids enough, and they deserve more.

"Caleb?" I whisper. "Are you awake?" He moans like he might've just fallen back to sleep. I wiggle his shoulder. "Come on. Get up."

His face is a mixture of surprise and confusion. He sits up slowly in bed. He raises his arms and puts his palms up as if to ask, *What are we doing?*

I speak quickly and quietly as I start throwing things he might need into his backpack. "Your dad hit Luna last night when he found out she went over to Kendra's to talk about the accident." His eyes widen in horror. "I know. It's awful. That's why she left. It's why we're leaving too."

He jumps out of bed and pulls on a pair of jeans crumpled on his floor. He searches the room for his shoes and slips them on after he finds them.

"We're going to Grandma's," I say, the plan coming to me as we move toward the door with his things. I stop him before we get to it and turn around so we're eye to eye. "And Caleb, honey, I'm so sorry that I ever made you come back into this house."

THIRTY-TWO
LINDSEY

I'm trying to get Jacob's arm around me, but it keeps falling off and flopping to his side, lifeless. It only stays if I hold it in place, so I give up and lay my head against his chest instead. The respirator moves his chest up and down in a steady rhythm. It's hypnotic and unnatural all at the same time.

"I wish you would've let me get this close to you," I say in a voice barely above a whisper. There has been some distance between us these past couple of years as he grew more independent. It's natural and means I'm doing my job right, since the point of parenting is to raise your children into healthy individuals, and pulling away is part of that, but it doesn't make the process any less painful.

I didn't plan on coming back to the hospital this late. I was going to grab a few hours of sleep and leave at five before everyone else was up, but I couldn't stay at home with Andrew after our conversation. There was no end or resolution to it. We just stopped talking.

"Your dad fell for somebody else. Can you believe that?" I let out a laugh. There's no mistaking the hysteria filling it. That only makes me let out another one. "Your dad. Of all people," I snort. Because that was his secret. He fell in love with an anonymous woman online. "He says there was nothing sexual about it and all they did was talk. They never exchanged pictures. Only words. And you know what? I believe him." This time it's a sob that escapes instead of my manic giggle. He was going to leave me. He wouldn't admit it. Not my Good Andrew, because good husbands don't leave their wives and families. "If any man could have an emotional affair, it's your dad. He said she made him feel things he's never felt before. What does that even mean? And who says that? It sounds like a cheesy romance novel." Tears stream unbidden down both cheeks.

I'm coming apart at the seams. My emotions are shredded. There's no resistance left. It's all gone. I'm destroyed.

"He was working out a way to tell me before you got hurt." Good Andrew couldn't live with what Bad Andrew had done. He would've left if this hadn't happened. That much I'm sure of, because if he fell that hard for somebody else, then he couldn't be in love with me, and he wouldn't think that was fair to either of us. He's so good even when he's bad. It makes me hate him more. "He kept saying that he was committed to me—to our family. He wants to stay." My Good Andrew. Of course he'll stay, because he couldn't live with himself if he left now. "What do you think?"

I strain my ears for any sound of life escaping from him. He was inside me for nine months. At some primal level he has to know I need him to give me a sign that he's still in there somewhere. That all of this isn't for nothing. That we didn't try our best to do everything right just to end up annihilated beyond recognition. The psst-tffff . . . pssst-tffff of his respirator, coupled with a few other beeps from the room across the hall, is all that answers back.

"You can't hear any of this, can you?" Anguished sobs work their way up my throat. I force them back down. "Can you hear me, Jacob? Answer me," I hiss in his ear.

Nothing.

I slap him, hard—harder than I meant to. I quickly scan the room, like someone might've walked in without me noticing and seen me hurt him. We're alone.

I take one last look around and then pull his hospital gown up until it exposes his pale thigh. I smack the meat of his thigh like it's a punching bag at the gym. My hand leaves a red mark. There will be a bruise tomorrow.

I jump off the bed and put my face within inches of his. "Did you feel that? Did you? Do something! Anything!" I backhand his cheek.

The same lifeless expression. His eyes are closed like he's in a deep sleep.

I stumble backward.

I just hit my son.

My back hits the bathroom door, and I slide down it until I reach the floor. I bite my cheek to keep from crying, but the sobs won't be ignored. They hit me like a violent ocean wave, and I tumble into them.

THIRTY-THREE
KENDRA

I hand Lindsey my phone. The video of Sawyer and Jacob that I found last night is already queued up and ready to go. "I'm telling you—Jacob and Sawyer were in a relationship."

"And you know that because of a video?" Lindsey asks in disbelief. Her eyes flit around the room like they don't know where to land.

I asked her to meet me in the south hospital cafeteria instead of Jacob's room. I told her I was hungry for breakfast because I couldn't handle watching her interact with him and I don't have the energy to muster up a fake conversation.

"Just watch. You'll see." I push around the soggy eggs on my plate and take a small bite of the toast while she watches the video. The more times I watch it, the more I'm convinced that something was going on between them.

She hands Sawyer's phone back to me with an absentminded shrug. Fatigue engraves her face. "Who knows what they were doing."

"Are you kidding?" I snatch it from her and point to the stilled video. "Jacob's trying to look sexy!"

"Maybe they were making it for a girl." She says it like she doesn't want it to be about the two of them. She's never been homophobic before. What's wrong with her? She glances at it again. "He'd look the same way if they were making a video for a girl. I don't see what the big deal is either way."

"It means our kids might have been hooking up." She has to see the significance that brings to things. It adds a huge piece to the puzzle. I don't want to come right out and say it, but messy love triangles are the oldest motive in the book.

"Everyone hooks up with everyone else now, Kendra. It's a completely different world than the one we grew up in." She says it in that enlightened mom voice that she developed after Sutton.

There's lots I could tell her about the world our kids lived in that she doesn't know, but there's no need to upset her more when it's obvious that she's having a rough day. Jacob must've kept her up most of the night.

"Okay, so whatever, everyone's hooking up. You don't have any reaction to Jacob and Sawyer possibly hooking up?" I can't imagine how that's possible. I can't stop thinking about it. I've been going back through all the pictures, and you can feel the connection between the two of them. How'd we miss that? Were they having sex when he was sleeping over? How long was it going on?

And what about the girls? They've been over at the house too. I've caught them in Sawyer's bed on more than one occasion. Was it a sexual free-for-all at my house? It couldn't have been, could it? The idea makes me nauseous.

I was always on Sawyer about using protection. Lindsey's super paranoid about Jacob getting a girl pregnant because it will ruin his college scholarship, but I'm the one who needed to worry. Jacob is as smart as he is athletic, so he'd figure out another opportunity if he screwed things up because of a girl, but Sawyer's never cared about school. Sports are the only thing that's ever kept him in school and out of trouble, so we've steered him toward them and away from girls. We encouraged him to date a lot of different girls and not settle down with a girlfriend. Maybe we pushed him too far in the other direction.

She gives me another nonchalant shrug. "I do my best not to think about my kids having sex with anyone."

That's an outright lie. She's really getting on my nerves. Her little I'm-not-bothered-with-anything act might work with other people but not me. Why is she even trying?

I set my fork down. "What's going on?"

"What do you mean?" She blinks twice in rapid succession.

I point to her. "This. You're acting like a robot. Everything I say, you're like, *Hmm . . . I don't know. Maybe . . . la-di-da.* But that's not you." I sweep my hand up and down the length of her body. "And you look awful. Have you been up all night?" Her lower lip quivers, and her eyes fill with tears. I didn't mean to make her cry. I jump up and rush to her side of the cafeteria table. I slide onto the bench next to her and throw my arm around her shoulders. "Tell me what's going on."

Her body is frail next to mine. She never eats when she's stressed. This better not kick up her eating disorder. She's a different person when that's going on. Maybe that's what all this is about. I'm going to text Dani as soon as I leave and see what she thinks. She's always so much better than me at spotting the signs. Plus, Lindsey will tell her things that she won't tell me. She thinks I don't understand weight issues because I've never had to struggle with mine, but whatever. She's always been skinnier than me.

Lindsey shakes her head. I reach over and tuck some of her unruly hair behind her ears. She furtively wipes at her tears, but they're coming faster than she can brush them away. "I'm just really tired. It gets overwhelming taking care of Jacob and being in the hospital all the time."

"You have to let people help you." She's been in her own world for nearly a month and has completely shut me out. She acts the same way with Dani. It was only a matter of time before she buckled underneath the pressure. "You're not alone."

She reaches over and grabs the napkin sitting beside my unfinished plate. She blows her nose and crumples it in her hand. She takes a few gasping breaths, struggling to regain her composure.

"Thanks," she says when she's finally in control of herself.

"I'm your best friend. I'm always here for you." I plant a kiss on her cheek. "No matter what." Even if Jacob killed Sawyer, because he's stuck in purgatory, which seems like a fitting punishment for gutting me and destroying my family.

THIRTY-FOUR

DANI

Mom sets a cup of coffee in front of me at the kitchen table. She didn't ask any questions when Caleb and I showed up on her doorstep at two a.m. this morning. She swooped us inside like she'd been expecting us and immediately went to work setting up the guest bedroom. I pull the creamer of milk toward me and pour in a teaspoon. I couldn't wait to be old enough to drink coffee so I could use this creamer. I always thought it was so cute and dainty with the small violet daisies printed on the side. Sometimes Mom let me use it to pour milk into my cereal, but it was never the same thing.

I stir my coffee while Mom pours herself a cup. She takes a seat across from me and clasps her hands around her mug the same way I hold mine. Her blood pressure medicine sits next to her allergy pills and a pile of unopened mail in the center of the table. Dad's letter opener rests beside it. It's been almost twenty years since cancer stole him from us, but his presence still fills the house like he's never left, like he might walk back through the door at any moment.

"Well?" Mom asks.

She might have been silent last night, but that doesn't mean she doesn't expect answers this morning. I wish I had some to give her. I didn't grow up in a violent home. I never saw my dad hit my mom. He rarely even got mad at her, and when he did, he tried his best not to raise his voice at her, at least in front of us. They loved each other in a mutually respectful way for thirty-seven years. Things like this aren't supposed to happen to people like me who grow up in good homes with loving parents. I'm not like the statistics. I have no idea how I ended up here.

"Whatever it is, honey, we'll get through it," Mom says after a few more beats pass and I still haven't answered. "All marriages hit rough times. Your daddy and I went through plenty of them over the years, especially when you kids were younger."

I shake my head. I told myself those exact words so many times that I've lost count. In the beginning, whenever I considered leaving, I reminded myself how I'd promised to love him in good times and bad, through it all, no matter what, because that's what being married meant. Bryan knew how seriously I took my vows and never failed to bring them up whenever he sensed I might be slipping away. If that didn't work, he threw statistics at me about the damaging effects of divorce on children. He preyed on my commitment to my family.

"Is somebody sick?" The color drains from her face at the possibility of having to meet another difficult challenge in the middle of this one.

I shake my head again and quickly speak before I lose my nerve and make up an alternate story to cover for him like I've done so many times before. "Two nights ago, Bryan hit Luna because she talked to Kendra after he told us not to. You know what? It doesn't matter why—it was wrong. He hit her and it's wrong. She left, probably assuming I'd do nothing about it because that's what I do—what I've done for her entire life. But I'm not doing any of it anymore. It's over." My words trip over each other, they're coming out so fast, and they're disjointed, but I can't put them together right. "I have no idea what happens now. Don't talk to him, please, or tell him I'm here. Although he'll figure out I'm here. But I still don't want you to talk to him." My eyes flit to the front door. They've never had an alarm system, always relying on an old-fashioned dead bolt. "Don't let him in." I'm running out of steam. I can't stop.

Not yet. "And my marriage was pretty bad. Like, the whole time. I'm sorry I lied about it. But I don't want to talk about any of this right now. Okay? That's what happened. That's why we're here, and if I talk about any of it in detail, then I might just fall apart, and I can't fall apart right now. I just can't—"

"Shhh . . . hush, okay, honey, okay. Settle down." Mom places her hand on top of mine. "You don't have to talk about anything that you don't want to talk about."

Breaking down isn't an option. Caleb's upstairs, and he needs me. Luna is somewhere in the world, and she needs me, too, even if she never responds to another one of my calls or texts.

"Okay." I take a deep breath, shoving my emotions back down, hoping they'll stay there. "Can we just focus on figuring out a way to make Caleb feel safe again?"

THIRTY-FIVE
LINDSEY

I hurry down the hallway to the conference room, where I've kept everyone waiting for almost ten minutes. I completely spaced the meeting with Jacob's medical team. I went back to his room after my breakfast with Kendra and lost all track of time. I almost told her about Andrew but chickened out at the last minute. He had an affair, but somehow, I feel like I'm the one who did something wrong and needs to hide. Do I call it an affair? He didn't really *do* anything. Or did he? Doubt and suspicion cloud everything he's said because I still haven't seen any of his conversations with May. I'm so jealous they have nicknames for each other. We've never had nicknames.

Earlier, I tilted my chair away from Jacob's bed because I couldn't stop staring at the spot on his thigh where the bruises from last night lay hidden underneath his white sheet. I can't believe I did that. I've always secretly wondered what would happen if you really hurt him. The nurses and doctors touch him so gently when they're examining his reflexes and responses, like he'll break if they press too hard. I've always wanted to ask them to apply more force during their examinations, but what kind of a mother asks a nurse to hurt their child? I got my answer, but it's not one I like—he didn't so much as flinch when I hurt him. I push the guilt away.

We used to have these meetings multiple times a day, but they've dwindled to once every two to three days since they moved us. I push open the door, muttering my apologies before I'm through the doorway. I grab the first open seat on the right.

Andrew sits next to Dr. Merck. Normally, Andrew and I would've coordinated our arrival so we could sit together, but I turned my phone off after Kendra left and haven't turned it back on since. Today might be one of those days I shut out the rest of the world.

"Hi, Lindsey, welcome." Dr. Merck stops the conversation he's having with Dr. Levlon to acknowledge me. Dr. Levlon occupies the seat on his left. He's Jacob's anesthesiologist and only comes to the meetings when we talk about surgery. Dread rises in my chest. I can't handle another surgery.

Andrew catches my eye and shoots me a tired smile. I shift my gaze to the other side of the table, ignoring him like I ignored his texts all morning before shutting my phone off. The doctors and specialists from the rehabilitation floor occupy the rest of the seats around the table, even though most of them aren't familiar with Jacob's case. I recognize the head of the human resources department, Diana, sitting across from Andrew.

"Hi, everyone," I say, letting my eyes travel around the room before settling on Dr. Merck, since he always leads these meetings. He's been with us since Jacob's admission to the hospital. He got there before we did and was already in surgery with him when we arrived during those awful hours when we hovered in limbo between then and now. As irritated as I can get with him, he's the reason Jacob's alive.

Dr. Merck folds his hands in front of him like he might be getting ready to lead us in a prayer. He's in his late fifties, wearing the lines of a seventy-year-old around his eyes. Years working with brain-injured kids would take their toll on anyone. As usual, he wastes no time getting down to business. "We'd like to talk about withdrawing Jacob from life support."

This is what I rushed down here for? How many times do we have to have this conversation? They've been trying to withdraw Jacob from support since he failed the coma recovery scale three days postaccident and every day since. The injuries to his brain stem mean that even if he does regain awareness, he might forget to swallow and choke to death on his own spit. At least that's what they say, but nobody can tell us with 100 percent certainty if that would be the case, and I've read plenty of stories where it wasn't. There's always a different reason for why they want to do it, but it all boils down to the same thing, no matter how they try to sugarcoat it with nice medical jargon—they've given up hope for his recovery. Today isn't a good day to talk to me about hope.

"We think it might be best—"

I interrupt the speech he's about to give. I've heard it enough to give it myself. "Why did we go through all the trouble of a tracheostomy if we were going to withdraw support? That seems really unnecessary."

Andrew nods in agreement.

"Long-term intubation is damaging after a certain amount of time has passed, and Jacob had far exceeded that window. As I explained then, the infections we had begun seeing were only going to continue and likely get worse. It's the standard medical recommendation for all brain-injured patients that have reached his vegetative state. And ultimately, we wanted him to be comfortable." He clears his throat like he's satisfied with his answer and ready to move on, which doesn't satisfy me at all because it has only been a few days. "There's no easy way to put this, and I'm so sorry that our current medical system often reduces patients to dollar amounts. However, your insurance company is refusing to pay to keep Jacob alive if he's brain dead."

"Can they do that?" Andrew asks. It's not the first time our insurance company has threatened to cut our funding or refuse to pay for certain procedures. Jacob's expenses far exceed anything they expect to pay.

"He's been declared medically brain dead, and after so many days without any significant changes, they can petition to end his services. Honestly, I'm surprised that they waited this long to file the paperwork." He pauses to glance at Diana, who nods her approval, before he continues. "Lots of insurance companies with clients in Jacob's state would do it within a matter of days, and his care would've been denied a long time ago."

"So we're supposed to feel lucky?" Andrew's eyes flare with anger.

"Again, I'm so sorry. I wish there was something that I could do, but I can't change the system, and we've done all we can do for him at this point." Dr. Merck's hands haven't moved from their folded position.

"What happens if we remove him from life support and he breathes on his own?" I ask, and everyone around the table looks at me like I'm a child who just asked how Santa Claus gets into houses that don't have chimneys.

"As I've explained before, the medical likelihood of that happening is very small," Dr. Merck says in the same matter-of-fact way he does each time.

Jacob's neurologist, Dr. Gervais, jumps in. "Your odds of winning the lottery are better than Jacob being able to sustain life on his own, given the extent of his brain injuries."

"We understand that," I say. She's not the first doctor to throw out the lottery statistic.

"We'll figure out a way to pay for his care out of pocket," Andrew says. He's been as adamantly opposed to shutting off Jacob's machines as me. We haven't wavered no matter what they've presented, even threatening to get lawyers involved if we needed to. It's never been a secret that most of Jacob's medical team doesn't agree with our decisions regarding his care.

Dr. Merck and Dr. Levlon exchange glances. The others are silent.

"Do you have any idea how much it costs to provide the round-the-clock medical care that Jacob requires?" Diana speaks up from the far end of the table. Her face is painted with makeup like she's going out to a club instead of working as a hospital administrator, and her fake eyelashes don't match the formal business suit stretched across her body.

Andrew shrugs. "Money isn't any issue when it comes to our son. Other families have been in our situation, and they've figured things out. We can have fundraisers. I can pick up an extra job." We've already been talking about refinancing the house to help pay for the medical bills that have started piling up and all Andrew's lost wages.

Diana glances at a report splayed open in front of her, but I suspect she already has the information memorized. "It's over eleven thousand dollars per day to care for Jacob. That's several hundred thousand dollars a month to artificially sustain a life when all external signs of life have ceased."

"You can't steamroll us into something we don't want to do," Andrew says as my heart sinks.

"I'm not sure we're being clear. It's the next indicated step in his medical care, and your insurance has refused to pay for anything beyond that, so we can't continue to treat him at this hospital once all the paperwork goes through." Dr. Merck's lips are set in a straight line.

Dr. Levlon's face is just as grim, and he nods curtly while Dr. Merck speaks to show his support. "We believe it's in his best interest," he says.

"Well, we're his parents, and we don't, so is there anything else we need to talk about?" Andrew pushes his chair back from the table like he might be getting up to leave.

"Your insurance company is refusing to pay for his continued support, and the hospital has a duty not to prolong his suffering," Dr. Merck repeats.

"Mr. and Mrs. Grant," Diana addresses us together, sitting up straight in her chair. "You can fight this if you want, and you have every right to seek legal counsel to help you do so. You can even contact our human resources department and initiate a court order to stop this process." She reaches into her suit pocket and pulls out a business card. She slides it across the table to Andrew. "There are families in your situation who choose to do just that. These are a few names of lawyers that they chose to help them with it. But please know, your fight might gain you a few extra weeks, maybe even a month or so, but eventually, you'll be court ordered to let him go. And do you know what happens next?" She doesn't wait for a reply. "You'll have drained every penny you have on lawyer costs and court fees. And you have to ask yourself this—is that in the best interest of the rest of your children? Your family?"

Andrew and I sit in stunned silence.

"Maybe we should hear the rest of what they have to say," I say softly after I've finally found my voice again. I can't believe I'm saying the words, but it doesn't seem like we have a choice, and I don't know what else to do. My life is unraveling in front of me, and there's nothing I can do to stop it.

Andrew stubbornly shakes his head and just keeps repeating, "No."

Dr. Merck unfolds his hands and places one of them on Andrew's back. "Listen to what your wife is trying to say."

Don't listen to me. I have no idea what I'm doing or saying. I've never felt so lost or alone. There's no ground underneath my feet.

"What are you talking about, Lindsey?" Andrew gets up and rushes over to me, crouching next to my chair. He puts his hand on my arm. "What are you doing? Do you really want to be making this kind of decision in the emotional state you're in?" His eyes are wide.

I jerk my arm away. "I'm not in any emotional state," I snap. Except that I am. I didn't sleep at all last night. My head pounds; my stomach twists with bile.

He points to my disheveled appearance. "Look at you. Clearly, you're not in the best spot emotionally after you found out—"

I cut him off, holding back tears. "Don't worry about my emotions." I can't handle the public humiliation of his affair on top of everything else. I'm already crumbling under the weight of it.

The room grows more uncomfortable.

"Are you serious? You really want to talk about letting him go?" Andrew's voice is thick with grief. All eyes are on us, but I can only see him. I give him a barely perceptible nod. He grabs both my hands to steady himself.

"Why don't we give the two of you a minute alone?" Dr. Merck suggests.

———

Our minute alone has grown into four hours, but we can't bring ourselves to leave this room because everything changes once we do. We're only prolonging the inevitable, but it doesn't matter. We're not ready.

We spent the first thirty minutes crying too hard to form words, let alone talk about anything. We clung to each other in a moment too intimate for words.

"What do we do?" Andrew asked when he finally pulled away. His voice was stripped to nothing but raw pain.

"We call Dan."

So that's what we did, because it seemed like the most logical thing to do, but his advice wasn't anything we wanted to hear. It matched what Diana had said. We could fight to stop the order, but it would be like trying to stop a moving train. Situations like ours are like divorce—nobody wins, and everybody gets hurt.

Dan's estimate of what it would cost to go to court was more than Diana's. Andrew and I couldn't help but admit that fighting would leave us financially ruined with two other kids to raise. Sutton just finished kindergarten, and it won't be long before Wyatt is in college, doubling our tuition costs. Is it fair to them? Whose needs are more important? All of it made my heart sick.

Our tears and conversation have stalled. Andrew lies with his head on his arms like he's in detention, too spent to do anything else. I twist a loose string from my shirt around my finger over and over again while staring at the hands on the clock. I remind myself to breathe whenever the minute hand gets to the twelve. Nobody's knocked on the door in fifty-four minutes. Maybe that means they've finally given up.

Andrew lifts his head, and his eyes are tunnels of unrelenting pain. "I'm so sorry, Lindsey." His voice cracks at the end.

Is he talking about Jacob or about our marriage? "This is not the time." I can't hear his apologies now no matter what they're about.

"I always knew I was going to be punished for it." There's no mistaking his reference. His leftover Catholic guilt runs deep, but we're not bringing her into this moment.

His stupid affair pales in comparison to losing our son. My guts are being ripped out. The weight of the loss makes it hard to breathe. We have to leave this room and face the world—a world that will never be the same again once we walk out those doors. My children's innocent lives are shattered. Their hearts broke once, and we have to do it again before they've had any chance to heal. How do we explain our decision after everything we've been saying about Jacob and not giving up?

There's a knock at the door. Before we have a chance to respond like before, Dr. Merck sticks his head through. "I'm sorry, but it's time to talk about next steps. We've waited as long as we can."

THIRTY-SIX
DANI

Caleb is sandwiched between Mom and me on the couch when my phone vibrates with a call. It's the third time in the last five minutes. "Sorry, guys, but I have to take this." I shrug out from underneath Caleb's arm and stand, wiping the chip crumbs off the front of my shirt.

"Is it Luna?" Mom glances up from the TV, instantly hopeful of a reunion. She has no clue how long Luna can ignore me if that's what she wants to do, and she expects her to come running over any second, but Luna can ghost me for weeks if she wants to.

I shake my head. "I wish. I'm thinking of driving by her apartment later tonight to see if her lights are on. Maybe I'll park on the sidewalk for a while." I pause for a second. "Or is that too stalkerish?"

A small giggle escapes Caleb's mouth. Mom and I freeze. It's the closest he's come to making a normal sound besides sobbing or yelling in his sleep. Did he notice it? Should I say something? He tosses popcorn in his mouth and stays focused on the movie. Mom's gaping at him too. I don't want to screw this up.

Mom blinks like she's suddenly come to her senses. "Yes, way too much, dear. Don't do that. Give that poor girl some space."

I nod, too shocked by Caleb's tiny outburst to form words.

Mom points to the phone in my hand. "Do you want us to wait for you while you make your phone call?"

"Oh yes," I say in a high-pitched voice that sounds nothing like me, but Caleb doesn't notice. "I was going to call Kendra back. She's called three times, so it must be important." I force myself to move into the kitchen. I catch Mom's eyes over my shoulder as I pass behind the couch and mouth *"Thank you"* to her. She smiles in return and snuggles closer to Caleb. One of her homemade quilts is spread across them. It's the most relaxed I've seen him since the accident. My heart melts with the first twinges of hope for his recovery.

I grab a bottle of water from the refrigerator and head outside to the backyard.

"I knew it! I knew it! I knew it!" I squeal as soon as the door shuts behind me and I'm out of their earshot. I twirl around, doing a happy dance underneath the stars. We've only been out of our house for a day, and he's already showing improvement. Mom's willing to let us stay for however long it takes to figure things out. She talks like reconciliation is possible, but that's only because she doesn't know the whole story.

I waited all day to hear from Bryan, but it was radio silence. That's the last thing I expected from him. He usually doesn't leave me alone after we've fought and refuses to be ignored. He leaves angry rants on my voice mail until he fills up my mailbox and spends hours rage texting, but there's been none of that. I don't trust his sudden absence, but I'm not going to let him spoil this moment.

I can't wait to tell Kendra about Caleb. She's going to be so excited. I tap her name. She cuts into the first ring without waiting for me to say anything or bothering to say hello. "They're taking Jacob off life support tomorrow," she blurts out.

"What?" Everything from the moment before vanishes in that instant. "That can't be right. There's no way Lindsey would do that. Something must've happened."

"I know." Kendra's concern comes through the phone. "It's so weird. It's like she changed her mind overnight, and that's so unlike her, especially after how hard she's fought for him. It doesn't make any sense."

There've been lots of medical emergencies with Jacob since he's been in the hospital and times when we were sure that we'd lose him. We used to get calls in the middle of the night all the time that his oxygen saturation levels had dropped so low they didn't think he would make it through the night or that fluid was building up on his brain and causing ministrokes, but it's been a while since we've had one.

"Maybe he took a turn for the worse, and she's just now getting a chance to tell people," I guess out loud.

"I have no idea. She just texted me an hour ago and told me to tell you."

She couldn't have sent a group text to both of us? How come I always have to find out important things from Kendra? Such childish thoughts, but that doesn't stop them. "Have you talked to her?" I ask, shoving my jealousy aside and trying to act like an adult.

"Nothing except the text. I have no idea what to do. That's why I'm calling you." She sounds fried.

"I don't think there's anything for us to do except be with her." I've become skilled at being with someone in incredible pain. I've sat through hours of grief and terror with Caleb. I felt so powerless in the beginning because I was driven to do something to make him feel better, but that's not what he wanted or needed. He'd experienced something awful, seen things no child should have to experience, and no words of comfort or support made it any less hideous or painful. It wasn't until I accepted that that I was able to be there for him.

A few beats of silence stretch between us before Kendra speaks. "Do you think she expects us to be there when it happens?"

"I would assume so."

I hear her sharp intake of breath.

"I'm not sure I can do that." Her voice trembles. "It's too close to . . . it's just . . ."

I don't make her finish the sentence. "Of course. I'm sure Lindsey will understand."

THIRTY-SEVEN
KENDRA

"Lindsey has to understand, right?" I ask Paul. He's hunched over Reese's algebra homework at our dining room table. He's trying to figure out the problem Reese gave up on an hour ago before he went upstairs to shower. Reese is still responsible for all his homework and assignments while he's suspended, which means we're filling in as his substitute teachers. Paul's done most of the work for him.

It's been almost two days without a pill, and I'm walking around like I'm covered in Teflon because one bump might send me into the abyss again. I don't listen to anything stimulating so that I can keep my emotions at bay. No music. No social media. Books. Pictures. None of it. Not when I'm trying to function in the world. Even then, I'm barely keeping it together. I had a meltdown at the gas station last night, and I still haven't made it through the grocery store without a panic attack. "There's no way I can be there for . . . see, I can't even say the words."

"You don't have to," Paul says, letting me off the hook like Dani did earlier.

I appreciate his understanding as much as I did hers. "Are you going to go?"

He shakes his head. "I texted Andrew and asked if he wanted me there, but he said no."

"I still can't get over how 'whatever' she was about the video." Paul agrees with me about the sexual tension between Sawyer and Jacob in the video. I showed it to him as soon as I found it, and his reaction was identical to mine. It's weird talking about it on the eve of Jacob's passing, but in my mind, he's been gone. It's just taken Lindsey this long to accept it. I told Paul to let me go immediately if I'm ever declared brain dead. I wouldn't want to live like that. It's not living.

"Speaking of videos, I've been wading through the videos and pictures from the Delta Tau house that night." He grins like a schoolkid. I don't wait for him to finish before butting in.

"You found something?" He has surprised me with his cyberstalking skills. He's been at it since Luna told us about the Delta Tau party, searching for anything from the party that has the boys in it. Paul wants someone to blame, and a college fraternity house with underage drinking gives him a perfect place to point his finger.

He pushes Reese's homework aside and grabs his MacBook, flipping it open. Social media images and videos are frozen on his screen. Videos are hard to come by since most of them are posted on people's stories and gone within twenty-four hours. "There's almost nothing from that night. Kids aren't stupid, and I guarantee they deleted everything once Detective Locke came around asking questions."

"I don't trust him." How could he know about the party and keep it from us? There is only one answer—he doesn't trust us, and it's impossible to trust someone who doesn't trust you.

"He's just doing his job. Anyway"—he clicks on one of the movies, bringing it to full screen—"I started thinking, and what are the chances that night was the first time the boys went to a party at the Delta Tau house?"

I nod eagerly. I like where he's going with this.

"Turns out the boys had been there quite a few times. Our kid really liked to party." He nudges my shoulder. "Kind of like his mom."

I shove him playfully. "Shut up!" The night we got back together after high school was at a college fraternity party after he barged in on me using the bathroom and threw up in the sink. He kisses me on my cheek, and I giggle in response, but my laughter stops in my throat like I've broken an unspoken rule—you're not allowed to have fun after your child dies, or you're disrespecting his memory. Paul doesn't notice and moves on like everything's okay. How does he do that?

"I've been working my way through other parties, and I finally got lucky. I stumbled on this one during my lunch break." He presses play. The screen fills with the frenetic movement of young people. Loud talking, laughter, and music playing in the background. A shirtless Sawyer dances into view, arms up, beer in one hand and the other fist pumping. His classic grin spreads wide across his face. A girl breaks through the crowd and grinds up against him. His smile gets bigger. Paul pauses the video and enlarges it. He doesn't say anything. Whatever it is, he wants to see if I can see it for myself and doesn't want to lead me.

At first, I can't take my eyes off Sawyer and the girl dancing on him, but there's nothing amiss about the two of them. They couldn't look happier. I shift my eyes to the rest of the photo. They quickly land on Jacob standing in the entryway of the same hallway that the couple just pranced through. He's leaning against the doorframe with his arms crossed, staring at Sawyer and the girl. Anger and rage contort his features. There's only one way to describe the glare in his eyes—it's murderous.

THIRTY-EIGHT

LINDSEY

It's been five hours since they turned off Jacob's life support, and Andrew and I are glued to our spots next to his bed. My back aches from being hunched over this way for so long, but I can't bring myself to move. Neither can Andrew. My left arm cradles Jacob's head while Andrew holds his shoulder, one of his hands lightly placed on his chest. We take turns talking to him. Sometimes we sing. Other times we read. Tears drench our faces; the white linens surrounding him are wet.

Jacob's nurse keeps coming in and asking if we need anything. Do we want water? Food? To use the restroom? Each time we decline, and each time she reminds us that it's okay to settle into our chairs or walk around to stretch our legs because this could be a long process. The last time she was in, Andrew snapped at her to leave us alone. Hopefully she'll listen.

The actual moment was quick. Once all the machines were unplugged and everything was ready, it was a swift upward movement, and the tube came out of his throat. They plugged his tracheostomy hole and stepped back while we held our breath and waited for what would happen next.

Andrew and I were on each side of his bed in the same positions we're in now. Wyatt and Sutton said their goodbyes before they removed Jacob from his support because we didn't want them in the room if he was one of those individuals who went quickly like they were choking to death. They're in the waiting room with the others. We kept it small. Only family and close friends.

Jacob's breathing and heart rate will slow and then stop. I listen to the sounds of him breathing on his own with amazement like I did when he was a newborn. He's my first baby, so everything was new, and like any first-time mother I was hyperfocused on everything he did. I spent hours staring at him while he slept, filled with equal parts fascination and fear. If he slept for too long, I held my finger underneath his nose to make sure he was still breathing. I've never spent a minute staring at Wyatt or Sutton sleeping. Not because I didn't want to but because there was never enough time for me to sit down long enough to watch them sleep.

Once again, I'm brought back to his infancy. The circle of life, except this circle is broken and moving backward. He's supposed to watch me crawl back into infancy, not the other way around.

"How long can he go on like this?" Andrew asks the nurse, Manuel, as soon as he walks into the room. Dark circles blacken Andrew's eyes like we've been up for days. These eight hours have been excruciatingly long. Last time Jacob teetered between life and death, we had the adrenaline boosts to sustain us. Desolation doesn't work the same way.

Manuel adjusts the pillows behind Jacob's head as if that will make some kind of difference, but I understand the need to do something other than sit in silence next to his bed. It's the second shift change, so Manuel will be with us for the next eight hours if Jacob decides to keep breathing.

"Like the doctors explained earlier this morning, most children take around six hours to pass. Some a bit less. Others a bit more," he says.

"Yes, but how long?" Andrew won't allow him to be vague. He likes to corner the nurses, as if they're likely to give him more information than the doctors.

"We can't predict that. There's no medical certainty about any of this." He's tall and sinewy with white-blond hair shaved on each side, a cowlick at the back of his head.

"What does it mean if he keeps breathing on his own?" There's a hint of hope in Andrew's voice.

Don't do that, Andrew. Please . . . don't.

"It could mean a lot of different things. These things take time. Sometimes the children fight to hold on, and it can be helpful if their loved ones give them permission to go—"

"We've been doing that," Andrew interjects.

He's been doing that. Not me. I can't bring myself to tell him to go when I want to yell at him to stay: *Don't leave me.*

"Oh, that's great," Manuel says like we've done something to be proud of. He takes another glance at the only machine left next to Jacob's bed. It's monitoring his vitals so we know when his respirations and heartbeat stop. "Dr. Merck will be in by the end of the evening to discuss what you'd like for us to do in the interim."

What a strange way to refer to the gap between now and his passing. I get more afraid to leave the wider it grows, because his passing is that much closer and I don't want to miss it. I can't stomach the idea of not holding his hand when he takes his final step. I held my pee for so long today that I'll probably end up with a UTI. Eventually, I didn't have a choice, and I raced down the hallway and back as quickly as possible, not even wasting time on washing my hands in the bathroom sink. I used the one in Jacob's room instead.

"Is there anything we can be doing to make things easier?" I hate the thought of him suffering.

"All you can do is wait," Manuel says as he gets ready to leave. "Dr. Merck will be here shortly to talk about next steps."

There's not supposed to be another step. This is supposed to be the end.

THIRTY-NINE
KENDRA

"First of all, who is the girl? Do we know that yet?" I blow up the picture we spliced from the video and examine her like I might have missed something the first ten times I enlarged the image. She's a beautiful girl with olive skin and dark, curly hair that she flips over her shoulders flirtatiously every few seconds. She wears a tight white tank, exposing a black bra underneath and a pair of ripped jeans that accentuate her long legs. I don't recognize her as any of the girls Sawyer brought home, but he didn't bring many girls to the house. I assumed it was because he didn't have a serious girlfriend, and that's how he played things off to me, but maybe that wasn't the case. He could've had a girlfriend.

Or a boyfriend. The thought comes a half second later. Maybe Jacob?

Paul taps on one of the other open tabs, bringing up screenshots from the girl's Instagram. Libby Walker. She's a freshman at Berkeley. Her pictures are everything I hate about Instagram—scantily clad and seductive poses with cheesy inspirational quotes about seizing the day and being your best self splashed across them.

"I've combed through all her social media accounts and the ones of her closest friends. Her and Sawyer don't have any other pictures together. I can't even find them in any group photos, so I'm pretty sure she's just some random chick that he happened to be dancing with at the party that night."

I zoom out and then go back in, centering on Jacob's face. "I can't tell if he's angry at Sawyer or her. Can you?"

He shakes his head and wrinkles his forehead. "I've blown this thing up and watched the video at least a hundred times since I found it. I've gone back and forth probably just as many. Honestly, I can't tell. The only thing for sure is that he's pissed off."

"I've never seen him that angry. Ever." Jacob favored Andrew that way—calm, even tempered.

"I wonder if Detective Locke has seen it," Paul says, thinking out loud.

I haven't talked to Detective Locke for almost twenty-four hours, which is the longest we've gone without speaking since he came into our lives, but what's the point if he's not going to tell us the whole truth? That's the same as lying to me. "Did you send it to him?" I ask.

"Not yet."

"Are you going to?"

He tilts his head to the side, eyeing me curiously. "I hadn't considered not doing it. I guess I didn't know that was an option."

I shrug. "It's not like he's being honest and up front with us."

"Nah. That's silly. Besides, what do we gain by keeping it a secret from him? There's nothing we can do about it on our own. It's not like we can go on a hunt and question the girl ourselves."

"You're right." I hate to concede, but he is.

"Besides, I still trust him."

I huff. "You would."

"What's that supposed to mean?" His eyebrows rise in offense.

"You always assume the best in people."

"O . . . kay." He draws out the word. "I'm sorry for being optimistic, I guess?"

My phone buzzes with an alert, and my heart stills. It's been like that all day. We've been waiting for news about Jacob since our morning coffee. Normally, I wouldn't reach for my phone in the middle of a conversation because it drives Paul nuts, but this could be the latest update. He pauses our conversation while I check my phone.

"Well?" he asks while I scan the text. He's been as anxious to hear something as me.

"He's still breathing on his own," I say with disbelief. "Maybe Lindsey will get her miracle after all."

FORTY
DANI

Waiting for someone to die is a lot like waiting for someone to be born. They've given us a private room while we wait for updates on Jacob. There are framed nature pictures on each wall; one has snow-capped mountaintops, and the others are all sandy beaches. A television is mounted in the corner on an endless loop of hospital infomercials because the channel is stuck, but someone turned it on earlier to have more than the silence to listen to. I liked the silence better. Two tables stacked with old magazines and a few donated books sit between the couches and chairs.

There's only a handful of us in the room—immediate family and close friends only—but we still overcrowd it. Wyatt looks miserable to be stuck in a room with only adults and his little sister. Poor Sutton. They really should just bring her home. We've taken turns keeping her occupied, and Lindsey's mom is walking the halls with her again.

What are we supposed to do if he's not gone soon? How do we decide who stays and who goes? It's almost six, and I arrived at eight. I never expected to be here all day. None of us did.

I can't stay any longer, though. I have to talk to Mom about Bryan. She's been nonstop texting me about him, and I need to get home before she tries to play matchmaker and arrange a secret meeting with the two of us to work things out. She's pulled that one before, since he's had her wrapped around his finger from day one and he can do no wrong in her eyes.

I was never supposed to be an only child. She wanted lots of kids—at least three, she always said—but my emergency cesarean section ended in an emergency hysterectomy for her. She swears my dad was her one true love, and she's never dated again, even after all this time has passed, so Bryan's flowering attention won her over immediately. Still does.

It shouldn't have been a surprise when I found out Bryan was texting her, but it dropped my stomach to the floor.

Don't talk to him!! I texted after she finally admitted they'd been communicating. I had to ask her about it three times before she came clean.

I got suspicious after she started asking questions about why we left and asking me if I was okay in a way that implied there was something slightly off with me. That was one of Bryan's favorite tactics—make everyone think I was the crazy one. I tried leaving Bryan shortly after Caleb was born. Bryan had spent an entire weekend drinking in front of the TV and unleashed a verbal assault on me that was as brutal as any punch and left me just as crippled. I showed up on her doorstep with the kids in almost the same way I did two nights ago, except it was the middle of the day, and I never told her I was leaving him. She thought I'd dropped by for an unannounced visit.

As the day wore on, I started second-guessing myself and wondering how I was going to raise two small children on my own. My doubts only grew as Caleb fussed and Luna refused to cooperate with anything since she was in the throes of her terrible twos. Bryan showed up around dinnertime, and Mom welcomed him in like she'd been expecting him all along. I didn't act surprised when he arrived that day, and I've always wondered what would've happened if I hadn't played along with him.

But I did, following him out the door when he left and telling Mom goodbye like the day had unfolded according to plan. As soon as we got in the car, I delivered my first ultimatum—"Stop drinking, or I'm gone." He laughed, and we went home without him ever agreeing to stop drinking. That was when I knew there was something seriously wrong with me, but not in the way he implied to everyone else.

Mom pestered me for hours because I wouldn't go into details about what was going on over text message. She kept saying that I didn't need to tell her everything and all she needed was an idea so she had a better understanding of how to act with him. But that's not the type of conversation you have over text message.

He's completely ignored me. That's the most unexpected move yet after years of threats about what would happen if I ever left him. Mom sent me screenshots of his texts to her, and they were sweet, filled with nothing but adoration and concern:

> I'm so grateful Dani has a place she can go right now.
>
> Thank you for taking care of my family during this difficult time. I hope you can help Dani sort through whatever she's going through.
>
> Please let me know if I can help or you want to talk. I'm here.

He makes me furious. How dare he try to turn Mom against me? I need to get home so I can explain everything to her. I glance at the clock, convinced another hour has passed, just to discover it's only been twelve minutes since the last time I checked. I gather my things and motion for Lindsey's dad. He's grateful for the distraction and hurries over to my side of the room.

"I have to go. I need to take care of some things at home. I'm so sorry," I whisper. There's something about a hospital waiting room that makes everyone speak in hushed tones whether it's necessary or not.

He gives me a huge hug. "Don't worry about it. This has been a long day. None of us expected to still be here."

I eye the hallway leading to Jacob's room. Still no sign of activity. The doctors barely go in there. "Will you tell her I love her when she comes out?"

The cool air blasts me as I step outside the hospital, and I swallow it hungrily. I'm so grateful that I've never had to live inside the walls of a hospital. I don't know how Lindsey does it. She's a special kind of superwoman. I hurry toward my car, anxious to get home and talk to Mom. I grab my phone to let her know I'm on my way.

"Hello, Dani." Bryan steps out from beside the minivan parked next to my car. I freeze as he walks around the front of it and into my space. "How are things going up there?" He points to the hospital.

Don't be fooled by his fake concern.

"What are you doing here?" I furtively scan the parking lot for cameras. I move to my left so I'm standing more directly in the light. He takes another step toward me, and I flinch. He laughs at my response like he's genuinely amused by it.

"What are you so jumpy for?"

"I'm tired. It's been a long day, and I want to go home."

"Well, come on, then. Why don't you leave your car, since you've had such a long day, and I can drive us home?" He tries to put his arm around me, but I step aside.

"Please, Bryan. I just want to leave." His body blocks the door. Checkmate.

The Best of Friends

The air between us is electric, thick.

"I'm really worried about you." His chest bulges with muscles underneath his white T-shirt. "Your friends are worried too."

"No, they're not. My friends have a lot going on. They don't have time to be worried about me." *Don't be fooled by his lies.*

"I'm not talking about Lindsey and Kendra."

Who else has he been talking to? I'm not close to anyone else. Is he talking about Mom?

I stop myself before I go any further down the rabbit hole of his delusional thinking.

"I would like you to move away from my door so that I can get in my car and go to my mom's." I speak with the same forced calmness and calculation that I used to speak to our kids with when they were toddlers.

"What do you think it's going to look like when the police find out you've had some kind of breakdown and taken Caleb from the house?" He raises his eyebrows and sneers at me with disgust.

My stomach heaves into my throat. White-hot fury pulses through me. *Breathe. Don't defend yourself. It doesn't matter, anyway. He'll only twist your words until they tell a story you don't recognize.*

"I've asked you to move, and I'm not going to ask you another time," I say with as much authority as I can muster, trying to keep my voice steady.

He bursts out laughing. "You're not going to ask me another time? What are you going to do, Dani?"

He feeds off your fear. Don't let him see it.

"Get away from me, or I'm calling 911."

"For what? Standing in a public parking lot?" He grabs my arm, digging his fingers into me. "You make me sick." He shoves me with his release, making me stumble backward. He turns around and starts walking away from my car.

I jump inside and slam the door, pressing the lock button as fast as I can. My teeth chatter like I'm cold. The tremors move their way through my entire body. I can't stop or control them. My leg shakes on the brake as I start the car. I put it in reverse, the rearview camera showing the back of him as he continues walking through the parking lot. I pull out quickly and head toward Mom's.

Please don't let him follow me there.

FORTY-ONE
LINDSEY

"If he makes it through the night, we'll want to order another CT scan," Dr. Merck explains. It's nine o'clock, and he finally made it in to see us. "We can—"

I raise my hand to stop him. "Are you saying there's a chance he could live through the night and pull through this?"

He shakes his head. "That's not what I'm saying. The likelihood of Jacob having any brain activity is very minimal."

He says the same thing before every scan, and the report is the same each time—pervasive brain damage—but he's already been wrong once about this. He sees me latching on to the possibility, grasping at it as my mind works backward, wondering, questioning. He loosens his tie.

"Then why are you bothering to do the scan?" Andrew asks. "What are you looking for?"

Dr. Merck appears flustered, and he never falters. Is he hiding something? Suddenly, none of this feels right.

"We want to make sure everything is the same as we move into the next phase." He clears his throat. "If Jacob continues to sustain his respiratory function, then he could begin experiencing muscle pain due to dehydration. That can be difficult to watch and, as you can imagine, quite difficult to experience as well. It's a stressful thing for parents and loved ones to go through."

What is he talking about? None of this is what we discussed. He's not supposed to be in pain. This is supposed to be quick, painless. That's what he said. He promised.

Andrew's concerned expression mirrors mine. "Why will he be in pain?"

"The muscles cramp within a few days of severe dehydration. The legs tend to be the worst, and his legs are quite muscular. The good news is that the cramps pass relatively quickly, and we can give pain medication to help."

The world is spinning, moving, and shifting underneath my feet. How does he feel pain if he's paralyzed? No brain stem activity. That's what the reports say. Damage to the left cerebral cortex.

"But he's breathing." My heart thumps; my pulse throbs in my ears. "And he's been breathing for over twelve hours."

"Yes, that was unexpected," he says with detached objectivity.

"So what can we expect?" Andrew wrings his hands together on his lap, desperate for something to hang on to in all of this.

"I'm sorry, but there's no medical certainty in end-of-life care."

FORTY-TWO
DANI

"I just don't know how you could be in *that kind* of a relationship for all these years and never tell me," Mom says. She was waiting for me with chamomile-and-lavender tea when I got home from the hospital. It took me ten minutes to calm down, but once I did, I started with Bryan confronting me in the parking lot tonight and worked my way backward, spilling all the secrets I've kept buried inside for all these years.

"There wasn't just one reason. There were so many. Mostly I didn't want to believe it myself, and telling anyone would make it real. I was so embarrassed and ashamed." And I loved him. But I don't say that part out loud because it makes me sound even more pathetic than I already feel. It's the truth, though. I've never fallen for someone the way I fell for Bryan.

For years, I thought I was supposed to end up with Paul. I harbored a secret crush on him all through high school, even though I never breathed a word about my feelings to anyone, especially not Kendra. She still calls herself the captain of the cheerleading squad whenever she talks about it now, but we were cocaptains. Paul was the star quarterback, so it made sense to set me up with his best friend, Josh, who also happened to be the star running back. Lindsey felt left out and wasn't thrilled about our pairings. It created all kinds of weird jealousy and tension, but our foursome was such an easy match. Besides, Lindsey could've joined, but she never had a steady boyfriend in high school. I didn't feel bad about it back then, but as I've watched Jacob and Sawyer edge Caleb out of the soccer equation over the years, it's made me realize how painful that must have been for her.

Being with Josh gave me a chance to be around Paul, and I was always searching for opportunities to be alone with him. He still felt like mine, and I never would've given Kendra permission to date him if I'd thought it would grow into anything serious.

Despite how things started out, Josh and I had an amazing last summer, and we talked about how we'd make things work despite going away to our colleges on separate coasts. I loved him the way you love when you're that young—wholeheartedly and with abandon. Josh broke up with me the second week of freshman year and proceeded to sleep his way through his freshman class at Tulane. I dated on and off but was never in a serious relationship again until I met Bryan at the end of my junior year. He was getting ready to graduate and nothing like Josh, which was the only relationship I had for comparison.

Bryan took me out on proper dates, and nobody had ever done that before, so right away it felt like I was stepping into an old romantic movie where men took the time to formally date women. He picked me up in his restored Porsche and brought me to dinner at expensive restaurants with pint-size portions that I'd never have been able to afford on my own. He didn't play any of the silly mind games that the other college boys did—pretending to like me one day and ignoring me the next. He showered me with attention and praise, and I soaked it up like a water-starved plant. It's hard to imagine I was ever that naive.

"Besides, he hit Luna," I say to Mom, pushing the memories away. "That trumps everything."

She surprises me by looking away. "Well, this is a very stressful time, and people can have unusual reactions when things are so chaotic."

She's been texting him back. This is why I told her not to communicate with him—because I knew he'd whittle his way into her brain and twist things around according to his disturbing logic.

"Hitting Luna wasn't because he was stressed—it was because he was pissed off." I try to control the trembling in my voice. "You know the biggest reason that I never told you or anyone else about what was going on in my marriage, Mom?" I glare at her without giving her a chance to respond. "I didn't tell anyone because I was afraid that they wouldn't believe me." I shove my chair back, coming up against the wall behind me.

"I'm not saying I don't believe you, honey. I'm just saying I . . . you seemed so happy to me. That's all." She takes a sip of her tea.

She's wrestling with how the man she's loved like a son for over twenty years could be the same guy who did all the horrible things I've spent the last hour describing. All his name-calling, spying on me, threatening to take the kids if I left, and the holes his fists put in the walls of our house during his rages. For some reason, she was especially horrified by the time I'd caught Bryan in a lie about his drinking back when I'd thought his drinking was responsible for stealing the man I'd married, and I'd spied on his bottle like it was a mistress. He'd gotten so upset, but his focus hadn't been on atoning for what he'd done or even admitting to the lie; he'd been furious because he hadn't known how I'd gotten my information and I'd refused to tell him. He had set an alarm and told me if I didn't tell him my source, then I would have to leave, because he couldn't live in the same house with someone who didn't trust him, as if I'd done something wrong by figuring out his lies. He'd circled me while the timer had ticked down, taunting me until I'd broken.

I don't expect her to wrap her brain around any of this in one discussion. It's taken me years to understand that the man I fell in love with was never real. He didn't exist and was just as much of a fairy tale as the ones I read to Luna when she was little. I'd fallen in love with the image he presented to the rest of the world and carefully used whenever it served him, but the man behind the mask was callous and mean. Accepting that truth didn't come easy.

I shift gears. "How'd Caleb do tonight?" I'm exhausted, but I can't go to bed without knowing how he did. I haven't spent this much time away from him since it happened.

"Good." She looks as relieved as I feel to move past talking about Bryan and into more familiar territory. "We played two games of gin rummy."

Flashbacks of sitting around the kitchen table on Friday nights flood my memory. Mom had a thing for family game nights when we were growing up, and she loved playing cards, so most of them were spent sitting right here. She's taught both my kids how to play gin, hearts, and poker. They played poker for M&M's when they were little. They've always played with her but never with me. I tried setting up family game nights like she did when Luna was in middle school and starting to pull away. Caleb loved the idea, but Bryan was never on board with them, so they never took at our house.

My house was never like the home where I'd grown up in so many different ways, no matter how hard I tried to re-create it. It didn't matter how beautiful I made it or how clean I kept it; the love that cocoons me in safety here never filled our home in the same way. Bryan's darkness grew larger until it eventually overtook the light. Maybe Sawyer died in our house because it was already filled with death.

FORTY-THREE

LINDSEY

My anxiety surges as I pace Jacob's floor, waiting for him to get back from his CT scan. Andrew went down to the cafeteria to get us coffee. The nurses bring you cups if you ask, but he needed to get away from here—from me, from this room. It's been twenty-eight hours since we left the room to do anything except use the restroom.

Every muscle aches from sitting in those uncomfortable chairs all night. We didn't sleep. We barely spoke. My brain has no battery left. Every time Andrew gets on his phone, I'm convinced he's messaging May. How many times over the last year have I been in the room while they were communicating? All those times that I thought he was combing through golf scores or reading excerpts from the *LA Times* could've been during one of their trysts.

Nothing scandalous is happening on my phone. All it does is buzz with questions about Jacob and with alerts whenever someone posts on the brain-injury-parenting blogs I follow. People have been texting me since seven, and I wish I had something to tell them. My thoughts chase themselves, plummeting from worries about Jacob to panic about my committed marriage being exposed as a lie.

The elevator at the end of the hall opens, and Andrew and Dr. Merck step out without Jacob.

"I had the nurses hold Jacob behind so that we could have a few minutes to speak in private," Dr. Merck says as they reach me. He motions to Jacob's room. "Why don't we talk in there?"

"Do you mind if we stay out here?" I ask. I've had enough of those four walls.

He eyes the empty hallway to make sure there's no one around before nodding his agreement. "I've had a look at Jacob's scans and already sent them over to Dr. Gervais for review, but I'm sure he'll agree with my determination that there's no changes in his brain activity."

He delivers the news, then gives it a chance to settle. So many emotions surge through me—relief, fear, guilt, hopelessness, love—the list is endless, and I flip through all of them without landing on any particular one.

"He's brain dead and the likelihood of any recovery is nil. You'll need to decide how to proceed from here." He says it in the mechanical way he does when he's checking an item off his mental to-do list.

How to proceed from here? We aren't supposed to be making any more difficult choices. Ours are done. We signed all the papers—the ones giving the team of doctors consent to withdraw his support and not provide any lifesaving measures. The risks of the procedure had been described in detail, and we'd initialed each line next to the warnings.

"What are we supposed to do?" Andrew asks.

"There's no right or wrong answer. All parents are different, and each situation is unique," he says in a noncommittal tone.

I look at Andrew's pained expression and grasp his hand. Our palms stick together with sweat. Neither of us wants to ask any of the hard questions.

"When they bring him back up, we can administer pain medication if you'd like, or we can wait until he begins exhibiting symptoms and see if he needs it. His contractions might be mild, and he won't even need the medication. The only issue with waiting is that the medication tends to be less effective if you wait until after he's in the throes of it."

"So are you saying it's better to give him the medication now?" I ask.

"It's up to you."

If it were up to me, Jacob would get up and start walking around the room. We would gather our things and go home like none of this had happened. That's what I want. I look to Andrew for help. He reads the agony in my eyes.

"We don't want him to be in pain," he says. He's unshaven and bleary eyed from being up all night.

Dr. Merck gives us a clipped nod. "We'll begin administering the pain medication, then."

The elevator sounds from the end of the hallway, and an orderly steps out with Jacob. He pushes him down the hallway to us. Jacob's orange *Naruto* socks poke out from underneath the blanket covering him. The floor rushes up to meet me as they get closer, and a sense of impending doom overtakes me at the thought of going back in his room. I lean against the wall, steadying myself until the world stops spinning.

"Can we take him outside?" I have no idea where the idea comes from. I just blurt it out without any thinking.

"There'd be no reason for you not to. He's—"

I don't wait for him to finish.

"I want to take him outside." The urgency in my voice grows more intense. I move in front of the gurney, making it difficult for them to pass by. "We'll take him from here," I announce in a commanding voice.

The orderly is a big, thick guy with a large, pockmarked nose and small green eyes that he quickly shifts to Dr. Merck for approval. Dr. Merck nods his consent, and the orderly retreats like a soldier who's just been given an order, leaving the three of us in a semicircle around Jacob's gurney. We stare down at him. New hair grows in patches around his scar.

"Hi, Jacob, we missed you," Andrew pipes up.

Maybe all he needs is to be out of this hospital and underneath the sky with the sun shining on his face. What if his soul left his body and is out there waiting for him in the open space? Tears work their way up my throat. "Please, can we just take him outside?"

FORTY-FOUR

KENDRA

Detective Locke came over this afternoon to go over the case, and Paul suggested I make lunch for us like he's an old family friend, even though he's destroyed my trust. Paul thinks it might bring us all back together again and help us share information. It seemed like a good idea at the time, but I'm second-guessing myself as I carry in dishes from the kitchen to the dining room, since Detective Locke has been nothing but awkward since he sat down. The food looks perfect, though. I ordered it from Cecconi's and put it in my best serving bowls. I smile at my secret as I bring in the last dish: salmon carpaccio. Delicious. This one always gets compliments.

Detective Locke and Paul sit at each end of our long dining table, and I sit in the middle, which only makes the table seem bigger. "Let's eat." I plaster a charming housewife smile on my face as I pass Detective Locke the salad bowl.

He takes it from me in the same formal way he does everything. "This all smells and looks delicious."

Paul doesn't miss a beat. "We thought it might be easier to talk about things with the case over lunch. At least then we can be more relaxed with each other and don't have to worry about anyone overhearing or misinterpreting what we're saying."

He's way off script, but I trust him. We've closed enough deals together over the years. The three of us pass food around the table, commenting on each dish as it changes hands.

"How are you feeling about things with the case?" I ask even though we just spoke about it this morning. It's different in an informal setting. Hopefully, he'll be more open.

"Leads slow down the more time goes on, but we got a good one today." He reaches for the water beside his plate instead of the wine and takes a sip before continuing. "The timing of our lunch couldn't be more perfect, because we just received the full toxicology report. It looks like all three of the boys were under the influence of alcohol, cannabis, and Adderall."

"So we know for sure the boys were on Adderall?" Paul asks like he's having a hard time believing it.

"Without a doubt," Detective Locke confirms. "It's quite the epidemic at Pine Grove. I swear half the teenagers are on it."

Including Reese, but neither of them knows that. Paul is adamantly opposed to giving kids psychotropic medication, and Reese's ADHD diagnosis from his pediatrician about a year ago did nothing to sway him on the issue. He was convinced Reese's academic problems were because he was stubborn and lazy, that he'd do better if he worked harder, but I didn't agree. He was a mess when it came to anything school related, no matter how hard he tried, and I got nervous he wasn't going to pass the high school entrance exams for Pine Grove. Siblings aren't automatically accepted like at many of the private schools in our area, and we needed him to get in with Sawyer. I filled the prescription from his pediatrician without telling Paul or Reese. I already made the boys take a multivitamin in the morning, so he didn't think anything of it when I added an additional pill to his morning routine. I noticed an immediate difference, and it wasn't long before his grades reflected it.

We're supposed to be talking about Sawyer, but all I can think about at the moment is Reese. What happens if he's taking Adderall on top of the Adderall I'm giving him in secret? Is that why he's been so difficult lately? How dangerous is it? I force myself to focus.

"Kids use it for all kinds of stuff. Lots of them take it during finals to help them stay focused or during SAT week so they can stay up and study. But mostly they use it to party." He takes a bite of the Caesar salad before reaching into the briefcase he placed next to his chair before lunch. He pulls out a stack of papers and thumbs through them. "The levels of chemicals in the boys' systems were off the charts. They weren't a little bit messed up—they were wasted. We might never know what happened because nothing makes sense when you're that loaded."

What was Sawyer thinking, playing with a gun in that condition? I can't be too mad at him, though, because how many times did I stumble through the neighbors' backyards on my way home from a Delta Tau party when I was the same age? We did so many stupid things, like competing over who was the best drunk driver and driving around on the outskirts of town, shooting BB guns at stop signs. We thought it was hilarious.

Detective Locke holds out the papers. "Which one of you wants to see it first?"

Paul jumps up and takes it from him. He crosses to the other side of the room and sits next to me on the bench seat so we can look at it together. He spreads the report out in front of us. All the official signatures and titles are splashed across the top like on all of the formal documents. The date reads two days ago. I point out the date to Paul without saying anything. Again, both of us talked to Detective Locke this morning, and he never mentioned anything about the toxicology report being back.

The first paragraph is a bunch of technical jargon about how the blood was drawn, transferred, and stored. Marijuana and alcohol are clearly positive even to my untrained eye. The amphetamines numbers are high from the Adderall. Nothing else spikes or dips.

"It's safe to say drugs and alcohol played a role in the incident, probably a major one," he says, and it's impossible not to feel like a scolded teenager, but it could've happened to anyone. Well, probably not him. I don't remember seeing Detective Locke at a single party all through high school, and there were parties that almost everyone went to, no matter what group they belonged to. How many times have I done something stupid because I was drunk? Too many to count. I don't know anyone who hasn't.

Why us? Is it because our lives were too perfect? I said that to Paul once when we were coming home from one of Sawyer's soccer games at sunset and traveling down the mountains during a rare moment when the boys were getting along in the back seat. I remember squeezing his thigh and telling him, "We have the perfect life." He smiled at me like we shared the world's greatest secret.

Silverware clinks as the men go back to eating, but I'm too nervous to swallow food. I push it around on my plate while I work up the courage to speak. It was different when I trusted Detective Locke. "I know Paul's mentioned the digging around that we've been doing on our end, and we wanted to talk to you about some of the things we've found." My confidence wavers. I was so sure about things when it was just the two of us, but now I'm not so certain. "I found pictures and videos on Sawyer's phone that hint at a sexual relationship between him and Jacob." I hand him Sawyer's phone—the moment I've been waiting for all day.

He takes it from me and taps play. The screen fills with the half-dressed image of Jacob. I wait for the realization to dawn on him, but he's unimpressed. "Do you have any others? I've seen this."

"You have?" How could he have seen this video and not suggested Sawyer and Jacob were in a relationship? Why didn't he ask us if they were in a sexual relationship?

"It was in a buried file," Paul adds.

The Best of Friends

"Yes, we went through all the files on his phone, even the hidden ones."

My cheeks burn with embarrassment. They've probably seen the Instagram video too. Paul takes the phone from him and pulls up the other video. "How about this?" he asks as he hands it back.

This time Detective Locke's forehead creases with curiosity. I grin like a kid and turn to Paul. He's wearing a matching face.

Detective Locke taps at the screen. "Do we know who this is?"

"Libby Walker," Paul and I say in unison.

"Is there—"

I jump in. "Paul's gone through everything in the month before and after the accident. They're not together in any other pictures. They don't tag each other in anything or even like similar posts. None of their friends are in the same circles. It was probably just a random dance they shared at a party."

He keeps blowing up Jacob's image, trying to figure out the focus of his glare, but there's no way to tell. His eyes reach the same conclusion as mine do every time. "As far as the pictures of Sawyer and Jacob on Sawyer's phone, I don't think it reveals anything meaningful or hints at a deeper relationship. Kids are much more fluid with their sexual expression and identities these days," he says. I can't help but feel like a prude, and it's weird to think of myself in those terms because nobody's ever defined me that way. "But I do find the angry expression on Jacob's face troubling, especially given the reports of all the arguing between them. The problem is that it's impossible to tell the focus of his fury in this picture." He hands Paul Sawyer's phone. "Speaking of Jacob, do we have any recent updates?"

"He's still hanging on," I say. And for a split second, I hate myself for wanting him to be gone.

FORTY-FIVE

LINDSEY

I absorb the air like I'm the one who's been indoors for twenty-five days. It doesn't matter that we're in a back alleyway with industrial-size dumpsters lining each side. Dr. Merck brought us through a side entrance that only gets used by the janitors and cleaning crews, but he didn't have time to think of a better plan. He's worked in the field long enough to spot an impending breakdown, and I was a half second away from crossing over. He quickly called together all personnel for an on-the-spot meeting to work out getting Jacob outside.

Jacob lies on his hospital bed. The thick plastic rails are raised on each side like there's a chance he might roll out. Doubled-up pairs of socks make his feet twice their normal size, but I didn't want him to get cold in the CT machine. His scalp shows signs of pressure sores, and it makes me start crying all over again.

"Don't put him directly in the sun," Andrew cautions. "He's not wearing any sunscreen."

The last thing we need is painful burns on his exposed skin, but I can't help myself. Maybe holding him under the sunlight will breathe life into his pale skin and limp, swollen body. I press my foot on the lever underneath and raise the back of his bed so he's tilted up without the sun beaming directly on his face. We couldn't do that before, but anything's possible now that his tubes are gone. Suddenly, his body falls forward, and Andrew swoops forward to catch him. He holds him against the bed, upright. My insides are being crushed, and I don't have to look at Andrew's face to know his are too. I lower the bed to its half position, where his body easily rests without falling forward.

It doesn't matter that we're outside. There's still not enough air getting to my lungs. I don't want to be here. I'm not sure I can do this anymore. An involuntary sob escapes my lips.

Andrew reaches across the bed and grabs my hands. "It's okay, Linds."

He hasn't called me Linds in years. She's from another lifetime. One that didn't include diapers and breastfeeding, meal planning, car pool, and doctor's appointments. It only makes me cry harder. I don't want to be here. I don't want to step foot back in that hospital. I don't want to take Jacob in there. I just want my life to go back to the way it was before.

"We need to go home. Please, can we go home?" Tears course their way down my cheeks. "I don't want to go through that again. I can't. Let's take him home and lay him in his bed. Or let him sit in the backyard underneath his tree house. Remember how happy he was when we built it?"

Andrew nods his head in agreement, his forehead lined with sweat. "Let's get out of here."

"Are you serious?" His response shocks me. I expected him to look at me like I'd lost my mind by suggesting such a thing. Maybe we both have, but I can't bring Jacob back inside, and I'm so glad he feels the same way.

"I don't want him to die in there. Maybe he doesn't want to either. That might be what he's trying to tell us." His eyes are endearing in the same way they were when he soothed the kids as babies after they had their first shots.

My heart swells with love for him. He is such a thoughtful man, and in the next instant it hits me that he might be a man who's no longer mine.

"We could take him to the soccer field." He spent more time there than he did at home, and he comes alive there in a way he doesn't anywhere else.

"Let's do it." Andrew grins.

"Are you sure?" Neither of us has done a single impulsive thing in our lives.

He nods and tries to swallow the lump of emotions in his throat. "Let's get out of here."

FORTY-SIX

DANI

"Turn on the TV," I blurt out as I rush into the living room, where Caleb's parked on the couch working his way through season two of *Sons of Anarchy*. He pauses the show and looks up at me with bewilderment. "Give me the remote," I order, too impatient to provide an explanation.

Mom hurries into the living room from the back bedroom, where she's spent most of the afternoon reading. "What's going on?" she asks as I fumble with buttons on the remote, trying to get the TV on the right input.

"I have no idea. Lindsey just texted and said they're taking Jacob out of the hospital. Then two seconds later Kendra texted me and told me to turn on the TV because their story is all over the news again."

"Where are they bringing him?" Mom asks.

"Home?" I shrug. "I can't imagine anywhere else they'd go."

Caleb gets up from the couch and grabs the remote from me, irritated at how long it's taking me to pull anything up. He has the cable on almost immediately and scrolls to KTLA. I grip his bicep while we listen to the evening news anchor describe how Lindsey and Andrew decided to discharge Jacob from the hospital against medical advice. Andrew's image swells onto the screen as they replay a clip of him standing outside of the north hospital entrance. He looks as bad as the parents of kidnapped children do when they beg for the kidnapper to bring their children home. My knees weaken. I lean into Caleb for support.

"Almost thirty-six hours ago, we removed our son Jacob from all life support because we determined that it was in his best interest at this time. His doctors told us it could take up to six hours for him to pass." He almost chokes on the words. "Jacob continues to breathe and fight, which my wife and I believe means that he's still in there somewhere. Maybe he's trying to tell us something. Who knows?" He shrugs in defeat, quickly losing steam. "We've decided to take him home, and we ask that you respect our family's privacy during this difficult time. Thank you." He steps away from the microphone as quickly as possible. Questions are lobbed at him from every direction. A man I've never seen before ushers him inside the hospital without giving him a chance to answer any of them.

Andrew's interview clip is quickly followed by a snippet of Lindsey and Andrew as they load Jacob into the back of a nonemergency medical transport vehicle. The video is cut short because someone steps in and blocks the camera with their hand, but it's enough to catch a glimpse of the side profile of Jacob's swollen face. I hope Lindsey doesn't see any of this. They've done such a good job of making sure there aren't any pictures of Jacob and his injuries leaked to the press. They have no desire to make his accident into a spectacle, and they're not the kind of people who enjoy being in the spotlight. They've turned down every interview request, even though they could use the money, because they refuse to profit from the tragedy. Suddenly turned superstitious, Lindsey swears it sets up a bad karmic reaction or something like that.

"How do they plan on getting him into their house?" Mom asks, having the same realization as me. "How are they going to take care of him on their own?"

Just as I turn to answer her, Caleb lets out a small whimper and drops to his knees on the floor. He grabs the coffee table and moans like he's in pain. I crouch beside him, careful not to touch him so I don't set him off any more than he already is. I glance at the TV. The image of Jacob is frozen on the screen while the news anchors remind viewers of the tragedy and the fact that there've been no arrests in the case. Caleb grips the remote, and I pry it out of his hands, shutting off the TV as fast as I can. What was I thinking? How could I forget that Caleb holds a bomb inside him that can be triggered by the slightest provocation?

FORTY-SEVEN
KENDRA

It feels strange being in my bedroom at night. I only come in here during the day to shower and get ready, but I rarely shower, so I don't spend much time here. Paul lies on his side with his arms tucked underneath him. He's kept my side of the bed completely intact. The pillows are still upright. He's only turned down his side. I guess I was responsible for the twisted sheets every morning.

Paul's lashes look even longer while he sleeps. I've never watched him sleep before. Lots of people get all sappy romantic and talk about how they love watching their lovers sleep, but I've never been one of those people. I don't know how much time has passed since I sat down on his side of our bed. I didn't come in here to watch him sleep, though. I came in here intending to tell him about Reese, but I can't bring myself to wake him.

I'm sick with fear. Paul will be furious, but that's not my biggest concern. What if he insists that I tell Reese what I've been doing? He'll be angrier with me than Paul will be, and unlike Paul, he's a lot less forgiving. My heart aches just thinking about it.

I lean over and gently shake Paul's shoulder. He moans and turns over, pulling the covers around him. I trace a circle on his back and whisper, "Wake up." He slowly opens his eyes, and it takes a second for the sleep to leave as he registers that it's me. He gives me a slow, tired smile and opens the covers with *that look* in his eyes. A wave of anxiety flips my stomach. I shake my head and pull away, quickly moving down the bed.

We were supposed to be having sex the night Sawyer died. We're like any couple who've been married forever and forget about sex because we're too busy with the delicate balancing act of managing work and kids while still trying to hold on to ourselves. Things had been especially hectic, and it had been a while since we'd been together, so I made sure Sawyer was gone with his friends and allowed Reese unlimited game time. I even bought new lingerie. I shudder at the memory, getting goose bumps and rubbing myself like I'm in the skimpy outfit now. Guilt is just one piece of my emotional chaos.

Paul sits up, rubbing the sleep from his eyes. "What's up?" he asks, finally semiawake. "Is everything okay?"

"Everything's fine." It's hard to speak around the lump of emotions in my throat. "I wanted to talk to you about Reese."

"Reese?" His eyebrows rise in genuine surprise. "In the middle of the night you needed to talk about Reese?"

I nod. I'm too nervous to speak. It didn't seem like what I was doing was all that bad until I had to say it out loud.

"What's going on, Kendra? You're starting to freak me out." He throws the covers off himself as if he's going to get out of bed.

I motion for him to stop. "You don't need to get up." It's better that he sits down for this. "Do you remember when I took Reese to Dr. Renault and he diagnosed him with ADHD?"

"Of course." His forehead wrinkles. He's instantly suspicious.

"And do you remember how he wrote him a prescription for Adderall?"

He narrows his eyes, trying to imagine where I'm going with all this. He's already sensed that wherever it is isn't good. "Yes." His response is curt.

"Well, last year he was really struggling right around the time he was getting ready to take his high school entrance exams and was almost failing math." I remind him like he doesn't monitor Reese's grades and school progress with more diligence than me. "I was afraid he wasn't going to get into Pine Grove and he was going to get stuck going to Huerte, so I decided to see if the medication that his doctor prescribed would help him focus." I stress that his doctor prescribed it. It's not like I gave him medication that he didn't need or forged a prescription to get some illicit drug. "I went to the pharmacy and had them fill the Adderall that Dr. Renault prescribed." My words slow at the part that comes next. "I started giving Reese the medication every morning." My hands shake. I twist them in front of me, trying to get them to stop. "And now I'm worried that he's using drugs on top of the Adderall that he's already taking. I'm scared that's why he's been even more difficult and unruly."

"You've been giving Reese Adderall?"

I nod.

"For an entire year, and you didn't tell me?"

"I'm sorry," I say, but my words don't mean much when we both know I'm only coming clean because everything's being exposed. The truth? I didn't ever plan on telling Paul or Reese.

He throws off the covers and stands, scanning the floor for the sweatpants he tossed somewhere before getting into bed. He spots them and slides them on. He works his jaw while he puts on a shirt. His socks are next.

"What are you doing?" I ask.

"Going for a run." He hurries to the closet to find his shoes. He hasn't run in four years. They might not even be there.

I glance at the clock. "Paul, it's three in the morning. You can't run now."

"I can do whatever I want." He turns around and shoots me a pointed glare. "You do."

FORTY-EIGHT
LINDSEY

"Why is Jacob sleeping in our living room?" Sutton asks for the third time. It doesn't matter how many times we explain it to her; she's still confused as to why the brother we made her say goodbye to the day before yesterday is alive on a hospital bed in our living room today.

I kneel next to her on the rug where she's been playing with her Barbie dolls for the last hour and pick up one of the Ken dolls, hoping to distract her. I twirl him around. I don't have the energy to explain things to her again. It's been over forty-eight hours since I last slept, and my eyes sting from being open so long.

"Mommy, why?" Her whine grates on my nerves.

"We decided to bring Jacob home so that he could be more comfortable and around people he loves when he goes to heaven."

"But he was already supposed to go to heaven." She sticks her lip out in an exaggerated pout.

"He was." A pounding headache grows at my temples. Where is Andrew? He's supposed to be back by now so he can get Sutton out of the house. I don't want her sitting here staring at Jacob and watching him die any more than I wanted her to do that when he was in the hospital. We never considered how any of this would work when we made the decision to leave the hospital, and we've been figuring it out as we go along, the repercussions of our decision weighing heavy on us. "He's going to heaven. It's just taking him a while to make his journey."

"Why is he taking so long? Can't he hurry up?" she asks in the blunt way all children do.

I want to call for Wyatt so that he can take her until Andrew gets back, but he wants nothing to do with Jacob dying in our house and won't do anything to help us. Pretty sure that includes not watching his sister. He completely freaked out last night when we told him our plans.

"What? No?" He shook his head like he was blocking the information from getting inside. "You can't bring him home."

It had never occurred to either of us that Wyatt would be opposed to the idea. We tried to assure him that it was a good idea and the best thing for Jacob, but he couldn't be as easily fooled as Sutton.

"You can't do this to me. How am I supposed to live in a house that my brother died in?" Hysteria filled his voice.

Andrew tried to calm him down, but he swore he wasn't coming downstairs until Jacob was out of the house, and so far, he's kept his word. I don't know what to do. I don't know what to do about any of this.

"Your brother will go when he's ready," I assure Sutton, and she picks up a different doll, satisfied for the moment.

I will Andrew to hurry before Jacob's throat fills with phlegm again. It needs to be suctioned out regularly. We spent most of the night trying to keep him from suffocating himself. We took turns holding his head to the side, and we used our turkey baster to suction out the corners of his mouth as best we could. Andrew looked at me like I was crazy when I suggested it, but it worked well enough to keep him from choking and making those horrible gurgling sounds. He's at the medical supply store picking up an EasyVac Aspirator.

I rest my head on the ottoman. Fatigue covers me like a thick blanket. Sutton prattles at me, but it's hard to keep up with what she's saying.

Something about a unicorn. Peaches. Where's Andrew? My thoughts drag in slow motion. Barbie dolls blur in front of me. Everything heavy. Maybe if I just close my eyes for a second.

"Mommy, look!" Sutton's voice startles me awake.

Was I dreaming? When did I fall asleep? Thoughts are cotton candy thick. Sutton's voice. She's still talking. That girl never stops talking. Where's Andrew?

My head throbs with pain. Too many days without sleep. I lift my head, and the movement makes me nauseous. Sutton's dolls are scattered in small piles on the floor.

"Mommy, look!" she calls again.

My eyes follow the sound of her voice. Her pink ballet tutu is spread out across Jacob's body as she straddles his chest. She smacks his cheeks like she's playing patty-cake with them. I leap to my feet.

"Sutton! Get off of him! What are you doing?" I race to Jacob's bed and grab her arm. "What are you doing?" The urge to shake her passes through me.

"Look! He woke up. Jacob woke up!"

I whip her off him in one swift movement, and she stumbles on the floor. "What were you thinking?" My voice shakes with fury as I glare down at her.

Her lower lip quivers as her eyes fill with tears. "I just wanted to see if he'd wake up."

"Don't you ever do something like that again! Do you hear me?" I push my finger into her chest. "You can't hit your brother like that."

"But Mommy, it worked. Jacob woke up."

"Stop saying that, Sutton. This is serious."

She points at him. This time her hand is the one to shake as she cries even harder and louder because I don't believe her story. Tears stream down her face. "But I'm not lying. He woke up from his nap. Jacob didn't wanna go to heaven, Mommy, he didn't."

Everything stills. I slowly release my hold on her skinny arms and stand. I turn around and look down at Jacob as if I'm sleepwalking.

Jacob's brown eyes stare back at me.

"Oh my God!" I grab his face and peer into his eyes. They're wide and unblinking. I smother his face with kisses. "Jacob?" This can't be happening. It's not real. His eyes are open.

Sutton slips her hand into mine.

"See, Mommy, I told you," she says softly.

"Wyatt!" I scream at the top of my lungs. "Get out of your room! Your brother isn't dying!"

FORTY-NINE

DANI

"Can you stay for tea?" I ask Luna as she gathers her stuff to leave Mom's house.

We called her this morning for help with Caleb because we couldn't do it by ourselves anymore. Mom and I had been up since four trying to ease his anxiety, but nothing we did made a difference. He only grew more agitated the harder we tried. We almost took him to the hospital, but we called Luna as a last-ditch effort to see if there was anything she could do. The small glimmer of hope I'd experienced the other day when he'd giggled was quickly extinguished after he'd been so triggered by the images on TV last night. He's almost as bad as he was when we brought him home from the hospital.

Sleep medication was the only thing that brought him relief, and luckily, we all got three hours of decent sleep before his screams penetrated the walls of the house. I tried everything I could think of, but nothing worked. Not even the Xanax we gave him at six.

My first call to Luna went ignored, but she called back immediately after she listened to my message. It took her a few hours, but she worked her magic, and he's been asleep on the couch for over two hours. Mom quietly stepped away to the back of the house to give Luna and me a chance to talk.

"I can't stay," she says when I point to the teakettle on the stove. "I have a history test tomorrow that I have to study for."

"Okay." I try to hide my disappointment. "I just like having you around. I miss you."

"God, Mom, it's only been three days. You act like I disappeared for weeks. I needed time to think." She adjusts her backpack on her back. "Did you read my letter?"

"Don't be mad, but I haven't read it yet." I reach out and grab both her hands before she has a chance to dart out the door. "I've been avoiding it, but not because I don't want to hear what you have to say." I search in her eyes for the little girl who used to be my best friend. "I already know what you have to say, and you're right. Whatever it is that you have to tell me about how I've damaged you, believe me when I tell you that I never meant to be like this and I'm so sorry for all the ways I've hurt you. I'd do things so differently if I could."

"That's not what I said." She smiles and wipes the tears off her cheeks. "Well, that's not entirely true. I did say some of that." We laugh. I squeeze her hands as she continues speaking. "But the moral of my story was that I was proud of you. You stood up to Dad over me, and you've never done that before."

"So you were so proud of me that you left?" She smiles, and the energy between us relaxes. "I've been so ashamed, and I haven't felt emotionally strong enough to read your letter. I'm barely holding on, and I was afraid it'd be the thing that pushed me off the emotional edge. I have to keep it together right now for Caleb." I quickly add, "And you."

She nods with understanding and shifts position, her bag getting heavy. "Do you have any idea what set him off?"

I shake my head. "Not a clue. There wasn't anything on the video that he hasn't seen before. It's not like it's the first time he's seen Jacob. Honestly, Jacob looked worse when he visited him at the hospital, and he didn't react to him then, so I'm not sure what it was about last night that did it."

His treatment team brought him down to Jacob's room for a visit while he was in the psychiatric ward. It was the only request he made while he was there, and despite their misgivings, they allowed it when he refused to let it go. Each room had a whiteboard on the wall that the nurses used, and he repeatedly scribbled, *I want to see Jacob.*

"What time is his therapy appointment?"

"Two. I'm hoping he sleeps until right before we have to leave. She's going to prepare him for their interview with Detective Locke." I lean forward. "Can I give you a hug?"

She nods and folds her body into mine. I wrap my arms around her despite her clunky bag. She rests her head on my shoulder. I inhale the faint smell of her lavender body soap. "Thanks for all your help today."

"No problem."

"I don't know what I would've done without you through all of this. You've been amazing, Luna. You really have."

Her body stiffens. "Do you know why I came home and stayed when Caleb came home from the hospital?"

"To help?" Isn't that what we're talking about?

"I wish I was doing it for this deep, heartfelt love for my baby brother like everyone makes it out to be and that I was the kind of big sister who took care of her little brother like that, but it's not." She struggles to talk through her tears and emotion. "A good big sister would've stayed with them that night. I knew they were way too messed up to be left alone, especially when they were so angry with each other." Her shoulders heave with the weight of her perceived responsibility. "If I had stayed that night . . . none of this would've happened. I—"

"Oh, honey, that's not true. You can't do that to yourself. Who knows what would've happened if you'd stayed?"

She shakes her head, unwilling to be swayed. "I know exactly what would've happened. I would've gotten all of them to go to bed. That's what would've happened."

"You don't know that."

"Yes, I do." She pulls away, and I wipe the smeared mascara from underneath her eyes with my thumbs. "All of us are to blame for this."

FIFTY

LINDSEY

Dr. Gervais shines her tiny light in Jacob's eyes a final time before completing her exam. I forgot to breathe during most of it. Feels like I've been holding my breath since Sutton slapped Jacob awake. Dr. Gervais turns to face Andrew and me.

"This is pretty remarkable," she says, shaking her head in disbelief like she's been doing since she arrived. It's strange seeing her outside of the hospital and in regular clothes. I feel the same way my kids do whenever they run into one of their teachers at the grocery store or Target.

Dr. Merck refused to come to our house when we called him with the news. He cut Andrew off short, barely giving him a chance to explain what happened. Maybe he's not allowed to speak with us because of all the drama surrounding the case. The hospitals are lawyered up like we're going to come after them with a lawsuit, but I can't imagine what we'd sue them for. It's not their fault our insurance sucks.

"There isn't any visual tracking, but his pupils respond to light." Her fingers fly on her phone while she talks. Is she sending an email? Texting? What's she saying about us? "I'm excited to monitor his progress over the next few days."

"Does this mean you're going to continue treating Jacob?" I ask. Diana told us that none of the doctors from Jacob's team would be able to follow his case once we left the hospital because it was against medical advice and there would be too many malpractice issues.

"My situation is unique because I'm independently contracted by the hospital. Therefore I'm not an actual employee, so some of the rules don't apply to me. I spoke with my attorney on the way here to make sure I wasn't breaking any rules." She tucks her phone away and brings her gaze back to Jacob.

"What do we do now?" Andrew asks. He was so happy to find Jacob awake when he got home that he picked Sutton up and twirled her around the living room. He hasn't stopped smiling since, and he's beaming like a little kid on Christmas morning.

"We wait," Dr. Gervais responds.

Back to that?

"Tell me exactly what was going on again when he opened his eyes." She's obsessed with the story. She was never this interested in him at the hospital.

Andrew is thrilled for an opportunity to retell it. He goes into dramatic detail about how we hadn't slept for days and were beyond exhausted. He grows more animated as he describes me falling asleep and waking up to the sound of Sutton slapping Jacob. All I can do while he talks is replay the slap I gave Jacob the night before they pulled him off life support. What if my slap rattled him without me knowing it, in the same way Sutton's did this afternoon?

"Could it have made him wake up?" I ask after Andrew finishes.

"Slapping him?" She laughs. "If that was the case, we'd just hit all our coma patients until they regained consciousness."

I laugh, too, like I'd only been kidding when I asked the question, but there's a small part of me still not convinced. Oh well. It doesn't matter. The important thing is that Jacob's alive. He's not just alive—he's awake.

FIFTY-ONE
KENDRA

I pour myself a glass of wine. Only a small one and just to calm my nerves. Paul didn't come home from his run until it was time for Reese to leave for school, and he barely spoke to me while he got him ready to go. I'm glad he's going back to school. Paul sent me a text after he dropped him off that he would be going to the office for the day. There wasn't an invitation for me to join him.

He texted me a few minutes ago that he'd pick Reese up from school but that he was stopping by the house beforehand to talk to me. I was disgusting—unshowered and in the same sweatpants I'd been in for three days. I hadn't bothered to brush my teeth, so they were covered in grime. I rushed into the shower and threw myself together as fast as I could, in and out of the shower within nine minutes. I put on makeup for the first time since Sawyer died. I can't lose Paul. That'll be it for me.

He walks in wearing the workout clothes he put on last night. He smells like sweat and old socks. His hair is disheveled and he's unshaven. There's no way he went to the office.

"Where have you been all day?" I ask.

"The office. I told you that already."

A sigh escapes. "Paul, you didn't go in there looking like that. I know you."

"I sent everyone home."

"Seriously? Why did you do that?" We can't lose an entire day's work for nothing during the busiest part of the week. Not after we've already missed so much. We've got great assistants, and our employees are the best in the state, but we're the face of our company, the ones people trust.

"I don't want to talk about work." His tone is barbed in anger. His eyes are cold when they meet mine. "Stop giving Reese Adderall immediately."

I clear my throat nervously. "Okay, I will . . . I'll just have to talk to his pediatrician about how to do it. You can't just go off those drugs. There's a process for weaning off."

"See?" he shrieks. "The drugs are perfectly harmless, but he can't stop taking them without tapering off them like he's a drug addict? You damaged his brain, Kendra. Irrevocably." The vein throbs in his forehead while he speaks. "And you did it knowing I was opposed to it. Not just on the fence. Absolutely against it."

"I know what I did was wrong. I should've told you."

"Should've told me?" He sounds disgusted. "You never should've done it in the first place. He's been on drugs that have the same exact chemical properties as crystal meth."

"Stop being so dramatic." I can't help myself. He acts like giving kids prescription drugs is the same as giving them heroin. It's not. I've done my research too.

"It's true. None of this is my opinion or about me overreacting. It's science. Pure neuroscience. Strip down Adderall or any of those other stimulant medications to their basic components, and they're identical." He runs his hand through his hair. "And for what? Why'd you give it to him, Kendra?"

"I . . . uh . . ." I'm too nervous to speak. I've never seen him this mad.

"You messed up his brain to get him into some yuppie private school. That's it. And then you kept giving it to him even after he got into school because, what? He annoys his teachers? He's not popular?" He cocks his head to the side. "You couldn't have a kid who wasn't as popular as you were in high school, huh?"

"It's not about him being popular. He's barely making it through high school, and he's been in trouble since preschool, so don't act like he's some perfect child whose innocent brain I'm messing with. I mean, he sells drugs, Paul."

"That was after you gave him the Adderall. It probably made him do it."

"I can't believe you're this angry."

"Really?" He glares at me. "And I can't believe you don't understand why I am." He steps back like he needs to gain control of himself, clenching and unclenching his fists at his sides. "I'm going to get Reese from school and take him somewhere fun. Maybe to the crack dealer over behind the 7-Eleven on Magnolia."

"Now you're being mean." I'm doing my best not to cry, but I'm wavering.

"I've been thinking," he says as he moves toward the door. "Maybe you should just keep sleeping in Sawyer's room since you like it so much in there."

FIFTY-TWO
DANI

Kendra sobs on the couch while I wait for the coffee to finish brewing. I was going to pour us a glass of wine but quickly decided against it when I got a whiff that she'd already been drinking. Her hair is greasy and piled in a messy bun on top of her head. She has a strange, hollowed-out expression on her face. She and Paul had a terrible fight.

I hug my knees up to my chest on the opposite end of the couch. She went to my house first and texted, *where are you?* when nobody answered the door. I told her I was at my mom's. She showed up twenty minutes later and hasn't stopped talking since. She's too self-absorbed to notice or wonder why I'm over at Mom's with my things in the guest bedroom. She can be really annoying and hurtful that way, but it's a blessing today, because I'm not ready to explain what's going on to her or anyone else yet, especially after the way things went when I told Mom.

"My marriage is falling apart. Did you know that most marriages don't survive a child's death? You'd think it'd be the opposite. Two people go through this horrible thing together that nobody else can possibly understand, so you assume it'd bring them closer, but that's not the case. Most of the time it rips them apart. What if we're one of those couples?"

"You're not," I say. "Paul adores you." I spent years wishing and waiting for them to break up. There were times when they were fighting and I purposefully gave her advice I knew would upset Paul instead of calm him down, but that was a long time ago, and Paul's done nothing but remain committed to her since college.

"He used to, but I don't know anymore. I don't know about anything anymore. None of my decisions make sense. They did at the time, but none of them do now. What if all this is somehow my fault?"

"Hush. None of this is your fault." I scoot down the couch.

"It is. You don't understand. There's stuff you don't know. Things I haven't told you."

Is she talking about her marriage with Paul or what happened with our kids? "I'm not following you," I say.

She gulps. "The reason Paul left was because he found out I've been giving Reese Adderall without telling him."

She conveniently left that part out of the story when she described how Paul had stormed out of their house at three in the morning to go running and hadn't come back until after the sun had come up. She made it sound like he was just upset, and they have plenty to be upset about, so I thought nothing of it.

She quickly adds, "And he is really against kids being on medication."

Of course he is. One of his cousins committed suicide when Paul was twelve after her doctor put her on Prozac for depression. His family swore she had a complete personality change from it and that was what pushed her over the edge. I never met his cousin. She didn't live around here, but he went to visit them for two weeks every summer up until the end of middle school. It devastated the entire family. His aunt never recovered.

"How long were you giving it to him?" I ask. It's difficult to keep the judgment out of my tone.

"A little over a year."

"And you were doing it behind his back the entire time?" This time the judgment creeps in.

She nods. Her face is broken with guilt, but I can't tell if she's sorry because she hurt him or because she got caught. It's never easy to tell with her.

I'd be furious if Bryan gave the kids psychiatric medication and I didn't know about it. I'm not opposed to kids being on it, but I would never want Caleb or Luna to take anything like that without my knowledge.

"Our boys were taking Adderall too," she says. "They tried to get it from Reese."

"But I thought Reese didn't know you were giving it to him?"

"He didn't. He was getting it from somewhere else."

"What makes you so sure our boys were taking it?" Caleb can't even have caffeine without getting ridiculously amped up. I can't imagine what Adderall would do to him.

"The toxicology reports are back. Detective Locke went over them with us yesterday. I'm sure he'll be calling you today to go over it with you."

"So you just saw Sawyer's report? You didn't see the reports for the other boys?"

"No, but Detective Locke was pretty clear that they were all wasted that night. He even admitted that alcohol played a role."

That doesn't mean anything. He could've just been saying that to make her feel better about Sawyer being so messed up. Caleb's report might be different than his.

"Does Lindsey know?"

"About the Adderall or what the toxicology report said?"

"All of it."

"I sent her a text that the toxicology report was in, but she never responded. I didn't tell anyone I was giving Reese Adderall."

It's a pretty big secret to keep for a year, but it's not surprising. She's always been good at keeping secrets.

"It isn't like I was hiding it from you guys. I just didn't want Paul to find out, and the only way to do that was to make sure I was the only person who knew about it. I couldn't risk someone else saying something if I told. I know it probably doesn't make sense to you." She turns her head to the side.

It makes perfect sense to me.

She's not the only one with secrets.

FIFTY-THREE
LINDSEY

I step outside onto our back patio to breathe. Being inside is more claustrophobic than being in the hospital. There's no place in our house to put Jacob except in the living room. All of the bedrooms in our house are upstairs, which is out of the question since we can't get him up there. The living room is the only space that's big enough to fit his hospital bed while still giving us enough room to move around. The smell of sickness is slowly seeping into our house. I opened the windows to air things out, but so far it hasn't done any good.

People keep stopping by. I swear Andrew texted everyone we know and told them Jacob has opened his eyes. It wasn't long before they started arriving on our doorsteps with food and random medical supplies that they thought we might need. Three different people showed up with gauze like Jacob has open wounds we have to bandage. Everyone makes their way through the house and peeks at Jacob like he's one of the displays at the Ripley's Believe It or Not museum on Hollywood Boulevard.

I grip one of the patio chairs and lean forward. "Breathe, Lindsey. Breathe," I instruct myself, hoping that saying it out loud makes it more effective.

Jacob's eyes are open. That's a good thing. What's wrong with me? I've spent hundreds of hours staring at his closed eyelids and praying to every god and form of divinity I could think of that he'd open them. I just kept thinking if he'd only open his eyes . . .

And now they're open. But they roll around like marbles, and I can't stand to look at them because they're more disturbing than when they were closed. Andrew holds his face and gazes into his eyes with complete rapture and awe, but I don't know how he does it. I thought if Jacob opened his eyes, I'd see my son staring back at me. But I can't see him in there. He's nowhere to be found.

Sutton's shrill voice carries outside into the crisp air. She tells anyone who will listen that she's responsible for waking him up. People keep feeding into her story, and if they're not careful, she's going to end up thinking she has some kind of superpowers. Wyatt asked to go to his best friend's house for the night, and I agreed. It'll be easier to figure things out if he's not here. Lots of friends have offered to take Sutton, too, but she doesn't sleep other places without us yet. My dad said he'd fly back out if we needed him to, but I hate to make him do that since he's only just gotten home.

The sliding glass door opens, and Andrew walks up behind me. His hand on my back makes me cringe and stiffen.

"Sorry," he mumbles.

I can't help it. I don't want him to touch me. I keep trying to pretend nothing has changed, but all I can think about whenever he touches me is that he's in love with another woman.

"Uncle Ross is talking about ordering pizza. How many do you think we should get?" he asks, moving quickly past the awkwardness of the moment.

"This isn't a party," I snap.

"Is there anything I can do to help?" He wears the same cautious expression as he does when I'm in the throes of PMS and waging war with my hormones.

"I just need everyone to leave and get out of my house."

His eyes widen in surprise. "Really?"

"I'm so tired I can barely stand. It hurts to think, and my eyes are burning, so yes, I'd like everyone to go home and stop wandering around my house like we're some circus freak show."

He instinctively goes to reach for me but quickly pulls back. "Everyone just wants to help. That's all." He tucks his hands in the front pockets of his jeans. "Why don't you go to sleep upstairs in our bedroom once everyone leaves, and I'll stay up with Jacob?"

I shake my head. I can't leave him. I'm his mom. He needs his mom.

"Maybe you'll feel differently after a shower. Do you want to do that?" he asks like I'm a feral cat he's trying to coax inside.

A shower might feel good. I can't remember the last time I took one. "I can take a shower," I say like I'm pumping myself up for a major task.

He gingerly takes my arm and leads me back inside the house.

―

My eyes snap open. Our mahogany dresser slowly takes shape in the dark. The closet door comes into focus next.

And then I remember.

It's like this whenever I wake up. In that instant between sleep and waking, I forget how my life has been destroyed. It's that brief second that destroys me because it makes me remember how happy I used to be, how perfect things were, everything I had, and the realization is like losing it all over again. I hate waking up now.

Andrew's side of the bed is empty. The bedding smooth, untouched. The red digits of his old-fashioned alarm clock that he refuses to give up read 3:12. The house is silent; everyone has gone home, and I revel in the quiet. I don't want anyone here tomorrow. I'm sending them all away if they come by uninvited or unannounced. I don't care what Andrew says. I need a day or two to breathe and put myself back together.

I throw the covers off and push my bare feet into the slippers underneath my bed. I grab my robe from the floral-printed chair underneath the window. My pages are still marked in the book I was reading before this happened, and it's tucked between the armrest and seat. I haven't read a word since no matter how many times I tried, and I spent hours forcing myself to read, especially in the hospital. People brought me so many different books to try and keep my mind occupied, and normally, I love to read, but my brain's too squirrelly to focus on anything. The words jumble together, or I read the same sentences over and over. I wrap the robe around myself and tighten the sash around my waist.

I open the door of our bedroom and tiptoe downstairs. The newly purchased night-lights glow in the outlets, lining a pathway to Jacob's bed and casting a strange glow on everything they touch. They lead from the kitchen into the living room and all the way to the bathroom. Andrew is asleep on the couch at the end of Jacob's bed.

I lightly wiggle his arm, and he opens his eyes.

"Go upstairs and sleep. I'll take over."

"Are you sure?"

I nod and point to the stairs. "Go."

He grabs his phone off the coffee table and shuffles upstairs. I perch on the edge of the couch, heated from his body. The couch is new. I had a decorator help me with the living room, since it's the first room everyone sees when they walk into the house, so I wanted it to set the tone for our home. It's a light blue and firm but still looks plump. It's the most expensive piece of furniture I've ever owned because I wanted it to look good, which it does, but I never expected people to sleep on it.

I carefully chose all the decor because I wanted the space to feel light and clean, airy. It's filled with soothing grays and pale whites. The couch faces a beautifully restored fireplace and the large wooden coffee table in front of it, which holds a collection of *Departures* magazines like we're the kind of family that takes luxury vacations. Above the fireplace is an enormous family portrait, and framed photographs of the kids line the mantelpiece. Every inch is familiar, but none of it feels that way anymore. The ease that I walked through my life with and how much I took it for granted washes over me, making me feel sick to my stomach.

I stare at Jacob's bulky hospital bed crowding the space between the coffee table and the fireplace. Someone changed his socks. Probably Sutton. I get up and move to his bed. I trail my hand along the rails of his bed while I circle it. All the lock mechanisms are in place and the extra safety strap engaged as if there's a chance Jacob might move and pitch himself out of bed. His eyes lie open, and if he were in there, they'd be staring up at the ceiling, but he's not staring at anything. His eyes are just open. They haven't shut yet other than reflexive blinks. Dr. Gervais said we should expect to see him moving into what appear to be sleep-wake cycles, but so far, there's only wake.

"Hey, honey. How was your day?" I bend over and kiss his forehead. His skin is waxy against my lips. "Mine was exhausting. I'm not even sure how I made it. I was about one step away from turning into Walgreens Mom." It's what he's called me ever since I went off on the pharmacy technician at the drive-through window when he filled my prescription wrong. "But your dad forced me to sleep for a while, and I'm feeling much better now. How about you?" I run my hand along his arm, dead weight next to his body. "Are you feeling any better?" I trail my hand along his feet as I move to the other side of his bed and run my arm up that side of his body until I've reached his head again.

I see the pink blur of my hand as it slaps his face. Those aren't my hands. They can't be. And then I watch as they do it another time, stunned as they connect. They're attached to my body, but a force outside my control has taken them over. I can't believe what they've done. How could they do that? Moonlight floods through the bay window and lands on my wedding ring. The diamonds wink at me mockingly like they know my secret. I grip the bed rails and continue circling his bed as I stifle the urge to scream.

FIFTY-FOUR
DANI

I'm frozen out of all my accounts. I went to the ATM to get cash for Mom to help with the groceries and bills, because we're a pretty big unexpected expense and she shouldn't have to handle it alone. I was going to have to find a way to slip it into her purse because she's too proud to take it outright, but none of that matters when I don't have any money to give her.

I immediately called my bank, but the customer service representative kept saying my name had been taken off the account and I needed to talk to my husband about it. She must've said it over ten times—"You need to talk to your husband, ma'am"—in a nasal voice that made me seethe with hot anger.

I've been on the phone with my credit card companies most of the morning, and he took me off those too. Which I think is illegal, but how am I supposed to get a retainer for a lawyer when I don't have any money?

I smack my hands on the steering wheel and let out a broken wail.

"This! Right here. The part that nobody understands. How do we actually get out? Somebody! Anybody. What am I going to do?" But there's nobody to answer me. There never is.

Thick tears cloud my vision as I keep driving in the direction of Mom's house. My childhood home. The one where my biggest problem was that my best friend was dating the guy I had a crush on. I'm not supposed to be here. This isn't supposed to be my life. I'm not one of those women.

But I am.

And I was right. He will do everything he ever threatened to do if I left him. This is only the beginning.

Caleb and I sit around the kitchen table. He's working on the math worksheets that I printed off the classroom website. I wish I could be more helpful with his math homework, but I've been lost since he was in fifth grade. He's frustrated and agitated, but I can't tell if it's with the equations or his inner state. He's so far behind in school that I don't know how he's ever going to catch up.

I've grown to appreciate his silence over these past few weeks because he can't ask me the hard questions that I'm not ready to answer. Or ramble with meaningless chatter just to fill up the silence that I never noticed ran through so much of daily life until he stopped talking.

A loud knock at the door makes us both jump. Kendra pops her head in front of the kitchen window and waves, holding up a Starbucks cup. I give her a smile, trying to hide my annoyance. She texted earlier, and I told her Caleb and I were going to be taking it easy at the house today, subtly implying that I didn't want to be bothered. She's come undone with Paul being mad at her. She's scrambling around even harder to put the pieces of the accident together, like that will make everything better.

I get up to answer the door and lean down to whisper in Caleb's ear as I pass, "Sorry. I'll try to get her to leave quickly."

She rushes inside when I open the door without giving me a chance to refuse, and now that she's inside, there's no telling how long she'll stay. I can't listen to her cry all day. I know that makes me a terrible friend, but I have my own problems going on. I have to talk to Bryan about money, and that terrifies me.

"Hi, Caleb!" she calls out to him. "Glad to see your mom has you keeping up on your homework." She reminds me of my college roommate when she went into her manic episodes. There's so much pressure to her speech, like the words can't get out fast enough.

He keeps his head down and waves at her while he keeps working. She hands me my coffee, even though I have a fresh cup of tea on the table. Oh well. There's no such thing as too much caffeine.

"I was in the neighborhood, and I'm headed back home but thought I'd stop by Lindsey's first. I figured you'd probably want to come with me since we haven't been over there since Jacob woke up, and it's already been a day. You know how she gets."

"But Lindsey texted this morning and asked everyone to stay away today. She said they needed a day to settle or something like that."

Kendra bats my arm. "She didn't mean us, goofball. Put your shoes on, and let's go."

She hasn't taken hers off. She stands in the entryway expectantly. I point to Caleb. She shrugs. "Bring him. Doesn't he want to see Jacob?" She raises her voice higher as if he didn't hear her. "Caleb? I bet you want to go see Jacob, don't you?"

I hide behind her back and shoot Caleb a helpless look. He shrugs noncommittally. She turns back to me.

"See, Caleb wants to go, too, so stop being such a stick-in-the-mud, and let's go."

"Okay, but we'll drive ourselves," I say. "I don't want you to have to come all the way back here to drop us off afterward. It's too inconvenient."

Really, I'm ensuring we get back here without her. I can't handle much Kendra time today.

FIFTY-FIVE
KENDRA

Dani rides my tailgate as she follows me to Lindsey's. I pretended my visit was about dragging them along with me so I didn't have to go alone, but it was the only way I could be sure Caleb came. Lindsey's been ignoring my texts for two days, and there's no way she'll make us leave if Caleb's with us.

I sent her the Instagram video of the party, and she never confirmed receipt. I understand she's got a lot on her plate right now, but she's not the only one who's going through things. I mean, come on—my son is gone, and her son is probably the one who killed him. I should be the most upset, but I'm not. I just want to know what happened so I can lay him to rest. Why is that so hard to understand? She'd be doing the same thing if the shoe were on the other foot.

I slow out of habit as I come around Pike's Bend. Yellow signs dot the sharp curve, warning people about falling over the cliff, just like the ones that warn about deer running across the road up north. They are done in the same way. Stick figures that Sawyer used to joke looked like they were doing cartwheels over the edge. He'd burst into giggles every time.

I miss his laugh. It's one of the things I miss the most. He never took anything too seriously, which made his grades a continual nightmare but our home a happy place. I had to get out of there today.

Paul's still barely talking to me. He acts like I gave Reese heroin. I get it, I do, but the medicine was prescribed for a real diagnosis by a doctor who's been his pediatrician since he was five days old, and I always gave it to him exactly as prescribed. I'm not saying it was the right thing to do, and I really am sorry that I didn't tell him, but it's not like I committed the worst crime on the planet.

It isn't long before we reach Lindsey's, and we pile out of our cars quickly. I hurry up the sidewalk and tap on the door, not too loud in case people are sleeping. There's no mistaking the annoyance on Lindsey's face when she opens the door. She stands with the door only slightly ajar and her body blocking the entrance into the house. Things obviously haven't gotten better since the last time I saw her. She might even look worse. Her eyes are red and watery. Skin gray and sallow like she might be getting sick. Her face is so gaunt.

I sneak a peek at Dani, and she's thinking the same thing—it's ten o'clock, and she's still in her bathrobe. Sleeping in for Lindsey is seven o'clock. She's been getting up at five since our sophomore year in high school. Her brown hair, normally meticulously done no matter what, lies flat and unwashed against her head. Maybe it's a good thing we stopped over to say hello.

"Hi, Lindsey, we were just in the neighborhood and thought we'd stop by," Dani says in an extra cheerful tone, stealing the line I used on her earlier to get inside her house.

Lindsey pulls her robe tighter. "Yeah, thanks, but I don't think we're in any shape for visitors. We're having a bit of a rough day."

"That's exactly why we're here," I say, stepping around her and into the house. I open the door wider to make room for everyone else to get through. Lindsey doesn't always know what's best for her.

FIFTY-SIX
LINDSEY

Kendra barges her way into my house like she forces her way into everything. She struts into the living room like she's the owner, and we automatically follow behind her like we've done so many times before. Caleb shuffles in with Dani. He's red faced with embarrassment, and his arms hang awkwardly by his sides like he doesn't know what to do with them.

I watch the three of them as they take in the scene. Kendra surveys the room, purposefully avoiding Jacob in the center. Dani pales instantly, and she swallows hard like she's choking on the air. Something's definitely going on with her. She won't say what it's about, but she's staying at her mom's with Caleb, so there's a reason she doesn't have him at home. Caleb's eyes fill with tears the way they do whenever he's around Jacob. Why do they do that to him? It's not fair when it clearly makes him so uncomfortable.

I move next to him and place my hand softly on his back. "You can sit in that chair over there if you want." I point to the leather ottoman on the other side of the room, the spot farthest away from Jacob and the one with the most obstructed view of his bed. His eyes speak gratitude, and he quickly moves around the foot of Jacob's bed. He takes a seat on the chair and curls his body up, wrapping his arms around himself.

"I like the setup you put together," Kendra says like we've redecorated the living room instead of making it into a hospital room.

"Thanks." I don't want them to get too comfortable. I only offered Caleb a seat because I feel sorry for him and he shouldn't have to be here.

"How are things going?" Dani asks. Her eyes radiate compassion and concern.

"It's not as easy as we hoped. We didn't think about any of this, and there's lots of challenges. For one"—I motion to the space around us—"this is the only place we can put him because his hospital bed doesn't fit anywhere else, and we don't have a handicap-accessible house, so we can't get him upstairs," I explain. "We can barely move him off his bed. There's a reason people train for that."

He's a five-foot-seven, 140-pound limp noodle. We can turn him left to right on the bed, but we can't get him safely out of bed or move him anywhere. We saw the nurses transfer him many times, but we nearly dropped him onto the wooden floor when we tried the techniques we'd seen them use. It's not like there is a quick way to learn, so we're poring through YouTube videos and earmarking the ones that look like they're made by reputable professionals.

Kendra turns around and locks eyes with me. "Can I ask what made you decide to leave the hospital?"

I hate when she poses questions that way. It's so manipulative. I dodged the question most of yesterday, but there's no way Kendra's letting me off the hook that easy, and Caleb probably wants to know too. It's mean not to tell him, except I don't know what came over me, which makes finding an explanation difficult.

"Honestly? I don't know." It's not the part of the story we tell others when they ask about it. We focus on what happened after we made our decision to take him out of the hospital, but the actual decision itself? We don't discuss that because it was a split-second idea that came out of nowhere. "Jacob had just finished his CT scan, and while Dr. Merck was explaining what they'd found—basically, no changes—I had this overwhelming urge to take him outside. I wasn't even thinking about it beforehand and just blurted it out. They let us take him outside, and as soon as we were outside with him, I couldn't go back inside. I don't know why. I just couldn't do it. I almost had a panic attack every time I looked at the building." Imagining it now makes me shudder with revulsion.

"What about Andrew?" Dani asks.

"He was the one that suggested it." Their faces fill with surprise, and I can't help but smile. "I know. I couldn't believe it either. I didn't think he was serious at first. We were standing in a back alleyway of the hospital, and I was totally freaking out. I'd been up for two days, so I just went with it when Andrew made the suggestion. Neither of us questioned it."

They shake their heads in disbelief. We're the last people anyone would imagine doing something like this, and I'm on board with them. Whatever impulse came over me two days ago has disappeared and left me with nothing but uncertainty and fear. This is why I think things through. It's exactly what I tell the kids.

"What are you going to do now?" Dani asks.

That's the next question everyone wants to know—what's the plan? We asked the doctors the same thing so many times in the hospital, and they were responsible for answering it. Now the responsibility rests solely on our shoulders, and I've never been so overwhelmed. We don't know what we're doing. We're two blind people trying to lead each other through a maze, and I'm forced to work with someone I don't trust anymore.

"Does it smell in here?" I blurt out in the same way I blurted that I wanted to take Jacob outside.

Kendra balks at the randomness of my question. "What?"

"Tell me the truth—don't lie. Does it stink when you walk in here?" I wave my hands around the room while I raise my head, sniffing the air.

"Remember when Sandra had cancer and her house smelled like cancer whenever we visited her? Does my house smell like death?"

The two of them exchange concerned glances like I'm not standing right in front of them. They can't tell me they don't smell it. Jacob's stench has infiltrated every room in our house. It's seeped into the walls. My house smelled like dirty diapers for years when my boys were in diapers, but it's different somehow.

Dani speaks first. "No, it's fine. I didn't notice anything."

Normally, I'd offer them something. A cup of tea or coffee. A glass of wine if it were past five, but giving them anything will only make them stay longer, and if I don't have some time to pull myself together, I don't know what I'm going to do. Their presence grates on me.

"I know you've had a million things to do, but did you get my text about the video Paul found on Instagram with Jacob and Sawyer at another Delta Tau party?" Kendra asks.

She keeps sending me that stupid video. The last thing I want to do is watch a video of Jacob smiling and alive. It hurts too much. Why can't she just let it go?

I shake my head. "I haven't had time."

Kendra reaches in her purse and pulls out her phone before hurrying over to me. She types in her pass code, and a video is already queued up on her screen. Anger shoots through me. This is the purpose of her visit. All of it makes sense now. I should've known she wanted something.

I step around her and begin folding Jacob's socks over his ankles like there's something important I need to do with his feet. She follows and stands behind me.

"You really should see this. There was definitely something going on with them." She tries to hand me the phone again. I ignore her. She tries again, reaching around me. I push her hand away. "What's wrong?" she asks.

"My child is a vegetable, Kendra!" I turn and scream at her. "Or haven't you noticed that because you're so wrapped up in your own damn pain that you can't see anybody else's? I lost my son too. The Jacob from before?" Rage shoots through my body, making it tremble. "He died that night. Right along with Sawyer. We might as well have buried them together. I'm never getting him back, and I'm left with an infant to raise for the rest of my life. Have you stopped to think that might be why I've been dodging your texts? Why I haven't dug into the latest investigation of Jacob and Sawyer's relationship?" I shake my head. Kendra backs up against the wall behind her like I'm going to attack her. "Don't say anything. I already know the answer. You don't think of anyone but yourself. Never have. The night of our junior prom? You could've—"

Dani steps forward and gently places her hand on my arm to stop me. We never talk about that night, didn't even the night it happened. "Lindsey, don't, please," she says softly.

"Don't give me that. You know I'm right. You even said so yourself, but you won't say it in front of Kendra, will you? You're just secretly glad she backed off of Caleb and started pointing her finger at Jacob." Horror crosses her face like I've slapped her. She drops my arm. "You know it's true. Come on, isn't that why Kendra marched in here? All in the name of truth telling? Truth finding? Well, how's this for truth—Caleb had a vicious temper. He hated being left out or told what to do. Maybe you guys should stop trying to write the next *Romeo and Juliet* and focus your attention on the kid who we all know would be voted most likely to go off and shoot his friends."

The room stills. I've crossed every line.

Dani rushes to Caleb and throws her arms around him, covering his ears with both hands to protect him from my words. Kendra stares at me like she's never seen me before. I lock eyes with her but can't bring myself to apologize. If I open my mouth, I'm only going to spill more poisonous venom. They never should've come to my house.

FIFTY-SEVEN

KENDRA

There's got to be something here—something I missed before—anything. I rip open Sawyer's dresser drawer and rummage through his T-shirts, tossing them out as I go, not caring where they land. Mounds of his clothes lie scattered in piles by my feet from the drawers I've already been through. I kick them aside and move on to his desk, jerking open the top drawer.

Paul startles me from behind. "What are you doing?" He stands in the doorway, eyeing me warily with his arms crossed.

He's supposed to be at the office. What's he doing home? I ignore him and tug open the other drawers. I grab random items and push them aside, making sure to dig all the way to the back for anything hidden or out of my reach.

"What are you doing?" he asks louder.

"Looking for something." I scurry away from the desk and drop to my knees next to Sawyer's bed. I peer underneath it like I used to look for monsters before turning the lights out for him to sleep at night. There's nothing but dust bunnies and scrunched-up socks.

I've never been so furious with Lindsey. How dare she make it sound like I'm being selfish by trying to piece together Sawyer's death? Like I'm supposed to feel bad when her kid probably killed mine? I deserve to know what happened to him. I've been doing her a favor by being nice and gentle. No more.

I had to get out of there before I did something terrible. I don't know how I drove home without crashing. One minute I was at her house, shaking with fury, and the next minute I was pulling into my driveway. I've been tearing apart Sawyer's room ever since, determined to find a clue that can bring him justice, and when I do, I'm going back over there and throwing it in her face.

"What are you looking for?" Paul asks.

"I don't know." I hop back to my feet and eye the posters taped on the walls of his room.

"What do you mean, you don't know?" He takes a step into the room.

I dart to the King Theta poster on the wall next to his bathroom door and grab a corner, ripping it off the wall. Parts of the paper stick to the wall, and I frantically scrape the last pieces off, clawing at them with my fingernails.

Paul races up behind me. "Stop it! What are you doing?"

I toss the poster on the floor and run my hand along the wall like there's a hidden spot behind it. Paul grabs my hands to stop me and pulls me close to him. He wraps his arms tightly around me. "Settle down."

I writhe against him. I don't want to settle down. I want to know what happened to my baby. He holds me tight, refusing to let go.

"It's okay. Just try to settle," he says in a calm, soothing voice.

My body trembles against his, and my voice shakes when I speak. "I need to know what happened to Sawyer. I don't care what Lindsey or anybody else thinks. I don't care if everybody else is like, *Oh, it's just an accident.* Nobody wants to say it out loud, Paul, but what if it wasn't?" I start crying as the questions tumble out of me. "What if Jacob shot Sawyer on purpose?"

"I care about what happened to Sawyer."

I lean into him; he's solid. "I'm sorry. I know you do. It's just we all tiptoe around it like there's no way it's a possibility, but I'm pretty sure Jacob killed Sawyer. As terrible as it is, it's the only explanation that makes sense. The only scenario where Jacob shoots himself is if he does it after he shoots Sawyer."

Paul traces lines on my back. "I know," he whispers into the top of my head.

"Why can't Lindsey admit that and move on? It's not like anything is going to happen to Jacob. No judge or jury is going to send him to jail. He's already lost his life." Unlike most people who lose their loved ones to violent crimes, I know my perpetrator will get the punishment and suffering that others only imagine in the dark corners of their minds.

"It's too hard for her or anyone else to think of him as a murderer. The kid was practically perfect. He's not supposed to be the type of kid who does something horrible, and if he could do something like that, then anybody could, so it's too terrifying for people to think about. Not to mention it's probably also not how she wants him remembered."

She doesn't want him remembered as a murderer any more than I want Sawyer remembered as a dumb jock who got drunk and made a stupid mistake, which is how he'll be remembered if I don't prove otherwise.

"Thank you for understanding." My breathing is slowly returning to normal.

"Believe me, I totally get it. Can we get out of here now?"

I eye the destruction I wreaked on the room. "I should pick this up." His eyes freeze with anxiety at the thought of having to stay in this room any longer. "And you should go downstairs and make us something to eat. I'll be hungry when I'm done."

I stare at the phone in disbelief. I was cleaning up my mess and putting things away after wreaking havoc on Sawyer's room when it tumbled out of a box of old clothes stacked in the back of his closet. I try his iPhone pass code first, hoping I'll get lucky and he used the same one, but the phone buzzes with denial. How did I miss this before? Guilt creeps its way up my stomach and inches its way up my throat. I was only in his closet if I was digging for bottles late at night when I was taking those pills. It's been five days since I took one, and I haven't been back here until today. Maybe I would've found it before if I hadn't been impaired, but I don't have time for regret. This is too important.

Getting into his iPhone was easy because I know both Sawyer's and Reese's pass codes. The only way the boys are allowed to have phones is if we have access to them. Obviously, there are still ways to hide things, but at least they know we monitor them. I keep trying different possible combinations, making sure to give the phone the proper time to reset between pass code fails so I don't get myself locked out, but no luck. I rack my brain, but the possibilities are endless. Hopelessness has started setting in when I suddenly have an idea. I type in Jacob's birth date and watch as the screen unlocks.

There's only one number he communicates with on the burner phone, and it's one that I don't recognize, but it's probably Jacob's. I bet if Lindsey searched his room, she would find a similar phone, and my suspicions are confirmed when I scroll to the beginning and find their first few texts are about buying the burner phones together. Their *Breaking Bad* references make me laugh.

I start reading the text stream between them like it's Sawyer's diary. They got the phone nine months ago, shortly after they started hooking up, because they didn't want anyone to know about their relationship. There's a level of intimacy I never imagined they had and certainly never saw, or I would've brought it up. They talk about how much pressure they feel on the soccer field. I had no idea Sawyer felt the level of stress he did or that Jacob was on a partial financial aid scholarship. Lindsey never breathed a word of that. Has that always been the case? There's tons of sex stuff, and I quickly scroll past it, wishing there were a way to filter it out, but there's not.

Their relationship was a secret. Nobody knew, not even Caleb. I wonder what he thinks now? Except their texts don't call it a relationship, and as soon as Jacob makes reference to the two of them being a couple, the pullback from Sawyer is immediate and obvious, even though it's clear Sawyer has feelings for him too. Jacob is head over heels in love with Sawyer and doesn't care who finds out. His texts move from brief misspelled shorthand, emojis, and videos to long, carefully drafted sentences.

> I know we said that we didn't want things to get serious because we're so young but we can't control the way we feel. I don't understand what you're so afraid of.

> I'm not gay.

> You can't control who you love.

> Who said anything about love?

His words stab me in the heart. What must they have done to Jacob? He doesn't respond after that, and there's a two-week gap between texts and FaceTime calls. I pull out his iPhone to see if they stop communicating on that, too, and interestingly, they communicate with each other in group chats, but there aren't any private communications between them. And then Sawyer breaks the silence with the oldest trick in the book:

> You looked hot in those jeans today.

Jacob bites within seconds like he's been waiting for contact.

Thanks!

It's not long before they're performing the dance that makes up almost every teenager's relationships with boys they like—*come closer, get away, come closer, get away.* Despite Sawyer being my son, I find myself rooting for Jacob in their emotional tug-of-war. It frustrates me that in addition to being your stereotypical jock, Sawyer's also your classic player, and at the expense of someone he so clearly cares about. Then something happens, and you can feel Sawyer's anger in his next text:

What you did today was wrong. I'm done with this.

What did Jacob do? There's no mention of it anywhere. Jacob doesn't respond. There's nothing for two weeks, and then Jacob starts derailing. He's every picture of teenage heartbreak and angst.

I can't sleep at night thinking about you.

I don't know how to breathe without you.

Please talk to me.

I can't go on like this.

But Sawyer doesn't. He ignores Jacob for another nine days. Jacob's last text to Sawyer was sent the day before the accident. My blood chills as I read his words:

I wanted to kill you when I saw you flirting with those girls at lunch.

FIFTY-EIGHT
LINDSEY

What's wrong with me? How could I say those things in front of Caleb? It doesn't matter if they were true; he's too shattered to hear them. I fuss with Jacob's sheets, going around his bed and meticulously tucking in the corners to have something to do with my hands. Kendra stormed out after my outburst, but Dani's still here, and she keeps digging in her purse like she's looking for something important. She doesn't want to be stuck in this room with me any more than I want to be in it with her, but we don't have much of a choice. Caleb cried for over an hour, and we just finally got him settled on the couch with Wyatt. There's no point in moving him and taking the risk of upsetting him again.

Wyatt was the one who got him to stop crying. Caleb wanted nothing to do with me or Dani, and nothing we said soothed him or provided him any relief. He just sat there plastered against his chair with a pained expression on his face while loud, racking sobs shook his body. The sounds brought Wyatt downstairs, and he coaxed Caleb into the TV room. Wyatt motioned for us to stay away, and we watched from the living room as he fervently whispered to Caleb like they were in a soccer huddle. His words reached him, and it wasn't much longer until Wyatt talked him into watching an Avengers movie.

"Look, I shouldn't have answered the door. I wasn't in the spot to talk to anyone today," I say, keeping my hands busy while I talk so I don't have to look at her. "It's why I sent the text and told everyone to stay away."

She can be mad at me all she wants, but both she and Kendra got my message. They each side-texted me and asked if there was anything they could do to help. I told them the same thing I told everyone:

I'm fine. Just need to rest.

She keeps her eyes glued to her purse. "I know you didn't want anyone here today. Kendra showed up at my house and dragged us with her."

And Dani went along with her, like we've been doing since we were ten years old. Are we ever going to stop? The only reason Kendra felt confident enough to barge into my house the way she did a few hours ago is because she knew I wouldn't try to stop her any more than Dani had stopped her when she'd forced her way into her house.

"I'm sorry I said all those awful things."

"Why be sorry? They're true. You don't think I knew you and Kendra thought Caleb was 'so aggressive' when the boys were younger?" She uses air quotes. "You guys couldn't wait for me to leave playdates so you could gossip about all the things Caleb had done to your boys while they played and how I failed miserably in controlling him."

"Dani, we—"

She puts her hand up to stop me. "Please, don't even try. It's okay. I've always been the one who made you guys feel better about your own parenting."

"Well, you sure made up for it after I had Sutton." I can't help myself. She and Kendra spend just as much time bashing me about the way I raise Sutton as we did talking about Caleb when the boys were younger. But there's a difference between then and now. We were legitimately concerned about Caleb because he kept injuring our kids, so we had to address things with each other. They're being judgmental and ignorant in all of their behind-my-back whispering about me and how I raise my kids. We didn't know half the things we knew about raising children when we had the boys, and we know a lot more these days about how to speak and act with our kids. Am I not entitled—no, obligated—to parent based on what the new research shows is the best way?

She's quiet because she knows I'm right. We listen to the sounds of the movie playing in the background, each lost in our own thoughts.

"I left Bryan," she blurts out.

"What are you talking about? When?"

"Four nights ago." She's on the verge of tears but desperately trying to keep it together.

I rush around Jacob's bed and grab her arms, staring into her eyes. "Are you okay? Did he do anything to you?"

I've been prepared for this moment for over a decade—the one where Dani shows up with a black eye or a fat lip in the middle of the night because Bryan beat her up. No amount of preparation equipped me for the amount of anger flooding my body, though.

She shakes her head. She's always been petite, barely over five feet, and she looks even tinier when she's upset. "He hit Luna."

"Oh my God."

She nods. "I know."

"Oh, honey." I pull her into my arms. "You did the right thing. It's going to be okay."

"I'm so terrified. Like, all the time. Every second. I have no idea what I'm doing. If he's going to come get me. If he'll hurt me or the kids. He's already ambushed me in the parking lot at the hospital." Her words come faster as she talks. "But he's their father. I have to see him. They have to see him. There's no getting away from him. I—"

A sharp knock at the door interrupts our conversation.

FIFTY-NINE
DANI

Lindsey and I quickly pull apart. I wipe the tears off my face as she hurries to the large bay window behind Jacob's bed and peeks out. She has a perfect view of the front porch. "Oh my God, Kendra's back."

Kendra pounds at the door again, louder this time.

"She's probably here to apologize," I say, but her knocks don't sound friendly at all. Just angry.

"What should we do?" Lindsey asks, turning to me with bewilderment in her eyes.

I get up from the couch, grateful for the distraction. "Let me handle it."

I unlatch the door and open it a crack. Kendra stands on the concrete, anxiously tapping her feet together. I drop my voice to a whisper like a baby is sleeping inside the house. "Hey, we just finally got things settled down, and we're trying not to stir them up again. Can you come back later? Maybe tomorrow?"

"I can't even believe you're still here," she hisses through gritted teeth. "How can you be here after she said those terrible things about Caleb?"

"Now is not the time," I snap at her and push the door shut, but she blocks it with her foot. "Are you serious, Kendra?"

She waves a phone in front of her. "I'm not leaving until she sees this." Her eyes are wild.

"Honestly, please stop. She already told you that she doesn't want to watch the video." She's gone too far. None of us can handle another confrontation.

"I'm not talking about that video. I'm talking about everything that's on this phone." She shoves the door open and pushes past me like I weigh nothing, hurrying inside.

Lindsey snaps the curtains closed and rushes over to her before she can make it into the living room. "You are ridiculous. This is over the line. You can't force your way into my house." She points to the door. "Leave."

Kendra shakes her head. "Oh no, I'm not going anywhere until you see this, and I'm not talking about a video." She frantically waves the phone around again. "I'm talking about secret burner phones that Jacob and Sawyer had. The ones that they texted privately on, and guess what? They also did a lot of sexting on them too."

Lindsey puts her hands over her ears. "Stop, Kendra. Please, stop. I don't want to hear about my son's sex life."

"It's not his sex life. This has never been about sex. Why don't you get that? Jacob was in love. He was head over heels for Sawyer. Don't believe me?" Kendra scrolls through the phone and then stops. She reads aloud, "'I've never felt love like this before. I can't stop thinking about you.'" She scrolls again. "Or how about this? 'We were meant to be together. I know everyone thinks that when they're young. But we're for real.' Tell me that doesn't sound like love to you? Tell me it doesn't?"

"You need to leave." I grab Kendra's arm and pull her back. She's getting into Lindsey's space. None of this is good.

"Leave me alone, Dani." She jerks away and takes another step toward Lindsey. "Just admit it so that we can start to move forward—your son killed mine."

Kendra says out loud what everyone's been thinking for the past week ever since hints of Sawyer and Jacob's relationship came to life, but it's still jarring hearing her say it out loud.

Lindsey moves within inches of Kendra's face. Their chests almost touch, like they're two men getting ready to fistfight. "My son didn't hurt your son, just like my son didn't hurt himself. What happened that night was an accident, and both our sons got hurt. I'm sorry it happened, and I'm really sorry that you can't move past it." Her voice sounds anything but sorry. She sounds angry in that calculated way that means you've thought about it and found yourself justified, which makes it almost more dangerous than the fly-off-the-handle kind.

"Stop it!" Caleb's voice cuts through the room. He stands in the entryway to the living room. Hands at his sides. His fists clenched. "Just stop it. Please."

The room comes to a standstill. Nobody moves. Nobody speaks. Wyatt stands beside him, but all eyes are on Caleb. His legs tremble like a baby deer's from the weight of his first words in over a month.

I rush toward him, but he quickly backs away. I freeze in my spot, careful not to startle him further. "I'm so sorry, honey. We didn't mean to upset you. We'll stop."

He starts rocking back and forth on his heels, running his hands up and down his arms.

"It's okay, Caleb. You're okay," I say soothingly, trying to mimic the way Luna calms him.

"N-no . . . no . . . it's not . . . Mom . . . it's . . . ," he whimpers. His face contorts like he's in physical pain. He takes another step backward into the doorway.

The Best of Friends

"Why don't you sit down again with Wyatt?" Lindsey says from behind me, but her words only seem to upset him more, as he starts shaking his head back and forth.

"Just leave him alone, Lindsey," I say without turning around. There's something off about his eyes.

"I did it." His voice is wobbly, unsure. "I killed Sawyer." His eyes furtively scan the room until they land on me, searching for connection. My mouth is too dry to speak. Limbs too frozen in shock to move toward him. My son. The one confessing murder in front of me. I'm not ready for what comes next, but I can't look away.

"I didn't mean to, Mom. I didn't." Each word is purposeful—deliberate and slow.

I nod at him because I can't speak. My words stripped from me in the same way his were. I'm sure he didn't. He couldn't. He wouldn't. Not my Caleb.

He slowly shifts his attention to Lindsey. He swallows a few times. "Jacob shot himself." Swallows again. "Not me. I had nothing to do with that."

Lindsey gives short, quick nods like she's trying to comprehend what he's telling her. Kendra and Lindsey hold each other up, leaning against each other like they might fall to the ground if they don't. Their fight from seconds ago forgotten that quickly. Nothing matters besides this moment.

"Why would you do that to Sawyer?" The emotion in Kendra's voice is so raw that it brings tears to my eyes.

For so long, I've waited for him to speak, but now all I want is for him to be quiet. I'm not sure I can handle hearing what drove him to shoot his best friend, no matter how badly I want answers. Bryan's voice pops into my head unbidden, like I'm being shocked out of a deep sleep: *Don't let him speak to anyone without a lawyer present.* I step forward. "Caleb, honey, I don't think you should say anything more."

"Dani, no, please, don't . . ." Kendra's desperation hits me like a real object. "Let him talk to me. It doesn't matter what he says." She shakes her head like a wild dog, so close to the truth she can smell it. "Nobody outside this room has to even know. We don't have to tell anyone. Just us. Please."

Caleb looks to me for permission. His dad's warnings to him as present as they are to me, like he's in the room with us.

And then I remember—I don't live by Bryan's rules anymore.

"Caleb, we're not keeping anything a secret. I'm done with secrets. So whatever you tell Kendra and Lindsey, just know that you're going to have to tell the detectives and police officers exactly what you told them. Do you understand that?"

He nods in consent, but I'm not sure he does. He's confessing to murder, and he's sixteen years old. Seventeen in five months. He's my little boy, but the court will only see him as a man. That much I'm sure of. Pain stabs my heart. *Please let it be an accident.*

"They never acted like they were in love. Nothing. Just regular. But they lied. All the time. I was so angry. Pissed off." His voice is deeper than I remember it. He struggles to find more words. "Not because they were hanging out together by themselves. They push me away all the time. I'm used to it. I thought they were leaving me out. Again. Like all the other times. You don't know what that feels like." He shifts his eyes away in embarrassment.

Except I do. I know exactly what that feels like. Kendra and Lindsey might not have been in love, but I was the one shoved aside in any third-wheel situation.

"I was so mad because they kept lying to me about things. That's what was driving me so crazy." His eyes glaze over like he's about to disappear. He can't disappear again.

The Best of Friends

"That night, Caleb. Tell us about that night." Kendra's voice is pressurized. She senses his departure too.

He slowly walks over to the couch and sits down. The three of us follow and hover around him in a semicircle, Jacob in his bed behind us. Wyatt hasn't moved from his spot in the doorway.

"We lied about what we were doing. Not about the whole thing. I had the video game, and we were going to play it, but not until we got home from the party. The two of them got into this huge fight before we even left. I thought it was about the Adderall, because Sawyer was mad that we got ripped off from his usual guy. That was probably a lie. I bet they were fighting about something that had to do with them. Anyway, we started drinking at the house." He looks at me again. "Sorry, Mom."

"It's okay," I say, but it isn't. My response happens automatically, and he needs to continue. None of this is okay.

"Sawyer got drunk fast, like, really fast." He twists his hands together on his lap. "But we were all drunk, even Jacob, and he never drinks like that. Maybe it was the pills."

My legs are so weak I have to sit down next to him, or they won't hold me up any longer. I take a seat next to Caleb and quickly realize that it looks like I'm supporting him, and I'm not sure I am.

"We got into a huge fight at the Delta Tau party and got thrown out. Luna showed up and got us an Uber home. I just remember lots of fighting in the car. Everyone was yelling. So loud." He cringes like he hears their voices now. "Sawyer kept trying to fight me and Jacob. Once we got back home, things got even worse. He started calling me and Jacob names."

They got into it over names? All of this—names? My brain won't wrap around what he's saying.

"What kind of names?" Kendra asks like that's important.

Caleb stalls. His lower lip quivers. This is where he wants to stop. But he can't. Every awful detail needs to come out. "He kept telling me to stop treating him like a faggot. I didn't know what he meant." His face turns red. "He went into detail about the things he'd do to Luna to prove it, and that's when I lost it. I don't even know what happened. But it was disgusting, and he wouldn't stop. I just remember he wouldn't shut up." His eyes glaze over.

Please don't leave now. I place my hand on his knee.

"I don't remember getting the gun. I remember being furious and running upstairs. I was just so angry. The next thing I know, I'm downstairs with the gun. Sawyer was still going off. He was screaming at Jacob, and Jacob was crying. It was like the saddest cry ever. And Sawyer wouldn't leave him alone. He was on him. I screamed at him to stop. He wouldn't stop. He just wouldn't stop." There's an eerie detachment to his voice. Pain too deep for tears. "I threatened him with the gun and—and . . . he said I was too big of a pussy to do it." Grief contorts his face as he wrestles with the memories. "And then I shoved the gun in his gut. I didn't mean for it to go off." He chokes on his sobs. "It wasn't supposed to go off." He puts his head in his hands, too racked with grief to continue. His shoulders hunch together, and he clutches his stomach like he's in pain while he sobs.

Lindsey breaks in with a tiny, quiet voice like she's scared to ask. "What about Jacob?"

Caleb raises his head. His face is covered in red blotches. Snot stains both cheeks. "I'm so sorry." He takes a few gasping breaths. "I dropped the gun and just started trying to help Sawyer. I was screaming at Jacob to call 911. There was just so much blood. I've never seen so much blood." The color drains from his face as he sees it again in his mind. "I kept trying to stop it. I put the couch pillow on top of it, and it just soaked through. It soaked through a pillow, Mom." His voice cracks. He struggles to go on. "And then there was a shot . . . I didn't do that one . . . Jacob . . . Jacob, he must've grabbed the gun when I dropped it, and he just shot himself."

I watch Lindsey as she turns to where Jacob lies comatose on the hospital bed, realizing that he did this to himself. She never considered the possibility any more than I considered the possibility Caleb had shot either of them. She swallows the truth like bile. It must leave the same awful taste in her mouth as it does mine.

SIXTY
LINDSEY

Kendra and I stand awkwardly next to each other in my driveway as we watch the taillights of Dani's car disappear around the corner of my block. They are headed to the police station. Bryan and their lawyer are meeting them there. I've never seen Dani look so scared.

Andrew's inside with the kids. I called him and told him to come home with Sutton as soon as Caleb's confession was over. After Kendra leaves, we're sitting down with the kids and telling them what happened. One single act of impulsivity, and Jacob's life was over. How could he have been in a relationship with Sawyer and not told me? And not just any relationship—he was in love and heartbroken. He would've gone on to love so many other people, but he didn't know that, and I could've told him that if he'd given me the chance. Why didn't he give me the chance? I might've been able to save him. How did I miss it? My head swirls with disbelief.

There's no sense going back inside the house since Paul's on his way to pick up Kendra and should be here soon. He still has no idea what's happened. She didn't want to tell him over the phone. She pushed so hard for answers. Is she satisfied with what she got? No answer brings Sawyer back, and the intensity of her sadness weighs on her face. She's aging by the minute.

"Dani left Bryan," I announce, hoping to shift the mood. I can't stand all the sadness. Maybe Dani setting herself free will be the light in all this darkness.

"What? Seriously? Is that why she's staying at her mom's?"

"Yeah."

I watch as the realization dawns on her.

"God, I'm such a moron. I didn't even ask her anything about why she was staying there."

"It's okay," I say, excusing her for what feels like the thousandth time for the same thing.

"It's not okay. It really isn't. I'm sorry that I'm such a shitty friend. I'm not a selfish idiot on purpose. I swear I'm not." Her eyes fill with tears.

The thing is—I know she's not. She loves her friends. She's been standing up for me whenever I couldn't since we were kids. She's chased every bully away and outplayed every mean girl who's ever threatened me.

I put my arm around her. "I still love you."

She lets out a small cry of relief and squeezes me back. "I love you too." She hugs me for another second before pulling away. "At least everything is finally out in the open. That part feels good, doesn't it?"

Not everything.

Andrew's in love with another woman. I still can't bring myself to say it out loud. Not to Kendra or anyone else. I'm too ashamed, even though I didn't do anything wrong, but his sin has already become mine. I never noticed anything going on with him in the same way I never noticed anything going on with Jacob. How long has my entire life been a lie?

I smile at Kendra despite the wails of anguish inside my body. "Yeah, it really does."

The house is finally quiet and still. Everyone has gone home, and my family is asleep. Andrew is tucked in bed with Sutton. He fell asleep out of sheer exhaustion after they finished reading. Wyatt's curled up with the dog in his room upstairs. My chest is heavy as I stand at the head of Jacob's bed, staring at his body and holding the burner phone I found in his bedroom this afternoon. I can't bring myself to sit down and settle in for the night.

I never bothered searching Jacob's room other than to give Detective Locke his phone and laptop. I figured any clues about what had happened lay hidden in his online world rather than in the real world, but it was the first thing I did today after Kendra left. I ransacked his room like I was the FBI, and my search revealed a cardboard box hidden underneath his bed filled with mementos of his relationship with Sawyer—movie stubs, concert tickets, dried flowers, and notes they'd scribbled to each other in class. I found the phone tucked inside an old blanket that I immediately recognized as the one Sawyer got when he was two weeks old. He called it his *mimi*, since he was never able to say *blankie*, and the name stuck. He carried it with him to playdates and sleepovers until he was too embarrassed to have it in public anymore, but he still slept with it every night until he was thirteen. I found the note that must've gone with it when he'd given it to Jacob:

So you can hold me when I'm not there.

Kendra was right.

Jacob was head over heels in love with Sawyer, and there's no mistaking Sawyer returned the feelings, even though he constantly pushed Jacob away, claiming he wasn't ready for a relationship. I didn't think there was any way Jacob could've been in a relationship with someone and not told me about it, but Sawyer swore him to secrecy. Somehow it makes me feel better that it wasn't just that he didn't think he could talk to me about it.

"I wish you would've told me about Sawyer," I whisper even though there's nobody there to hear me. "I could've helped you through it."

The Best of Friends

I grab his hand, noticing his fingernails are turning black, the skin wrinkled and flat like an elderly man's hand. There's no warmth left. His wide-open eyes stare into my aching heart without connecting. There's a strange odor that's never been there before. He's gone from body to ghost.

I lift my eyes to the mantel and our family photo framed in gold at the center. His wide grin spreads across his face with an arm wrapped around each sibling. Andrew and I stand behind them with matching smiles. We took it last year during our trip to Hawaii, and it's one of my favorite pictures because the happiness in our smiles is real, not posed. All the kids agree that it was our best family trip. The days in the sun and sand gave us all a much-needed reprieve from our busy lives and a chance to connect with each other without all the distractions.

His face is filled with so much love and light. It reaches out to me from behind the frame, more alive in the picture than he is in this room. "Do you want to go?" I ask, and in the next instant, it hits me that he's already gone. For the first time, my mind grasps what it's fought so hard to deny—he's not in there.

His shallow breaths rise and fall, followed by a rattling sound, because each exhale takes work. During the hours we waited for him to pass at the hospital, Andrew told me he'd read somewhere that people often wait to die alone because they don't want to put their loved ones through that pain, or they wait until all the people closest to them have had a chance to say goodbye and make their peace.

Maybe today was it.

"Is this what you were waiting for?" I return my gaze to his face, almost unrecognizable as the boy in the picture. My throat catches with a sob.

I could never bring myself to give him permission to go like Andrew. Not when all I wanted him to do was stay. I couldn't imagine living with the hole in my heart that he'd leave. I'd seen the grief over losing a child take Kendra to places I wasn't willing to go.

But my son is gone. That's the reality. The only reality that stares me in the face as I watch him struggle to swallow the phlegm that's built up in his throat. His brain unable to complete basic tasks.

I brush my other hand against his cheek. I've walked him through every important milestone since he was born, from teaching him how to tie his shoes to driving a car and filling out college applications. But I don't know if I can do this. I'm not strong enough. My eyes rise to meet his in the photo; they sear into my soul.

What if he's hanging on for me?

"You don't have to stay any longer." Grief thickens the sound of my voice. "I'm going to be okay," I assure him even though I don't know how I'll live life without him. "I love you so much, Jacob." Deep sobs overtake me, and it takes time for them to settle before I can speak again. I watch his chest as he struggles to breathe. I grab Sawyer's blanket from the couch and lay it next to Jacob's face so he can feel the softness and smell whatever scent of security might still be there. "You can go now." I rub the blanket softly against his cheek. "You don't have to be afraid. Sawyer is waiting for you. Go to him."

Time stands still as I watch his chest rise and fall. I don't move from his bedside until the sun begins peeking through the curtains, casting its first rays of light into our living room. His body releases a long exhale, and I wait for the next inhale, but this time it doesn't come. His chest no longer moves. A calm fills the room. I imagine him walking toward the light and Sawyer waving at him and telling him to hurry up.

I reach down and close his eyes.

EPILOGUE

DANI

TWO WEEKS LATER

I shut the door behind me and slide into Mom's desk. I push aside all her accounting and bills along with her itemized grocery list. I jiggle the mouse, waking up the computer. I have to hurry before Mom gets back. She scooped up Luna on her way home from the grocery store, and we're cooking dinner together tonight. Mom's been an amazing bridge between us.

Caleb's with Bryan tonight. We've worked out a temporary visitation schedule with him until we can figure out something more permanent. Caleb's confession created a huge shift in Bryan's attention toward me. His sole focus is on making sure Caleb doesn't do jail time. Bryan got rid of Ted and hired a cutthroat defense attorney to get him off. But Caleb killed his best friend because he was drunk and angry—I'm not sure he should.

If Caleb had his way, he'd be sent to death row. His therapist says he has a "disproportionate amount of guilt" over that night. My goal is to get him into as many therapy sessions as I can before his court date, because there's no specialized trauma therapy in jail. What innocence he has left will be stripped away. The thought of going to visit him there makes me sick to my stomach.

I wait for the website to load while I pull out my phone to respond to the group text Lindsey sent earlier about making a dinner date. She wants to tell Kendra and me something about Andrew. She was all cryptic about it over the phone. She said it was important but that she hadn't wanted to burden us with it when everything was going down. I can't imagine what she wants to say. I've barely seen her since Jacob's funeral. Her journey is only beginning, but she's finding a way to go on every day, just like we all are.

Kendra started attending support groups about parenting children on the other side, and it's simultaneously the saddest and creepiest thing I've ever heard. She's met all these new friends in her groups, and she talks about them like they've known each other forever instead of only a few weeks. But I guess that's how it is when you've lost a child. Nobody else can understand what that's like. She's tried getting Lindsey to go with her, but she's not ready for that yet.

Things between her and Paul are slowly improving. They've banded together since they've found a common enemy to fight—an enemy that just happens to be my husband. A huge part of the defense Bryan and his lawyer have built for Caleb is directed at them for allowing the easy access to the alcohol that night. They also claim that Caleb's erratic and violent behavior was because of the Adderall he'd been taking on a regular basis. They want to blame that on them, too, since there were times Caleb got it from Reese. It's a jumbled-up legal mess, but the two of them are committed to get through it, and it has renewed their commitment to each other. At least for now. It's a delicate balancing act trying to support Caleb and Kendra at the same time, but Kendra and I agreed not to talk about the case together, which makes it easier.

The home page fills my screen. Mom's Wi-Fi is dinosaur speed. It's been weeks since I logged in, but I checked my messages yesterday, and there was one in my in-box waiting for me. My heart leaped when I saw it was from him. He sent it two days ago. I select the message and stare at the blinking cursor as I get ready to type my response.

I stumbled on the site a few years ago after one of my fights with Bryan, when I was at my lowest. I had never felt so alone and just wanted someone to talk to. I created a profile based on the person I've always imagined I'd be if I'd never met Bryan—a successful woman living on the East Coast with a husband who adored me instead of hurting me, with children who respected me, and running my own interior design business. It gave me a chance to be the person I never got to become. I never expected to meet someone I cared about or to develop the feelings that have grown out of our relationship.

We can go weeks without being able to coordinate our schedules to be online at the same time, so most of our communication in the beginning was through long emails to each other that read like old-fashioned letters sent through the mail. I loved everything about it, and it gave me something to look forward to that was only mine—a treat at the end of my day, an escape from the suffocating walls of my home. I set things up through an old email account of Luna's rather than my own. Bryan knew how paranoid and diligent I was about monitoring the kids' online activity, so he left all that up to me, and he stopped paying attention to any of Luna's stuff after she moved out. I was so proud of myself for exerting the first piece of independence I'd had in years.

It's weird to feel so strongly about someone whose face I've never seen, but I liked it that way. I could imagine him as whoever I needed him to be at the moment. It has kept me going when I wanted to give up and allowed me to find the self I discarded years ago. Now that I've found her, I'm never letting her go again.

I'm going to miss him. That's for sure, but I don't need him like I did, because there's nothing left to escape from anymore. I finally read Luna's letter, and one of the things she described was how living a lie was the hardest part of being in our family. I can't do anything about the past, but I can do things differently going forward, and I promised her an authentic life. It's as important for her as it is to me.

This is a new beginning, and it's time to let go of anything that stands in the way of my fresh start. I hope he understands.

> *L—*
> *I've missed you too and I hope you're well. Can we chat soon? There's something I need to tell you.*
> *Love,*
> *May*

ACKNOWLEDGMENTS

A book is only as strong as the team behind it, and I'm so grateful for my team. Forever grateful to call Thomas & Mercer my publishing home. To my brilliant editor, Charlotte Herscher, who always takes my work to the next level and finds the holes I miss. To Megha Parekh, who stands at the top supervising us all and keeping me in line. Whose words, "Make sure the suspense drives the story," will forever reign in my mind while I write. To all the copyeditors, proofreaders, cover designers, and marketing managers who make sure the finished product shines—thank you. To my agent extraordinaire, Christina Hogrebe, who knew exactly how to pursue me and came into my life when I needed her the most. And lastly, my readers, because where would I be without you? Thank you from the bottom of my heart for all your support.

ABOUT THE AUTHOR

Dr. Lucinda Berry is a former psychologist and leading researcher in childhood trauma. Now, she spends her time writing full-time where she uses her clinical experience to blur the line between fiction and nonfiction. She enjoys taking her readers on a journey through the dark recesses of the human psyche.

If Berry isn't chasing after her son, you can find her running through Los Angeles, prepping for her next marathon. To hear about her upcoming releases, visit her on Facebook or sign up for her newsletter at https://lucindaberry.com/.